# THE NEFARIOUS TRIANGLE OF LOVE PART 2

**CHEROKEE GREY**

# THE NEFARIOUS TRIANGLE OF LOVE

# PART 2

## BY CHEROKEE GREY

WE SHINE MEDIA SOLUTIONS

Copyright © 2024 Cherokee Grey

All rights reserved under International Copyright Law. Except as permitted under the U.S. Copyright Act of 1976, no part of this publication may be reproduced, distributed, or transmitted in any form or by any means or stored in a database or retrieval system without the prior written permission of the publisher.

Publishing Company: WE Shine Media Solutions

Book Cover Design: Cherokee Grey

ISBN 979-8-876-97584-3

Printed in: The United States, First Edition

# TABLE OF CONTENTS

CHAPTER 1:   THE BOLD & BEAUTIFUL          6

CHAPTER 2:   PRIORITIES                    25

CHAPTER 3:   MOVING ON                     35

CHAPTER 4:   TIME KEEPS PASSING            52

CHAPTER 5:   MENDING FENCES                59

CHAPTER 6:   DRAMA AT ITS FINEST           73

CHAPTER 7:   ACCIDENTS HAPPEN              86

CHAPTER 8:   CORDERO HOLDS NO PUNCHES      129

CHAPTER 9:   WEDDING BLISS OR MAYHEM?      140

CHAPTER 10:  THE LUAU SHOWDOWN             157

CHAPTER 11:  THE SENTENCING                171

CHAPTER 12:  JOYOUS MOMENTS                181

CHAPTER 13:  RANDOM INCIDENTS              188

CHAPTER 14:  DIGGING DEEPER                206

CHAPTER 15:  THE SETUP                     221

CHAPTER 16:  GETTING TO THE BOTTOM OF IT   235

| | |
|---|---|
| CHAPTER 17: BABY? ON BOARD | 243 |
| CHAPTER 18: HOME ALONE | 248 |
| CHAPTER 19: THE MASSACRE | 253 |
| CHAPTER 20: THE AFTERMATH | 266 |
| CHAPTER 21: CHRISTMAS | 274 |
| CHAPTER 22: THE HAPPILY EVER AFTER | 276 |
| EPILOGUE: LESSONS | 278 |
| ABOUT THE AUTHOR | 279 |

## CHAPTER 1: THE BOLD & BEAUTIFUL

As the holidays approached, more and more people were piling into the hospital. Yanira picked up extra hours in the evenings, working until 10 p.m. Monday through Thursday over the next several weeks leading up to Christmas. She missed Kaeo, especially at night. She was lonely, but she was working to accomplish her goals. He understood and respected her decisions—it allowed him to spend time with Clariana as they prepared for her move.

On Friday night, Anais came to pick up her daughter. As Clariana packed, she turned to Kaeo, "Hey, I need to speak with you privately in your bedroom."

Kaeo declined, "Nah, we can step outside." He got up off the couch, walked towards the door, and waited outside the door; he really didn't want her there, but for Clariana, he allowed it.

Anais followed him out. Once she was outside, she shut the door, then turned to look him in the eyes, saying, "Kaeo, my love, look at me. Can you not look at me lover?"

Kaeo looked up from the ground and glared at Anais directly in the eye as she asked. He knew she was about to say something stupid or something he didn't want to hear. Making sure to lean against the window as far away from her as he could, he asked, "What's up Anais?"

"Listen, I am thinking about moving, and I was wondering if you could live without me in your life permanently? I am trying to give you another chance before I make my final decision."

Kaeo laughed at her; the words coming out of her mouth tickled him. "Please, by all means, take your foolishness and games elsewhere. There is nothing inside of me that wants to be with you anymore. Too much has transpired, Anais, and I want to live my life without your drama, and your recklessness. Go do whatever makes you happy because I am ecstatic."

Anais admonished, "Baby, don't say that. You know all those things I have done have been out of anger. I am just furious because of this stupid relationship you and that Yanira girl are building, not to mention putting my daughter in the equation. It is killing me, lover. Let's just put all this behind us and start over. This time will be different." She walked over to touch him.

Kaeo shook his head and held up his hand for her not to come any closer, "Clariana is building her own relationship with Yanira. I have not forced anything. Anais, you need to consider how I felt when you cheated, lied, and disrespected me by using our son and your brother, whom I raised, to beat me. You didn't forget about the metal pipe, did you? I didn't."

"Lover, that's all old news. You should be over that by now."

"You are a joke, and for you to even think I want to be with you after all this is stupid. By all means, move on! Move out of town so Yanira and I can move on with our lives together."

Kaeo opened the door and told Clariana her mother was waiting outside. He could hear Anais through the door. She was enraged, but he did not care. Kaeo was ready to rid himself of her so he could move in with Yanira and start their life together. Yanira had been patient with him when it came to Anais, and he did not want to mess that up.

The following weekend after Kaeo's exchange with Anias, Clariana had no plans and remained at home. Kaeo thought this meant limited time with Yanira, but to his surprise, it was the total opposite. Yanira came over Friday night, and Clariana asked if they could all go to a movie. Kaeo and Yanira both were shocked. The trio went to dinner, then a movie, the grocery store and afterward, they all went back to Kaeo's to make banana splits; it was a good day. Kaeo couldn't have asked for anything more than the woman he loved and his daughter to be cordial and enjoy time with one another.

After spending the next couple of weekends with Yanira, Clariana began engaging even more with her, and the two built a tighter bond. Clariana would often ask for advice on school, boys, and friends, even confiding in her about her hopes and dreams of attending school. Yanira was proud of Clariana. She had a good head on her shoulders, and with the proper support, love, and guidance, Clariana could go far. The only thing is, if they left it up to Anais, she would use her mind and body to become a weapon instead of her brain. It was sad but true. Anais never really wanted to do much. She was a nanny and often slept with the men she nannied for, while the mothers of the children were clueless. Anais was unphased by her actions; she was a single mother and didn't see why anyone else should have a dream life if she couldn't.

Anais was the type of woman who would watch you, befriend you, then steal your dreams, man, and your patience. Anais had no regard for anyone who had more than she did. She would often tell Clariana to make sure to watch her figure because it would take her places when she got older. Besides advising Clariana to wear makeup, she wanted her in tight clothes so she would look just like her, but Clariana was the total opposite of her mother. She was loyal and full of dreams and aspirations, along with the will to make it on her own. Never would she ever want to harm another person for her own gain.

After finding out her mother had lied and betrayed them all, she started to open her eyes and see Yanira for who she was, a kindhearted, hardworking Boss of a woman who loved her dad. For these reasons alone, she admired Yanira. This made her want to change her ways, knowing she needed to apologize to Yanira and make every effort to make amends.

The recent change and shift in Clariana made Kaeo happy; he only wanted peace in his life, and as long as Anais was around, he knew he would not get it. These days, when Yanira came over, Clariana did not leave; she was cordial and smiled. Sadly, just as they were warming up, soon his daughter would have to leave. Although she made things right with Yanira, Anais still had a hold on her and often made her choose. Yanira always took the high road, encouraging her to go and be with her mother; she only had one, and whether she was right or wrong, it was still her mother. This is something Clariana would never understand because Anias constantly called Yanira out of her name, often referring to her as "The Bitch." Clariana had to remain quiet because if she did not, it would cause a fight between her and her mother, so she humbled herself just as Yanira did to save herself from scrutiny and argument.

Much to their surprise, by Christmas time, Clariana was still living with Kaeo. She and Yanira had become almost like family. The two of them worked out their issues, and Clariana treated her just as a stepchild should, with respect and affection. So, for the holiday, they decided to have decorate and celebrate Christmas Eve together since she would be going with her mother on Christmas morning.

Somehow, Yanira was off on Christmas Eve, Christmas Day, and the day after. Arriving at Kaeo's place while he was at work, she and Clariana cooked a delicious meal together, put decorations on the Christmas tree, and made Christmas cookies and ice cream sandwiches. When Kaeo came home, he was so happy that his two girls were bonding and even more floored by the wonderful job they had done together with the house and dinner. The tree was gorgeous, and the dinner looked even more scrumptious because he had skipped lunch. They decided to binge-watch movies until midnight and allow Clariana to open her gifts before she left in the morning.

Yanira gave her several gift cards and clothes from her favorite stores for Christmas, while Kaeo bought her a diamond bracelet with the inscription, "Daddy's Girl Always and Forever" and gift cards. Clariana was a happy teenager with $600 in gift cards to do whatever she wanted, new clothes, and a new diamond bracelet. Before she went to bed, Yanira said,

"Hey Clariana, it may be a good idea to state all the gifts came from your dad, ok. I don't want you to deal with any drama about me with your mother. You deserve those things, and I do not want them taken away from you because of me."

Clariana agreed, "Sorry, but I had planned on doing that anyway. It would be easier for me." Yanira smiled and nodded. Kaeo, however, was disappointed. He knew they were trying to keep the peace, but the fact that his daughter had to lie about gifts made him mad and disgusted. He walked to the kitchen to clean the remaining dishes and wipe down the counters.

Yanira walked over to hug him from behind without uttering a word, simply because they both knew it was best. Anais would cause drama if she didn't. Clariana hugged Yanira and thanked her for everything. Yanira was happy. The hug felt genuine and like it lasted for eternity. She had grown to love this young woman, even though they had a rocky start.

*********************************************

After finishing up in the living room and kitchen, Yanira followed Kaeo into the restroom, determined to pleasure her man with a little oral love. As he stood in the bathroom with a towel wrapped around his waist, she grazed his chest with her hands then dropped down low to put him inside her mouth. Her tongue circled around his fat juicy head, then she softly but quickly deep throated him which caused him to suck in air and hum. Yanira moved back and forth with massive suction as she played with his handles below and slightly tugged on his dick with the other.

Kaeo was taken off guard; the amount of pressure was making him cave in much faster than he wanted, and he began to tug on his own hair. She slowed down to let him catch his wind, but she was not done sucking and slurping just yet. She wanted five more minutes. As soon as she felt his tension was gone, she began again, full throttle. Kaeo was too excited, "Baby, hold on for me; Yanira, please baby, just one min." He didn't finish, because Yanira didn't stop sucking her pop sickle and playing with his handles. Before he could finish his plea, Yanira pulled him in for one big gulp and he released, filling her throat with his hearty cum. His body shook as he released, and Yanira sucked him dry.

Kaeo looked down at her as she freed him and shook his head. She smiled as she stood up and walked over to the sink to brush and gargle. Kaeo tapped her bottom and told her, "I will be waiting on you in the bedroom; please don't keep me waiting too long. I have something I need to give you!" The two made love for the next hour and a half, then Kaeo caressed and held her all night.

The next morning, as Clariana dressed to go with her mother, Kaeo told Yanira it was time for her to receive her gifts.

Yanira gave a beautiful smile, "I thought I had my gift last night."

Kaeo laughed as he walked over to her, planting a sweet kiss on her forehead then her lips. "Baby, that's not a gift to you, that is a gift you give me, and I will give that to you every day for the rest of your life if I can."

Yanira blushed. They walked into the living room and sat near the tree. Kaeo gave Yanira a box. When she opened it, she saw a 7-karat white gold diamond engagement ring shaped like an egg; he then proposed to the love of his life. Getting on his knee, he grabbed her hand, saying, "Yanira, would you do me the honor of marrying me? I would love to spend the rest of my days with you and give you exactly what you deserve."

Yanira was ecstatic and began screaming loudly. "Yes! Yes!" She felt all the trouble with Anais was worth it at that point. Due to all the screaming, Clariana rushed in, and she saw the ring. Yanira pulled her hand back in an attempt to hide it.

Kaeo noticed. He held her hand out, and with a big grin, he told Clariana, "She said yes!"

Months before, he had told his family and had even asked Yanira's father for permission. He just wanted to marry her: when and where did not matter as long as he was with her.

"Congratulations, Yanira. You deserve it!" Clariana hugged her again, saying, "I knew for a week, but I had to keep it a secret."

Yanira smiled. "Well, this is the best-kept secret, and I am grateful to you both. Clariana, I am actually more relieved that you are ok with the proposal."

Clariana explained, "Honestly, because of you two, I see love differently. I can see love and happiness in your relationship. It is unlike what I saw between Dad and my Mom. I guess they were happy when I was a kid, but for a long time, he was unhappy unless my brother and I were around. I can tell you have true love; it seems special. These last few weeks, I have been able to experience you and your kindness. I am grateful, and my eyes and heart are open because of you especially."

Yanira teared up. Clariana's words warmed her heart and relieved her soul because she knew then that she and Kaeo could now move on with their lives. She hugged Clariana with all her might.

Later that morning, Clariana left with her mom. An hour later, Anais called and told Kaeo she would not be back, as Yanira had tampered and played with her daughter's emotions. Anais vowed never to speak with him again, stating she would be coming to pick up Clariana's things when they returned in two weeks. She was hurt, declaring he was only with Yanira to get back at her for what she had done, but now he had gone too far, and it was over. She was moving to California to be with her family, claiming she needed the support of her children. She hated him and ended with calling Kaeo a sorry individual and a poor excuse for a man.

It was a bittersweet moment for Kaeo. He would miss his daughter, but he was glad to get rid of Anais. He found out the true power of manipulation she had over him. Now, however, he felt blessed; he knew what it felt like to truly be loved by someone, and it had not taken ten years, only three. He was in love with Yanira and wanted to spend the rest of his life with her.

That night Kaeo picked up several items of clothing, shoes, and everyday personal items and took them to Yanira's. When he arrived, she noticed the large bag. Kaeo grinned, "I'm going to stay with you for a few days, and we can rotate if you want to, or we can get a break in."

"No explanation needed, I am good with you being here and I do not need a break. We are engaged and we should try living together all the time. Maybe we should think about renting out or selling your condo by the end of February." He agreed.

The week was off to a great start, both were elated to be alone, and Yanira couldn't keep her eyes off the ring. Every moment she had, her head was down admiring her ring, then her future husband. They worked, came home, took turns cooking, and cleaning, and often in the midst of cooking or cleaning Kaeo would get aroused and bend her over in the kitchen.

On Wednesday, as Yanira stood in the kitchen, she took a moment to admire her hand. Kaeo caught her admiring the ring from the couch in the living room. He walked over and kissed her. When she kissed back, something surged through his body with that one kiss and all hell broke loose. Kaeo wanted Yanira badly; he couldn't help himself. He picked her up and took her aside. He snatched her pants down, lifted her body and plastered her ass cheeks against the backdoor. Removing her body away from the stove, he inserted his third leg into her hot kitty, fucking life into her. It was so unexpectedly pleasing, she kept yelling, "I love you, baby!"

The sound of her words made him go harder. He pumped at a rapid pace; it was a whirl wind. She didn't know if she was making love or fucking but it felt phenomenal. The encounter was so intense they never paid attention to the burning chicken. Kaeo began to growl as he was rising to the occasion. Yanira wrapped her legs around him and clinched her walls, trying to hold out but Kaeo was giving her so much dick she couldn't help but cave. When he felt the splatter, he helped flush her out and himself too. Kaeo had to carry her to the couch as Yanira couldn't stand. The smoke detectors started going off, but they took their time. The chicken was burnt to a crisp, so they had to order out.

Unfortunately, the premarital bliss was short lived. One week and two days later, Anais called; he didn't answer, so she sent a text message saying, "It is important that we speak. Things have not worked out as planned, and I have already given up everything. Your daughter needs to return home to finish her last month of school, and I will be homeless because I didn't plan on returning." After reading the text, he placed his hand on his face in frustration and handed the phone to Yanira for her to read. Yanira was not surprised. She knew this would not be the end of Anais. Kaeo, however, was dazed; he thought he would be able to live peacefully.

"Yanira, what do you think I should do?" Kaeo asked. "I do not want to go back to living separately because of my daughter; I want to focus on us."

Yanira said, "Well, give her the last two months, then you move in. If her mother does not find a place for her by then, Clariana can move in here with you, but her mother is not welcome in my home or on my property because I do not trust her, nor do I care for her."

Kaeo asked, "What do I do about Anais? I do not want her coming in between us."

Yanira firmly stated, "Then don't let her; she is not your problem. We can help your daughter, but Anais, on the other hand, she is a grown-ass woman and I'm not taking care of her, nor will I support you helping her. Burning bridges and being irresponsible do not constitute help on my behalf. You have done enough, and anything else will give her the idea or hope that she still has a chance with you. As I said before, I will never make you choose between your children, family, and business, but when it comes to Anais, there is no option other than me or her period."

Kaeo responded, "I understand that, and you are right. The last thing I want is for another woman to cause issues within our relationship. You are the one for me, Yani, 100%. I will let Anais figure it out."

Kaeo texted Anais back, stating, "Anais, Clariana staying with me is not a problem. She is welcome and can stay as long as she needs to. But understand I plan on moving by the end of February, and I will not change my plans. I will be moving in with Yanira, and if Clariana is with me at that point, she will be too. I am giving you a heads-up so there will be no surprises."

"Ok, that is fine, but what about me?"

Laughing out loud, he replied, "Please secure your plans in finding a place for yourself."

Anais texted back, "So you do not care if I have a place or not, only your daughter? What kind of lover says something like this? Did our love mean nothing to you?"

Kaeo responded, "Anais, our love meant everything to me but nothing to you; you ruined it with your lies and deceit. There is nothing left in my heart for you, and it's all your fault. It has nothing to do with Yanira. Your cheating broke me, along with the lies about the miscarriages; I cannot move on with you or forget that ever."

"Kaeo, Lover, please understand those were mistakes. I am sorry I hurt you; it will never happen again. I miss you, and I want to try once more. It will be better. I promise!"

"Anais, I changed my entire life for you and left my family only for you to lie, cheat, and deceive me. There is nothing more left between us. I will not text you again if it has nothing to do with my daughter."

Anais was livid, sending messages saying, "Fuck you, Kaeo! You are nothing to me any longer. I am done pleading with you and trying to win your love. You both will pay for what you are doing to me. Trust me; you will not be happy without me."

"Fuck you Kaeo;" "You are an ass;" "You have no right to treat me this way." The messages kept coming. He finally responded to her.

"Ok, Anais, that's all good. I will make it my business to continue to be happy and live a peaceful life without your foolishness. Now please do what you need to do and stop texting me before I block you."

Anais continued to text, but Kaeo ignored her calls and text messages. He had nothing left to say, and after the 14$^{th}$ call, he blocked her number. He genuinely cared for Anais, but everything she had done was unforgivable. The miscarriages changed him. He could not believe how she had lied to him and faked having children with him, knowing that all he desired was to have children of his own one day. At this point, it was water under the bridge; he knew he would have children with Yanira once they were married and settled in.

The couple tried their best to enjoy the remainder of their last week together at Yanira's house without any interruptions. They both left for work at the same time, and whoever got home first cooked dinner; then, on Friday, their date night, they ordered in and made love throughout the night. It started in the living room after they showered and had dinner.

Kaeo took Yanira, lifting her off her feet and placing her on the counter, snatching her panties off and pulling her pussy into his face. Kaeo devoured his dessert. He made sure his tongue touched every wall it could reach, and when the tongue went as far as it could, he took his fingers and massaged her insides while his tongue sucked her clitoris, curving at an angle where the entire clitoris was covered with his tongue and lips.

Yanira leaned back and open her legs wider to let him fill his mouth and hands with ass and pussycat. His free hand gripped her ass, pulling her in more and more, sucking more vigorously than before. Yanira was panting as she began to erupt! His finger went in for the last time, and she filled his mouth with her sweet buttercream!

The next evening, for their couple's night out with Ryleigh and Marshall, Kaeo made reservations at the Grille Restaurant for Saturday. Throughout the entire dinner, they kept making eyes at one another. Yanira was thinking to herself how she would not have him at home with her tonight to make love to, and it was unfortunate because he looked so damn good in his button-down. She took her leg and placed it on his, rubbing it up and down his legs, and felt him growing underneath his pants. She got up and excused herself. Kaeo waited five minutes and followed her.

Just as she was coming out of the restroom, he pushed her back in. "So, you think you can tease me and not follow through?"

She giggled. "So, what are you trying to do, Mr. Iosua?"

"Let me show you!" He hijacked her legs from the ground. She had already taken her panties off because she wanted to tease him; when he felt her ass, he noticed and smiled, murmuring, "Umm hmm," as he pushed her into the wall and bent her over. She watched him through the glass as he smashed into her, and she let out a little squirm. He pounded her from the back, taking a fist full of her hair and holding on to it, not pulling but allowing her to feel the grip he had.

This small gesture gave Yanira power, and she began to throw it back at him. Surprised, he lifted her left leg so he could dive deeper. Her leg was so high she touched her own belly while he continued to send chills through her vagina. There was a knock at the door. Kaeo yelled, "Go away!" Yanira pushed faster to get his mind back on her; he refocused, continuing to drill into her, and 9 deep thrusts later, both surrendered their orgasms.

They went back to the table where Marshall and Ryleigh were waiting patiently; Ryleigh smiled and mouthed, "You nasty!" Yanira stuck out her tongue, mouthing, "Don't be jealous." They sat for another twenty minutes then went their separate ways.

*****************************************************

On Sunday, Kaeo went back to his condo. After two hours of being there, he called Yanira, telling her he felt she should be there too. He wanted to set the tone for his relationship with Anais. Yanira liked that he was stepping up, so she agreed to meet him there and spend a few nights.

When Clariana arrived, she hugged her dad and Yanira, then went to her bedroom. Just as Kaeo was about to shut the door, Anais stepped in, bringing in more bags for her daughter, and looked around his condo. She saw Yanira at the entrance of the kitchen doorway.

Anais said, "Kaeo, we need to speak privately."

Kaeo shook his head. He knew where this was going since he had blocked her after her last rant. "Anais, anything you have to say to me, you can say in front of Yanira. She is my fiancé now, and truthfully, whatever we discuss, I will only share it with her later. So, it makes no sense to hide it now or repeat it later on." Yanira smiled at his words and flipped her hair with a pompous grin while Anais boiled inside, rolling her eyes.

Anais went off. "Fiancé! You bitch! What have you done to him? He doesn't love me because of you. This is your fault; you have turned him against me! Kaeo, is she pregnant? That is the only way you will stay with her; she must be pregnant. I know you will never leave the woman who gives you a child; you promised me this before. Oh, my goodness. Don't do this; kill it! I will kill it for you. I will untie my tubes. Please, Kaeo, this is not right."

Clariana came from her bedroom to witness what was going on. She was hurt and disappointed in her mother. Yanira was good to her, and there was no need for name-calling or her trying to push past her dad to fight with Yanira. She heard her say kill the baby, and she knew now that her mother must have antagonized all the issues and fights that had transpired before. She shook her head and slammed her bedroom door. Hoping her mother would leave.

Kaeo said, "Anais, get a hold of yourself. You are upsetting Clariana. I have already told you never to disrespect Yanira. This is her house now. You need to leave and never step foot in this door again unless you apologize and act like a person with some sense. And I will never leave her, pregnant or not; you made sure of that, so thank yourself. To answer your question, she is not pregnant yet, but trust me, I will make sure that she will be as soon as she marries me."

Kaeo shut the door. He looked in the direction of Yanira, who signaled him to go and check on his daughter as she finished her walk into the kitchen. He headed to do as he was told, but not before he planted a kiss on her cheek, then lips, and hugged her tightly. He was melancholy and said, "I am sorry, Yani, really I am, but I am trying."

She answered back, "Don't be sorry. I do not expect you to be mean to her or mistreat her, just to respect our love and relationship, and you are. (Kissing him sweetly) Now, please, Clariana needs you."

His daughter looked up as he walked into her bedroom; she wept and sat on the bed. Clariana now utterly understood the magnitude of her mother's manipulation. She would go to any lengths to get her way. Sadly, Yanira would see more venom from her mother. The only question is when and where would it be.

Kaeo sighed, "Clariana, I am sorry you had to witness that. I do not want you to think for one second that this relationship ended because of Yanira. It ended because your mother and I were on different pages. Sometimes we make choices for ourselves, and it's not what's best for our families. I am with Yanira because I love her and what we share. I never cheated on your mother nor lied to her. We just grew apart over time."

Clariana looked up. "I know, Dad. It just hurts to see her without you. I like Yanira, and she is a good person. I know this, but my mom is my mom. I know she cheated, lied, and faked babies, and I can understand how she hurt you. My brother told me everything that happened that night, and I, in turn, told him about what I knew. They were wrong for what they did to you, and I am so sorry. I hate that she wants you back and you don't want her, but again I get it. I wouldn't want her back if I were you either; she has done too much. Honestly, she has someone, and she also has somewhere to stay; he is just not you. I know she just wants you to end your relationship with Yanira and has no plans to be faithful. I don't want you or Yanira to suffer anymore, but you know, like I know, that my mom is not giving up."

Kaeo looked at Clariana in disbelief. His daughter was confiding in him and telling him her mother's plans. He knew it was hard for her to betray her mother, but he was grateful. He held her in his arms and rocked her as she was crying. Both were feeling the wrath of Anais. He told her, "It is going to be ok. We'll get through it together."

Yanira was in the kitchen cooking dinner: steaks smothered with onions and peppers, potatoes, rice, and green beans. She heard Clariana crying, and it hurt to hear how much pain she was in. Clariana was torn, knowing her mother was wrong but also knowing that she was petty enough to do anything to hurt him. Anais had used her own daughter.

As she set the table for dinner, they both walked in. Respecting her feelings and space, Yanira did not say a word; she wanted Clariana to be the first to speak, which she was.

"So, what did you guys do while I was away?"

Kaeo responded, "Just chilled out, nothing special."

Yanira said, "Well, your dad took me to a great restaurant called "Grille Bistro." It was amazing. We need to take you."

"I'd like that, Yani," Clariana said with a smile. After that, the room became silent as they ate.

"Don't get too stuffed," Yanira demanded. "Save room for dessert. I made three hot fudge sundaes and placed them in the freezer until after dinner." She got up from the table and headed to the freezer.

Kaeo and Clariana smiled, looking around. Yanira beamed, "Look at these!" She opened the freezer door to show them the sundaes.

Simultaneously, they both said, "I'm finished."

Yanira burst into laughter, "No finish, just save a little room. They have a new episode of our show "Lioness" so we can watch it together as we eat dessert!"

Clariana was just like Kaeo; she had a great sense of humor. After dinner, they all went and showered, then met back in the living room thirty minutes later. They listened to Clariana talk about her trip and her time with her brother. She seemed to genuinely enjoy every aspect of the vacation outside of her mother's manipulation. That was the hard part, knowing a child was suffering unnecessarily because of a selfish woman who betrayed everyone she came across. Once the conversation finished, they ate their sundaes and watched their TV show. Three episodes later, they were all caught up and ready to climb into bed.

## CHAPTER 2: PRIORITIES

The month of January went fast! The couple and daughter became a family of three, and their date night was on Thursdays. Yanira would meet them at the restaurant of the week after everyone was home from work and school. On the weekends that Clariana was home, they dined out and always went to do something fun or adventurous, like a movie, ziplining, go-cart racing, or bowling, and on rainy days they binged-watched TV shows and ate all day.

This time together brought them closer, and Clariana opened up to Yanira about many challenges in her life. Yanira tried to give the best advice possible and always informed Kaeo of their conversations, except about personal stuff she vowed to keep secret. On the weekends, Clariana was with her mother or friends, while Yanira and Kaeo went back to Yanira's place to enjoy time with Ryleigh and Marshall on Friday nights.

On the first Friday in February, Clariana called and said she was at her friend's, and her mother was supposed to pick her up, but she had not shown up. She was panicking as she had called her mother five times, and her friend's family had plans, so she needed to leave. Since Yanira and Kaeo had plans to attend a gathering, Yanira told him, "Baby, just pick her up and bring her to the house while I get our things together." Kaeo didn't question her and left to pick up his daughter.

Yanira's plan was to allow her to stay at the house alone for a couple of hours, and then they would go back to his place if Clariana was not comfortable after the event. Once Kaeo returned and saw she was still getting dressed, he was excited. He thought she would be mad and would want to change their plans. He had already told Clariana that they had something to do, and she would possibly stay at the house; then they would leave after the event. He had given her specific instructions not to tell her mother where Yanira lived or allow her to pick her up. Clariana agreed.

When Clariana arrived, they placed her in the guest room on the main floor. Immediately she fell in love with the house. Yanira took her on a tour of the home first, then went outside to the pool and hot tub. Clariana was amazed. She had never been to someone's home that had their own pool. She told Kaeo, "Dad, you've been holding out. We should have been staying here the entire time."

He laughed and kissed her forehead. The couple finished preparing for their evening and ordered Clariana a pizza for dinner. Once it arrived, they headed out and locked all the doors, checked the windows, and set the alarm. Yanira wanted to make sure Clariana felt safe and was as comfortable as she could possibly be alone in the house.

Finally, they reached the club for the all-white party to see the famous West Coast rappers. To avoid the large crowd, they entered through the back door and were escorted to VIP. The two partied and mingled with the stars, but around 12:30 a.m., Yanira looked at her watch and stated to Kaeo and Ryleigh, "Hey we need to head home and check on Clariana." Kaeo grinned from ear to ear and stood. They said their goodbyes while Marshall called for a valet to meet them at the door with their car.

As they exited and waited for the valet, they saw Anais standing across from them with some man. Her arm was wrapped around him, and she smiled as if she was the happiest woman in the world. Kaeo lost it. "Can you believe this shit? How can you hang out and party knowing you only get your daughter two days out of seven? You stood her up, but your ass is in a line to get into a club?"

Anais looked at Kaeo and didn't say anything. She was embarrassed. He was extremely loud, not holding his composure well at all. Kaeo kept talking to Yanira, and finally, Anais walked up. Yanira stood in between them.

Anais spoke quietly, "I thought she would have called you to pick her up. I was busy."

Kaeo responded, "You were busy? You were busy? You had plans with a man. Did you not think that we had plans too?"

Anais snarked, "Yes, but you could have canceled them. I knew she would call, but I figured you would change your plans so you could sit at home with your daughter."

It was plain and simple. She hoped that Kaeo would change his plans and Yanira would be upset Kaeo was canceling or leaving due to his responsibilities with Clariana.

Kaeo looked Anais in the eye and said, "You are sorry and a poor excuse for a mother! Unlike you, Yanira made arrangements for our daughter, and now we are leaving to check on her. You are pitiful, Anais."

Yanira pulled him away; she didn't want to draw any more of a crowd than was already there. She turned his face to look at hers, then she whispered to him, advising, "Hey, it is ok. We got her. You took her to a safe place, and she is ok. Just calm down, and let's go so we can finish our night at home!"

At that moment, the valet pulled up with their car. Kaeo allowed Yanira to enter; then, he closed it. Before he got in, he took one last look of disgust at Anais, got in, and drove off.

When they arrived home, Clariana was in bed sleeping like a baby. Kaeo was still pissed; he talked about Anais for an hour. Finally, after allowing him to vent his frustration, Yanira went downstairs to fix him a drink so he could relax.

Clariana walked into the kitchen, rubbing the sleep out of her eyes. "Hey, Yani, is everything ok? Why are you guys fighting?"

Yanira explained, "No, everything is fine between us. He is a little upset; he just needs to relax and sleep it off."

Clariana looked at her and then said, "You can tell me. I already heard my dad say my mom was there. She wanted him to change his plans, so that's why she didn't answer me. She is trying to do anything and everything to break him. Guess it backfired," (she smirked as she thought about her words). Yanira could not help but grin herself. She knew Clariana could probably hear Kaeo; he was not calm or quiet about his feelings.

Clariana broke Yanira's thoughts by saying, "I know you are trying to protect her even though you shouldn't. Remember, we promised to be honest with one another. It's ok to tell me when my mother is wrong. I just don't want you to disrespect her, and I know that is hard to ask, considering all that she has done to you."

Yanira looked in amazement. "I would never disrespect anyone who didn't deserve it, and yes, your mother deserves it, but she is your mother, and I will always respect you enough to be the bigger person until I can't. And you are right; I am sorry. I will not hide things from you again. Deal?"

"Deal," Clariana responded and went back to the guest room.

The next morning Clariana's phone was buzzing during breakfast. It was her mother. She answered, "Hey mom. I tried to call you. I was supposed to leave Laine's house, but you never answered. I was worried."

Anais asked, "Where are you guys? I am at the condo door, and no one is answering. Get up and let me in."

Clariana said, "Oh, I am not there." In a low tone, she said, "Dad picked me up and brought me to Yanira's house because they had plans, but they came back early to make sure I was safe."

Anais yelled, "What!!"

Clariana countered, "I was safe. She has a house alarm with cameras and everything."

"What is the address? I will pick you up now," Anais calmly said into the phone.

"Oh, well, I do not know the address, but I am not allowed to give it to you. Sorry, Mom. Dad, when will I be home? Mom is at the condo."

"Let me speak to him, Clariana," Anais demanded; she was ready to pick a fight.

"Mom wants to speak with you, Dad." She tried to hand Kaeo the phone, but he refused.

Yanira said, "We will have you home within an hour, as soon as you can finish your breakfast and get dressed."

Clariana said, "We will leave as soon as I finish breakfast and get dressed, Mom. I will see you in about an hour." Anais didn't say another word as she disconnected the call. She was furious. Her plan really did backfire, and now her daughter was at the house of the enemy eating breakfast.

Clariana finished her breakfast and headed to get dressed. Kaeo looked at Yanira and said, "She is a sorry-ass excuse for a mother. She leaves my daughter stranded so she can go clubbing with another man. And now you want to know where she is. What kind of bullshit is that? Now you want her all of a sudden. I am done, Yanira. I do not want to see her face; I do not want to be bothered."

Yanira told him, "Look, just relax; I will drop her off so you can chill and calm down. If it's ok, I will drive your truck."

"Thank you, my love. I appreciate that because I am liable to end up in jail if I go there today. Yes, drive my truck because I parked behind you last night."

As they drove to Kaeo's condo. Clariana asked, "Yanira, did you see my mom on a date last night?"

Yanira didn't want to answer, but she promised to always be honest with her. "Yes, dear, we did. She was on a date. We left early because we didn't want you home too long by yourself since it was your first time at the house, and we didn't know if you would feel comfortable. We knew you were old enough, but it was just the principle."

"Well, what happened? Why is Dad so mad?"

"Well, while we were waiting for the valet to bring the car around, we saw your mother with a gentleman friend. Your dad was a tad bit upset because she ignored your calls while she was out. He did not mind getting you; he just did not like how it played out. You could have been hurt or harmed, and she would not have known. He takes fatherhood very seriously."

Clariana sighed a little but said, "Thank you for allowing me to stay and dropping me off. I don't want them to fight. Once we move and are out of state, I think it will be better for her and you guys too."

Yanira was surprised at the maturity of this young woman. She was sacrificing her feelings and happiness for her parents.

Yanira asked, "What are you doing for college? Have you decided yet? I think we should get you prepared so you can have a plan—dorm room, expenses paid, etc. Remember I told you I have some co-workers who are looking for teenagers to sponsor? Would you be interested in that? You can go to the University of California and at least get your core classes paid for, and of course, Kaeo and I will help."

"You would help me?"

"Of course, I would."

"Well, I still want to be a nurse. I feel like I will always have a job opportunity as a nurse."

"Ok, well, since you are 100% sure, I will see what I can do," Yanira said. Clariana was full of excitement.

Yanira did not tell her, but she had already inquired and was in the final stages of getting her financial help. She was hoping to get the papers back within the next week. She knew that her mother would be taking her away and wanted her to have something to look forward to when she arrived in California. She also didn't want Clariana to succumb to the ways of her mother and her environment, causing her to give up on school due to financial responsibilities.

When they arrived at the apartment, Anais was there waiting for them. Clariana got out of the car, and Anais walked to the driver's side door just as Yanira was putting the car in reverse to pull out.

Yanira rolled down the window and said, "Hello Anais," with a big Olympic smile on her face.

Anais was shocked and pissed. "I was expecting to see Kaeo, not you."

"Well, Anais, he does not want to see you. He is still a little upset about last night. Maybe you can call him later to discuss whatever you need to."

Anais looked at her as if she wanted to say thank you, but she also could not understand why she was being so nice. Just a while ago, she had blacked her eyes, broken her nose, and bashed her head on the floor. Anais looked at her ring and snickered, then turned her back and went to get her daughter.

Yanira was not phased at all; she had long ago realized that Anais had some mental issues, and she had used her beauty to hustle people for a long time. Maybe it was done to her, or perhaps she was taught to act this way, but either way, it no longer worked on Kaeo, and she knew there was nothing to worry about. She and her man were fully committed to one another, and Anais was no longer a threat. She had hung herself with her actions.

When she arrived home, Kaeo was waiting in the living room for her. He greeted her and asked, "How did it go?"

She explained, "It was fine. Anais wanted to speak with you but realized it was me in the truck, so I told her to try you later."

Kaeo looked at her with his handsome face, and at that moment, he understood why he loved her so much. She was nurturing, mature, respectful, intelligent, outgoing, and feisty; he loved it all. He picked her up and decided to carry her to their bedroom for a lovemaking session. He wanted to give her undeniable pleasure.

Once in the room, Kaeo turned on the alarm, stripped her down, and ate her for brunch. Gobbling her wetness, he kept her ass up high to ensure he tasted everything she shed. After 15 minutes of wolfing down her pussy and juice, he pulled her toward the edge of the bed. He stood there, lifted her legs, spread them wide, then pulled them up to his shoulder and inserted his thick, caramel cock into her still warm and wet pussy. She let out a sigh as she prepared herself for the hard steel that entered her. Kaeo drove full throttle into her like a crash car dummy. He was on the go, giving her all he had to give, bending down and resting his arms on the bed as he continued to plow into her, giving her sex and all his love.

Yanira couldn't hold back the flooding from her body; she felt him deep inside her walls. It was magnificent, and she let out squeals and light screams. Kaeo smiled as he knew she loved to have sex with him; he climbed on top of her, kissing all over her lips and breasts and scraping into her as intensely as her body allowed. Kaeo started to feel more excited. His movements began to come more swiftly. He could feel her walls; they were tight and closing in on him. Each time he entered and exited all but the head of his penis, he heard a swishing noise escaping from her. He continued pouncing in and out, going deeper and deeper. At every entry, he dropped his head but kept fucking. She felt so good; he smelled the sweet scent of her perfume, and it drove him wild. Kaeo stopped and rolled her over; he wanted a ride from his woman. Yanira was ready. She took hold of him and slid down his pole. Working her magic, she pushed forward while her ass cheeks surrounded his lower half, grinding on his dick as if she wanted him to reach her throat from below.

Kaeo released but regained full hardness in seconds. Yanira rolled her ass with more intent, milling into his hips until she felt her walls crash; Kaeo flipped her over again and went so deep she screamed out and grabbed his shoulders, scratching his back with her nails. He loved this; his stroke game was vigorous.

Deeper, harder, and stronger, Kaeo leaned in and kept digging until he yelled out, "Damn, Yani, Shit, ahh Fuck!!"

Yanira felt him even more as he began to explode. She, too, had reached her pinnacle point, yelling, "Kaeo ahh, umm," as he plowed one last time.

The two lay naked and tapped out. They fell asleep with him lying on her belly as she rubbed his hair until she dozed off too. Their sessions always got the best of them, tiring them out and taking up all of their energy.

## CHAPTER 3: MOVING ON

On Tuesday, Yanira received good news. The inquiry and paperwork she previously filled out for Clariana came back, and she would receive a $35k scholarship for her first two years of college. Clariana was smart, and her grades allowed her to receive the highest amount as long as she went to school for clinical education.

Time was moving fast, and Clariana ended up staying in school to take additional core classes for college during the last three months of the school year. She tested so well that she only had one core class per day because math was not her strong suit. Kaeo allowed her to drive his truck while he drove Yanira's Jaguar, and she drove her new Audi. The family dynamic was well in place, and they all strived to make the others happy and go with the flow.

On Clariana's last day of school, Yanira asked her not to make any plans for Friday night because they would be going out to dinner in her honor. She could bring two guests of her choice. Yanira knew one would be her mother and the other her best friend. She was hoping that Anais would be on her best behavior; however, Ryleigh knew where she would be just in case things went left and she ended up going to jail.

The trio met at the condo around 4 pm; it was not only Clariana's last day of school but also her birthday, and she was as happy as ever. Shortly after, the friend she invited to dinner arrived; it was her best friend, Laine, with whom she hung out every weekend in some form or fashion. Yanira had a surprise for them both.

Yanira asked Clariana, "Where is your second guest?"

Clariana answered, "One was busy, and I didn't invite the other."

Yanira gave her a look, then said, "Listen, if it is your mother, it is ok. I don't want you to feel like you can't have her around, and I will never tell you not to include your mother on such a special occasion. It is your night. We just want you to enjoy it and be happy and proud of your accomplishment. So really, it's ok; invite her."

Clariana screamed happily. She picked up her phone to invite her mother, asking her to please come and celebrate her special night. She wanted everyone to be supportive and make this one night special. Her mother agreed and said she would meet her there at 6 pm. Kaeo looked at Yanira and shook his head in disbelief that she would be humble enough after everything Anais had put them through to allow her to share this moment with them. He was definitely not thrilled to spend the evening with Anais, but for his daughter's sake, he would.

Yanira said, "Ok, we have one hour to get dressed and make this happen. Here are our outfits for the night."

Clariana had a puzzled look on her face, and so did Kaeo; he was surprised himself. Yanira bought a new dress for Clariana: a pink, four-strapped, flowing dress that came to her thighs with her back out. She also had matching pink heels and a blue jacket to cover herself. Clariana screamed even louder than before. She was so excited, hugging Yanira as if she had bought her a new convertible.

It was cute and sexy, yet not too much for an 18-year-old young woman. For Kaeo, she bought him a blue suit with a pink bowtie; he smiled at her taste. It was something he would not have picked, but he loved it and would wear it proudly for his daughter.

After much inspection, he countered, "I can work with that."

Yanira had gotten herself a long, blue, off-shoulder, sleeveless dress with pink and blue stilettos and a matching pink clutch purse. She had already warned her friends to wear pink. She had also told the other friend to meet them at dinner one week ago, which is why she was busy.

Sixty-two minutes later, everyone was dressed and ready to go. Before leaving the house, they took turns taking pictures of one another and in groups. When they arrived at Kaye La Chino's new Italian American Steakhouse, which specialized in steaks, gourmet gelato, ice cream, and coffee, Clariana's other friend, Sierra, was waiting for them at the entrance. Anais had not arrived.

The reservations were made for the VIP table with a view of the entire restaurant. The girls were amazed at how high the ceilings were and all the lavish décor, plus they saw a few celebrities and their kids in the building as they walked in. Some of the celebrities knew Kaeo and Yanira from the club, so they spoke briefly and allowed the girls to take pictures with them since it was Clariana's birthday.

While at dinner, everything was perfect, although Anais still had not shown up. Clariana was not mad because she had met celebrities and posted on her Instagram, Facebook, and Snapchat. All the kids from school began liking her posts, and the ones she was not associated with, who saw others liking and commenting, had now sent her friend requests. She was the talk of the school and graduation class on social media.

The group sat at the restaurant for 2 hours, enjoying photos, appetizers, salads, entrees, and desserts mixed with coffee. Kaeo was annoyed that Anais was late and couldn't even be on time for her daughter's birthday. After two hours and twenty minutes and all the social media posts, Anais decided to show up. She called her daughter to come out and get her, but Clariana told her they were about to leave the table and exit the restaurant, so they would all meet her out front.

Anais hugged her and smiled at her beautiful attire. "Oh, mami, you are gorgeous. I love this dress! Where did you get it?"

Clariana was hesitant to answer but knew her mother expected a response. "I don't know. Yanira bought our outfits; it was a surprise to dad and I."

Anais looked at her once more, then at Kaeo and Yanira. "Hmm, she would try to dress you like her. Well, it is cute." She was smug and turned her head.

"Well, on that note, it is time to go," Kaeo demanded. He promised Yanira that he would be on his best behavior regardless of what Anais said or did, for Clariana's sake, so it was best that he did not comment further on any of Anais' antics.

"Clariana, your mother is welcome to meet us at the next location. It is the same place we saw her a few weeks ago," Yanira chimed in, throwing her own shade.

Kaeo looked at his woman, but this time he was annoyed. He could not believe she was taking the high road yet again and inviting Anais to anything after her smart-ass comment, but he knew it was all for his daughter. This was a testament of true love for him.

They left the restaurant and headed to the club to meet Ryleigh and Marshall. No one was there yet, but they had a photoshoot surprise with a personal photographer. Yanira had to call ahead to let her know that Anais would be there to take pictures with her daughter and not to panic or beat the hell out of her. Ryleigh was not happy, sending all types of fists, smacking, and bruised emojis. Yanira could not help but laugh; she showed Kaeo, and he said,

"I feel the same way. If it was not my baby's birthday, I wouldn't be mad at all."

Once they arrived, the valet opened their doors and let them out at the front of the club. They screamed yet again. Ryleigh and Marshall had set up photo booths on each floor with different themes. The photographer took over 200 photos of the group, several of just Clariana, then pics with her dad, her mom, and her friends. Anais asked Kaeo for a family photo, so Kaeo grabbed Yanira and placed her right in front of him next to Clariana.

Anais was pissed, but Kaeo didn't care. It was his way of letting her know that whatever they had was dead. This was his family. They hit the other floors, taking selfies and photos with the Latin theme, then posting online again. Her social status had gone up a couple of notches, with 200 new friends and 1500 new likes all in one day. The girls were excited.

They were prepared to leave once the club opened at 10 pm but paused to take selfies in front of the line as if they were going in; IG and FB messages were coming in left and right. Once they exited, they made sure that Anais was held back just a few minutes so she would not follow them, then made both girls turn off their location now that they were done celebrating. The girls thought nothing of it because they were in the clouds.

Entering the door at Yanira's place, the girls noticed she had decorated the living room and kitchen in pink and blue with balloons everywhere. On the couch, she had bags with each of their names on them, containing swimsuits and large beach towels so they could enjoy the hot tub and make all the noise they wanted. Yanira and Kaeo made sure they had plenty of snacks, sodas, candy, chips, and ice cream. The trio stayed up until 2:30 am when their sugar rush ended; all three crashed in Clariana's room after a spectacular evening.

In the bedroom, Kaeo told Yanira, "You are amazing, you know! I cannot believe all you've done for Clariana, considering all that she and her mother have put you through, especially Anais. I mean I am at a loss for words."

Yanira responded, "Sometimes, as adults, we have to lead by example; children are often a product of their environment. Clariana was only acting out towards me as a result of her mother and her negative connotations about me and our relationship. I mean, Clariana has worked hard in school and has changed her attitude, so she deserved everything she received."

Kaeo took her tongue and snatched her soul from her. He grabbed her by the waist, pulling her into him, then grasping each item covering her body and taking it off her skin. Starting with her nipples, he stroked them both and began gnawing on them, kissing and sucking. He made his way to the bed and pleasured her with his hands as he continued groping her upper body.

Yanira was reaching her breaking point when Kaeo paused. He looked up at her, whispering, "No, not yet. I want to feel that." He tore off his clothes, climbed on top of her, and entered her dam; it was wet and slushy. Kaeo gave her 5 pumps of good wood, and she conceded, freeing her flow.

Once she poured out, he followed suit. She was so wet he couldn't wait or hold on to his explosion any longer. He collapsed on her body, breathing heavily. Yanira could not help but smile as she lay underneath him; she felt the same way. Their sex was so extraordinary that she felt like she had found the best lover in the world—no other man could please her like Kaeo.

She smiled as he rolled over to look at her, saying, "What?"

"Yanira, I am so glad you said yes. I have never had so much pleasure in pleasing a woman the way I do with you. I thought I had great sex before, but with you, nothing compares to what and how I feel when we make love or have talks, even as simple as me just admiring your beauty. I just love you so much. I can't imagine having my life and not spending it with you. You truly are the woman of my dreams."

Tears rolled from her eyes. No one had ever said anything so sweet to her, and it made her melt. "Baby, I love you too; I can't imagine life without you either. I have loved you for so long, and I know that I will only love you for the rest of my life; even resting in heaven, I know you will still be the love of my life. Thank you for loving me the way you do!"

Kaeo held and cuddled with Yanira for the rest of the night. Anytime she moved he adjusted his body to her comfort; he would never allow her to know what it felt like to not be in his arms. He loved this woman and the man she was teaching him to be. He thought to himself as he watched her drift off to sleep, "Where was she 12-plus years ago when he needed a good woman? He suffered so much with Anais and missed out on so many intricate pieces in a relationship that he never knew existed. Anais had groomed him to be the man she wanted him to be; however, he had not once thought about the kind of woman he wanted until he met Yanira.

At that moment, he remembered his mother saying, "He will allow you to see what you can endure, give you strength to endure it, and then he will bless you with things far beyond your imagination. Always wait on him, son, and never question his choices for you. He knows what is best more so than you!" He could only smile at the thought.

The next day, Yanira and Kaeo woke up around 10 am, tired and hungry from their long night of lovemaking. While the girls were still asleep, they made brunch: Waffles, eggs, bacon, sausages, chicken tenders, mac n cheese, French toast, and fruit. The girls woke up from the smell of the food around 11:30 am. The girls ate just about everything that was cooked. Kaeo looked at them. "How can you eat so much and be so little." They all laughed and shrugged their shoulders. Each one of them was small and petite!

Shortly after brunch, Clariana asked, "Yanira, would you mind if the girls could stay with me one more night after graduation? We don't want to go to any of the parties!"

Yanira looked at Kaeo, and he smiled. "Yes, they can as long as their parents are ok with it."

The girls had already told their parents, and both were ok with them staying. Yanira changed their reservations from 4 to 6 people. This was the last surprise she had for Clariana, but it was a surprise for Kaeo as well. She advised her to invite her mother again if she wanted to. Everyone helped clean the kitchen, and then they all went back down for a nap and promised to be ready for dinner. After partying so much, they just wanted to get more rest.

\*\*\*\*\*\*\*\*\*\*\*\*\*\*\*\*\*\*\*\*\*\*\*\*\*\*\*\*\*\*\*\*\*\*\*\*\*\*\*\*\*\*\*\*\*\*\*\*\*\*\*\*\*

After an hour and a half of prepping they went to the graduation. Yanira had out done herself again with their outfits. Clariana had on a white dress similar to the one she wore yesterday with gold high heels and a gold clutch purse. Kaeo had on a linen suit with a collared shirt that matched Yanira's gold shoes. The girls also wore gold as well. Yanira had on white to match their friend. The graduation started at 4 pm and since there were only 80 students, they were hopefully going to make their 7:30 pm reservation.

Graduation was amazing! The children's speeches, along with the words of encouragement from the commencement speakers, were very well received by those young and old. It was not long and drawn out but went by in a flash. They were out of the parking lot by 6:47 pm heading to Top Sea & Spice Thai Seafood for dinner, arriving with five minutes to spare. Kaeo pulled up to valet and they all exited. As usual the girls posted every moment of the day. Anything they could take a picture in front of they did. The girls sat down and ordered all sorts of appetizers and a meal each and one to share. Kaeo laughed at their appetite, they were not shy girls who worried about their size 6 figures.

As usual, Anais was super late, showing up just as they were ordering dessert. Once dessert was over, Yanira stood, tapped on her glass, and began to speak.

"May I have everyone's attention please. Now that Anais is here, I think we can provide you with your final gift and I think it will seal the deal on this purposeful celebration. Clariana, you have worked so hard since I've known you, and we have had plenty of conversations regarding your future. You have expressed consistently that you want to become a nurse and get into the nursing program at

California University once you leave us here in MIA. (Clariana was shaking her head yes and smiling. She had no clue as to what was next.) Remember when I told you I have a few people that may be willing to invest in your future? Well, they made good on their promise. Dr. Rodriguez, Dr. Manuel, Dr. Simons, Dr. Moore, and I, along with our hospital organization, would like to extend to you your first step into college. I present to you on behalf of those individuals named a scholarship check for $35k for your education, books, room, and board!!"

Clariana screamed loudly as the restaurant erupted into a round of applause. The waiter was videoing the entire time. Clariana cried, then rushed across the table to hug, and thank her.

Yanira told her, "Look into the camera and tell all those people who helped you thank you, along with your father, and your mother. I did not do this alone."

Clariana dried her face, then said, "To everyone who made this possible, thank you!! I cannot tell you how grateful I am to be in this position. You don't know how much this means to me. I am blessed; thank you. Hopefully, you will give me a job one day or an internship when I return with my degree!" Her friends laughed at her future plug for a job when she hadn't even started yet.

The restaurant gave her a standing ovation. Once they sat down, Yanira told her she would receive the same amount next year if she remained in school, so she must promise to go, make the grades, and make good on her promise. Kaeo had tears in his eyes, bewildered by what Yanira had done, by not even letting him know but giving him and Anais credit. His heart was overjoyed.

Clariana said, "Seriously? I don't even know what to say?"

Yanira said, "The university has also approved your grants and gave you a scholarship, plus you qualify for additional funds as well; however, you must maintain your grades and GPA. It has to be where it is now, a 3.4 or higher. That's the only catch, but it has already been arranged."

Anais sat there in amazement yet filled with anger. Yanira had outshined her again by making her daughter want to attend college, be a nurse like her, and by making her this happy over the money for school. She was pissed. Here it is this woman was trying to take her daughter away and make her a mini version of herself. That bitch! There was no way she would allow her to get away with this; she had gone way to far, stealing her man and her daughter. She was an all-around thief in her eyes and Yanira would surely pay for butting into her family and her business.

*****************************************************

The girls enjoyed their second night at Yanira's, pigging out on food and delighting in the hot tub with a million selfies. Kaeo and Yanira had some quiet time upstairs while the girls partied like rock stars downstairs. The night became morning, and eventually, they crashed.

The following day, they went to breakfast before Kaeo and Yanira dropped off the girls at their homes. Clariana was going with her mother as they were finally moving to Cali. Kaeo and Yanira hated to see her go but it was good because now she had her place solidified. She did not have to depend on anyone because she had a place of her own, and money in her bank account. Clariana was also not taking any time off. She was starting school that following week. Yanira was excited because she wanted Clariana to be stable and nothing like her mother. Although she could not say it without offending her, for some reason, she believed that Clariana knew her purpose as well.

Finally, Kaeo moved in with Yanira. He had packed up his condo and sold everything except for living room furniture and a few décor pieces he loved. He received a couple thousand for his items and gave it all to Yanira. In addition, he sold his condo for $23,000 more than he owed. Much to her surprise, his plan was to use those funds to build an indoor/outdoor patio for her. He had already hired a company to build them an enclosed living room deck on her back porch. They gave him an estimate of $15,000. Kaeo told them to get started as soon as possible and that he would be available to oversee the project.

On his first night, they decided to watch a movie, excited to officially be together under one roof. The movie had a sex scene, and Kaeo became aroused. Yanira watched him as he attempted to adjust himself underneath her.

"Baby, you, ok?"

"Yes, I just imagined that being you right there. Made me want to take you to the bedroom."

Yanira stood and tugged his hand. When they got to the stairwell, she said, "Wait, let me turn off the TV."

He sat on the last step and waited patiently. She returned and noticed his dick was now pointing at 12. As she leaned down to kiss him, she fell into him, and he pulled her into his lap. He pushed her legs open and with only a T-shirt on, her lips were easily accessible. Lifting up, he pulled his dick out of his pants and glided into her. He gave her a few thumps and realized he couldn't do what he needed to on the stairwell. He told her to "Hold on tight" while still inside of her, then he stood and held on to her cheeks so he could give her a stroke every step of the way.

He took his time making it to the top to ensure he stayed inside her as he fondled her from behind with his hands, giving her double pleasure. Once Kaeo got his woman to the master bedroom, he stood her up, bent her over, placed her knees on the bed, and directed her face down. He took charge satisfying her from behind, then flipped her over for the finale some hour and a half later!

*****************************************************

One week later, the work began; it took two and a half weeks. The crew did an amazing job installing all four glass windows, and a solar power light system, with heat for cold winter nights and ac for hot summer days. They installed a wide door that opened automatically when there was movement but was controlled at night with locks when not in use. The team also added an outdoor kitchen on the other side of the pool for cooking and grilling for an additional $2650.00.

Kaeo intended to pay for it all, at least he thought, until he handed the remaining balance to the gentleman, who said, "Sir, your balance is only $3000; your wife gave us funds a week ago for $4650.00."

Kaeo smiled. "She did, did she? Ok, hang on."

Kaeo wrote him another check for $3000, giving them a $300 cash tip for lunch that day. He knew they had given him a deal on all the hard work they had done. The men were all thankful and happy. Kaeo could not wait for Yanira to get home and see the finished product; he made her promise not to go out and look while the men worked.

That night Kaeo made Yanira a three-course dinner, picked up dessert, chilled a bottle of wine, and placed a candle in the new outdoor living room space. It was 6 pm when she got home after doing a couple of anesthetic preps that afternoon. All she wanted was to rest. When she walked in, she saw Kaeo holding a glass of wine in his hand. He grabbed her bags and told her to shower and head down when she could; dinner was ready. Yanira smiled. This warmed her heart after such a long day. She gave him three smooches and headed to shower.

Twenty minutes later, she went downstairs, where Kaeo was waiting patiently. He took her outside and into their new space. It was magnificent. She could not believe how beautiful her backyard looked. As she walked into the outdoor living space, the glass doors opened, and she was in awe. Kaeo had prepared a beautiful dinner for two with wine, candles, and all of her favorite things. He sat her down and served her as she smiled from ear to ear; their dinner date was fantastic.

After the meal and two bottles of wine, Yanira was feeling hot and horny. She mounted her man and gave him steamy kisses on his lips and upper body. She felt him rising beneath her, as she continued to melt him with kisses. She untied his pajama pants, pulled his dick out, and inserted it into her soaking-wet hot spot, ready and willing to take a long ride to K Town. Yanira rode Kaeo softly, with a medium glide, twirling her hips and ass as he gripped her for stamina and stability.

His eyes rolled to the ceiling as he squeezed her cheeks. His head fell back, and he couldn't help but let one off. He gave it to her hard, pulling and pushing into her as he quickly hardened again. He flipped her body and excavated into her walls gently while consuming her breasts. Yanira let out a whine; he felt so damn good. She pulled him down further to get more even though she struggled with what she had already; he made her want more.

Kaeo stood and spun her over, hitting it from the back. She immediately threw it back, but she began to pant as he was much deeper than she had expected. She let out a cry as she reached back, tugging at his hips. He slowed down to let her catch her breath. As she relaxed, he picked up speed, giving more power in each thrust. He could feel her tightening around him; she was ready to explode again, and so was he. Six more strokes were all he thought he needed, but she released in four, and when she released her ocean, so did he.

They ran to the shower to clean up, but the night didn't end there. Yanira went downstairs for a late-night snack and watched a little TV. She made a mini bed out of the sectional chaise and lay there watching a movie. Kaeo soon followed and snuggled with her on the chaise. Within ten minutes he was all over her saying, "Since there is no chicken to burn, let's go for round two."

He took her right there in the living room, and she didn't resist. Round two sounded like music to her ears. She hit the remote to turn on the slow jams music channel and intertwined her body with her man's. The rest of the night was one for the history books!

• • • • • • • • • • • • • • • • • • • • • • • • • • • • • • • • • • • • • • • • • • • • •

That Friday night the weather was gloomy and rainy. Yanira invited Ryleigh over for dinner to have a quiet night under the stars with wine, appetizers, and a full course meal. She cooked bruschetta, crab dip, lamb chops, grilled chicken breasts, garlic mashed potatoes and asparagus, her favorite; lastly, she made brownies, and red velvet cupcakes. When they arrived, Ryleigh was floored by the outdoor patio and backyard; she could not believe how it turned out. She was even kept away so she would not tell her cousin what was going on. Only her father and mother had gotten away with a sneak peek. The guys pounded one another and went on to grab drinks and chop it up about work and future plans.

"Righteous Kaeo! You did your thing. You make it hard for me, man. I may need to get some ideas from you because I can only imagine what type of shenanigans will go on out here after dark!" Marshall chuckled as he uttered the last words from his mouth.

Kaeo did the same. "Too late bro; we took full advantage already." Kaeo was visualizing it in just that instant.

"Man, I understand. You are so happy these days!"

"It's her Marshall; she is my world, and I am so glad that she is as patient and loving as she is and has been. I would have crumbled without her."

"Righteous words man. Our ladies are amazing seriously and I can't imagine any other way. Ry is the same. Like my businesses are flourishing because of her ideas. Our new ventures are coming into fruition because of her. I am so lucky I found her when I did. Otherwise, I would have just been lonely man. I couldn't settle."

"That's real talk. To us and our come up!" The men toasted one another, cheerful about their love and finding the right ones.

Their rainy night turned into a night of drinking, trash talking, board games, and having fun. They were so wasted off wine and Hennessy that Marshall and Ryleigh stayed over, since neither could make it out the door to drive home. Yanira missed those nights with her cousin and was super delighted to host her at their home. The club scene was great, but quality personal time was much more her speed.

# CHAPTER 4: TIME KEEPS PASSING

Yanira was pleasantly surprised to hear from Kalia, asking when they were visiting again. Kalia told her the family was having a reunion during spring break, and it would be nice if they could attend. She had already spoken with Kaeo but wanted to communicate with her, too, just in case he forgot. When Kaeo arrived home later that evening, Yanira had dinner waiting. They discussed going home for the week of spring break since the office was closed and she could take off from the hospital. Kaeo agreed; he said if she was cool with it, so was he, admitting it would be nice to see the family again, but this time they would stay at a hotel or rent a house on the beach. That was music to her ears.

Kaeo asked what she thought about Ryleigh and Marshall tagging along and she loved the idea. His family loved Ryleigh as she was often around when they Facetimed on Sundays, not to mention Kalia, and the young adults bragged about all the wonderful places Marshall and Ryleigh had taken them to when they visited. She called Ryleigh right after dinner, asking her if she and Marshall were interested and could get away; they were in. It would be a couple's vacation in Hawaii in one month's time.

The following day Yanira arrived home a little early; she had a slow day at work. Ryleigh and Marshall were coming over for dinner to hang out and discuss the upcoming trip to Hawaii. After a shower, she cooked a four-course meal, set the table outside for four, and chilled some Hennessy and wine. Ryleigh and Marshall arrived around 6:30 pm, and Kaeo around 6:45 pm. He told her he had forgotten that Ryleigh and Marshall were joining them for dinner and rushed to shower.

Kaeo had terrific news that he could not wait to share with everyone. He and his partner had bought another truck for business, and now he was the proud owner of four. Things were going great for him financially and romantically, not to mention his partner wanted to open another furniture store and have his son run it now that he had graduated from college. Life was coming together; they were making good business decisions, and he had been saving money since he was no longer with Anais. Yanira had her own and never asked him for money, so he saved thousands every month with no one to beg and take.

Together, he and Yanira were saving money on rent by staying in one household where he paid the mortgage and bills. They rarely ate out unless it was a weekend, and occasionally, he let her pay, unlike with Anais. She never offered nor had the money to pay for their family meals unless it was his money. Kaeo was all about family, and he was ready for Yanira to start planning their wedding.

Dinner started around 7:10 pm, but they began drinking immediately as they looked at homes to rent on the beach while waiting on Kaeo. Once he came down and noticed they were searching, he told them there was no need to look. His mother had spoken to his aunt, and her rental was available, so they were booked and ready; he had also made reservations for an SUV. His aunt and Kalia agreed to stop and grab some groceries and beverages for them before their arrival. Ryleigh was excited. She had been to many places, but neither she nor Marshall had ever been to Hawaii.

After they finished dinner, Marshall asked, "How is everything working with the new truck?"

Kaeo replied excitedly, "Man, I was going to announce the good news. I purchased a new one, and now we are also opening a new furniture store. We're hoping to get my partner's son to run it. If not, my sister can run it or at least help him."

They all toasted to his good news. Ryleigh also had good news. She and Marshall were going to start planning for a winter wedding this upcoming December in Jamaica and a baby, hopefully, next year. They were in love and had been together for four years now. It was time to slow down on the clubbing and do something different.

Kaeo said, "Aww man! Well, hey, with all that investing you are doing, you can chill for a while."

Marshall smiled at him and responded, "That is the plan."

They celebrated each other's good news and good fortune. Ryleigh and Marshall ended up staying the night because they had drunk too much Henny and wine.

Around 2 am, Yanira and Kaeo must have had the same idea because they both woke up. It seems they were up trying to put in some work. Yanira had Kaeo in the room howling as she rode him like she was riding a roller coaster with her hand up in the air taking the highs and lows. She had her back turned from him, slow motioning her ass on his pelvis. As she leaned down to grip the bed, she felt him getting harder, and proceeded to brace herself.

Kaeo softly ran his hands over her cheeks, squeezing that ass tight every time she came down on his shaft. When it was really good and she didn't go down far enough, he took one hand and cuffed her right breasts and held it so she would go deeper. Yanira cried out and lost control as Kaeo hit her spot. She felt him all in her stomach! Unable to help herself, Yanira splattered all over him.

She could feel the orgasm pouring out of her, but she continued to ride through it. She wanted more, so she grinded faster, then she did a slow grind, as Kaeo squeezed even more. They both were ready. Yanira leaned down closer to the bed, lifting her ass up and gliding back down with force. Kaeo couldn't help but bust one off, rising up off the bed to put it all in and so did she, releasing another water flood.

After this session, Yanira tapped out and within 4 minutes she was out. Kaeo knew anytime she went to sleep immediately he had done his job. He nestled next to her until he fell asleep himself.

Yanira slept in the next morning but woke up around 10 am to fix everyone's breakfast before they started their day. Ryleigh and Marshall left shortly after they finished the delicious meal.

••••••••••••••••••••••••••••••••••••••••

Thursday morning the group met at the airport for an early morning flight. They were scheduled to land at 6:45 pm in Hawaii, which allowed them to bypass any traffic and get plenty of time to sleep. When they arrived at the house it was breathtaking. The view made Marshall feel like he was home, beautiful trees, the smell of the ocean, and a cool breeze. They picked their rooms and came back down to check out the rest of the home.

No one was hungry until they smelled the food in the kitchen. Kaeo's mother and Kalia had dinner ready on the stove for them. There was chicken and steak, macaroni salad, steamed white rice, and poke. Kaeo warmed up the food while the rest of them spent time on the deck. Once he finished, they ate, chatted, took a walk on the beach enjoying the smell of the ocean and the cool breeze, then headed to bed. The reunion started the following day at 4 pm and would last until Sunday at 5 pm. The morning would be theirs to tour the islands. Kalia left a list of tours and places they could visit.

Friday morning, the group woke up to Kaeo's mother and father cooking breakfast. They were all so grateful and pleased to see one another again. Kaeo's father began the conversation by advising the group of the family reunion itinerary by saying, "We will start with an opening Luau to include dancing, traditional toga, and fireworks today, then Saturday we will have outdoor family games, family competition, BBQ, and a bonfire out on the private family beach. Sunday, everyone will attend lunch and a closing show with more fireworks."

The plan sounded good to Marshall. He loved family and gatherings, and all the traditions made him think of home. One thing about being in Jamaica, his family can and will have a party out of any event, and their family loved to celebrate one another. Just as his father described, the weekend went just as planned, and the rest of the trip went even better.

The group toured the entire island in five days, visiting different sides of the beach, along with shopping at all the family shops and local stores, tours, and museums. The island was beautiful; there were so many different people and cultures that co-existed in one place.

Kaeo's mother was the sweetest woman. She made dinner for three nights during the week and gave them a final sendoff dinner on their last night at her house with all of Kaeo's siblings.

Returning home from the trip was twofold; they had fun and loved the beach but knew it was short-lived as they all dreaded returning to work. Kaeo made sure everyone came back on Saturday as Sunday would be too much of a time adjustment knowing they had a long week ahead.

By Monday, Yanira was back to business with surgery preps, patients, and now planning for Ryleigh's upcoming wedding in just a few months and their wedding for next year. Kaeo and Yanira had talked with his mother, and they wanted to have a wedding there in Hawaii. Yanira would only concern herself with her parents, aunt, and uncle (Ryleigh's parents), and Ryleigh and Marshall. Anyone else could attend, but they would have to pay for their own accommodation. With the family property and advantages in Hawaii, the cost would be minimal because they owned land and had the perfect space for an outdoor wedding.

••••••••••••••••••••••••••••••••••••••••••

The summer months pushed past like the wind, and in a hurry. The couple tried to enjoy every ounce of fun they could at the house or the club with Ryleigh and Marshall. Clariana even came to visit for two weeks and stayed with them. They threw a pool party in her honor to celebrate how well she was doing in school with a 3.75 GPA.

The party was a success as she invited her two close friends, a few others, and the doctors from her practice with their young adult children. Marshall invited some of his nieces and nephews as well. There was BBQ and seafood on the menu. Yanira's mom and Aunt cooked up all sorts of side dishes, while Kaeo, her father, uncle, and Marshall manned the grills and the seafood boil.

Clariana and her friends had matured just a little so social media was not the big deal that it had previously been, nor was it that cool in college; they did, however, post everything under the sun except the address.

## CHAPTER 5: MENDING FENCES

The time for Ryleigh and Marshall's wedding in Jamaica had finally arrived. Yanira was her maid of honor, and Marshall's sisters and two of her friends were the bridesmaids. Marshall's brother was his best man, his business partner, and close friends, along with Kaeo were his groomsmen. The wedding took place on a beach at a beautiful resort in Ocho Rios. Marshall took over the resort, renting out just about every room since all the family and friends that traveled to celebrate their union stayed on site. The resort planned it all under Ryleigh's detailed instructions.

The wedding was phenomenal. Ryleigh was stunning; she wore a white wedding gown that fit her body perfectly, showing curves for days. Her veil was simple, covering only the top portion of her face. Ryleigh was naturally gorgeous, so she only needed light makeup, and since she was an AKA, her colors were accented with green and salmon. Her stilettos were one-of-a-kind, made by one of her sorority sisters, with a pink and green design. The men matched her in her color scheme as well. There was not a dry eye in the hotel during the ceremony.

The reception was incredible; they had all sorts of foods, pastries, and beverages. There was dancing and different genres of music, along with toasts, surprises, and gifts for the couple. Following the reception was the after-party with all of Marshall's friends and the few of her sorority sisters Ryleigh invited. It was a night to remember, with twerking, popping, shaking, grinding, and riding.

As the crowd continued to get wild and dirty, Yanira and Kaeo snuck off to a cabana right in front of the beach on the far side, where they had nothing but privacy. The two snuggled up, listening to the waves, staring into each other's eyes as they discussed how beautiful the wedding was. They began to talk about their event and how it would be good if it were nothing but family. They wanted the ceremony to be small and intimate with less than 50 people, but the reception would be open to everyone. Just the thought of their special day made Kaeo hunger for love from Yanira. He crawled under her dress, hiding his head between the fabric and her legs, sucking the juice right out of her, allowing her to bust two, as he rose to the occasion to bust a couple of his own.

Not stopping there, he manhandled her pussy in the cabana, making the wooden rods shake, rattle, and rock as he drilled into her insides. Yanira let out so many sounds that Kaeo couldn't help but resume pulsating her body even after the first two rounds. Her soft voice made him eager to please. Kaeo knew he was doing his job, but he had to slow down as he had become so excited. It was easy to quickly let go of a series of orgasms when he was with Yanira, so he decided to pace himself and allow his heart rate to slow down.

She came again, and he pumped more intensely after he felt her warmth. No longer able to control the passion that he had worked so hard to maintain, Kaeo burst instantly, and much to his surprise, it was a great one because she let go of another. The two lay there breathless, trying to catch their wind. They lay watching the sunset and the waves crash against one another for another hour. Kaeo held her closely. Soon after, they sneaked back to the party before anyone noticed they were gone or before anyone had the same thoughts.

On Tuesday night Kaeo received a strange call from an unlisted number and sent it to voicemail. Yanira told him that if it was from California, he should answer in case it was Clariana. They went to shower, and when he returned, the number had called back again, leaving a message this time. It was his son, well Anais's son, Cordero. Kaeo had not spoken with him since the altercation at the gas station. Her son stated that he was in town and wanted to meet with him for lunch or maybe dinner.

After hearing the voicemail, Yanira commented, "Well, that was sweet. You should go so that you can have closure. He was a kid listening to his mother and was given false information. Besides, Clariana already told you she explained what she knew from that night, and so did he; so, you might be surprised by this meeting. I think you should go, baby."

Kaeo was hesitant, telling her, "Baby, I am not sure if that is a good idea. I mean I love Cordero, and he is my son, but I do not want to argue over the incident or rehash old wounds."

Yanira looked at her man and simply said, "Go!"

Kaeo listened to his woman and met up with his son the following day for lunch.

During lunch, Cordero apologized to Kaeo for the way he had acted toward him that night of the fight. He explained that his mother had convinced him and his uncle that Kaeo was cheating, lying, and taking from her. Anais said he was taking her money and not paying the bills but giving it to another woman, and the woman was the one he was riding with that evening. He claimed only recently did he find out the entire truth when Clariana visited him.

Cordero stated they talked more when she came to see his newborn son. She told him of the fake pregnancies, all the lies, the fight between her and Yanira and how she left her hanging and they changed their plans. He added that Clariana told him about the entire incident and how his mother failed to be a motherly figure for her, how she used her, and how Yanira helped her get a scholarship and gave her money for school. He said Clariana tried to tell him before, but he truly realized the magnitude of his mother's selfish and manipulating ways when she turned against him, his wife, and his mother-in-law.

Cordero told Kaeo that he was the first man to teach him how to be a man and many other life lessons that he always took for granted. He wanted to apologize and make amends because he was the only father he had known since his father passed away. Kaeo was amazed at the maturity of Cordero and how he took the time to meet with him on his family vacation. Cordero asked if he could introduce him to his family as they would be arriving soon. Kaeo was honored.

Cordero was married now with a son, and when they arrived, he noticed the little boy looked just like him. His wife took photos of their reunion and told him it was nice to meet him. Kaeo told him if he had time again before they left to call him, maybe he could meet his fiancé Yanira, and they could all do lunch or dinner. They agreed before parting ways, stating they were only there for a wedding and had no other plans so it would be great to have something else to do.

On the other side of town, Yanira waited patiently for Kaeo to arrive home that night; she was worried about his meeting with Cordero and if everything was okay. She had been busy most of the afternoon and could not call. Kaeo came home around 6 pm; he brought her flowers and a card, greeting her with a kiss and a thank you. She did not know what he was thanking her for, just that he must have had a good day.

Kaeo explained that everything in his life was coming together, both old and new. His son had a son and asked for forgiveness for what he had done to him almost four years ago, admitting that he was under his mother's thumb, and only until recently had he realized how bad she was. He thanked her for being his motivation, his rock, convincing him to take the call, agreeing to be his wife, and loving him unconditionally.

Yanira was elated with his news. She was glad to see Kaeo bringing closure to his life. Whether he stayed connected or not, that time of his life was now over, and the baggage he was carrying had been removed. Yanira shared his joy and thought it was extremely sweet that he found happiness in his closure and found a way to incorporate her. Kaeo ended the conversation by telling her that he wanted her to meet his son and maybe have lunch with him if they had time before returning to California.

She asked, "Are you sure he is up for that? Or better yet, what will Anais think or do?"

Kaeo replied, "Yes, he is. He wants to thank you for what you did for his sister. He and his mother are not on speaking terms; he finally sees her for who she is like the rest of us."

*************************************************

Yanira made sure she was mentally prepared for the lunch meeting with Kaeo's son and his family in case things went left. Since he had a son, she recommended taking them to The Candy Factory; they had great food and plenty of good choices for adults, along with treats and ambiance for kids.

Much to her surprise, the young man was the male version of his sister but very handsome, sweet, and kind. His wife was just as beautiful inside and out. Immediately upon seeing her, Cordero shook her hand and told her it was genuinely nice to meet her, thanking her for all she had done.

As they dined, Cordero told her all the stories of how Kaeo was such a good father figure in his life and always took care of him, his uncle, and his sister. It was only in the last year of their relationship that his mother had planted seeds in his head about Kaeo and all the things he had supposedly done; he was too naïve to know or think his mother was the problem all along. Stating even though he never seen his father do anything bad, he noticed there were always woman throwing themselves at him or trying to get his attention. He thought that maybe he had given into one of them because his mother was so convincing.

Cordero explained how he remembered the night Kaeo was attacked by Anais.

"That night, she came home asking how we got to school and how dad got to work. We explained we were not sure, but he woke us up, fixed breakfast, and made sure we got on the bus. He was still at home when we left. My uncle told her that someone picked him up in a fancy car. Mom told us that he was cheating on her and abusive towards her, and that is why she didn't come home. My uncle and I were enraged and couldn't believe Dad would hit her; he had told us never to do it, so we told her that didn't seem right. She showed us a bruise, so we wanted to make him pay for what he had done. We hid in the car, and she told us when to get out to help her hit him because he would attack her for sure. When we got out and started wrestling with him, he never hit us, nor her. We didn't think about it at the time. We just wanted to protect her. Not for one minute did we know she was the one cheating, lying to us, and using us as pawns.

I heard my uncle arguing with her two nights after the attack, saying if he cheated, then why do you keep calling him? Then he asked her if she had seen him? She told us no, so he asked her how come she had another bruise, this time it was on her face. It was then we knew it was not from my dad, so my uncle felt ashamed. He told her that he didn't trust her anymore and that he had ruined a relationship with his brother-in-law because of her. He later told me if I was smart, I would get away from her as soon as I could. Soon after he left for California to live with his cousin and then I followed him and left a year later."

It was the beginning and end for Kaeo; he was able to truly get closure on how things went down in detail with Anais and why his son and brother-in-law would attack him. If all he had was his children, he was fine with that. The group took pictures and Cordero agreed to see them if they were ever in town again and promised to stay in touch.

************************************************

A few days later, as Kaeo exited the building and walked to his car for lunch, he felt a hand brush up against him and squeeze him from the back. It was Anais, stating,

"Hey Lover. I want to talk with you if you have the time," in a tone she considered her sexy voice.

Kaeo agreed, "Sure Anais. Talk and walk, I'm listening, but I do not have much time."

"Can we go inside your workplace?"

Kaeo retorted quickly, "No, we cannot. We can speak here in public, not privately, nor in my place of business."

Anais did not like his answer, but she knew she had to butter him up first to break down the wall.

"Well lover, I just wanted to apologize to you for the way things happened. I have thought over everything, my actions, and the mistakes I've made many times, and I am sorry for all that I have put you through."

Kaeo was surprised because usually she would manipulate him, but never had she ever said the words I am sorry. He thought maybe, after all this time, she was finally realizing that she was the problem.

"This is very surprising to hear, Anais. I do not think I have ever heard you apologize and being genuine about it at that. I appreciate your kind words and your time, the apology especially. It was nice of you, but I need to get going."

Anais stated, "We should have lunch together."

Kaeo declined saying, "No, we shouldn't, and you know I am with Yanira."

At that moment, Anais lashed out, saying, "You can make time for everyone else but not me? You parade your stupid girlfriend around with my children, but you refuse to have lunch with me? I saw the pictures of our son on social media with you and her. You continue to disrespect me all for this girl. You allow her to insult me. Why would you do this? She hit me and embarrassed me. Why do you allow her to? She should be in jail for what she did to me!"

Kaeo was not surprised to see the real scheme Anais was cooking up. He replied to her,

"Anais, I was doing fine after you left me. You brought Clariana to me, knowing that I had moved on; that's on you. As far as Cordero, you are the reason he and Yanira met. You, your lies, and your manipulation are the reason they are open to loving their dad again. As a matter of fact, how could you lie to Cordero and your brother, allowing them to think I would hit you? What is wrong with you? You have burned your bridges in California, and now he is coming to me for forgiveness because you wronged us all. You did this to yourself. No one forced you to become this evil of a person. Please just leave me alone, Anais."

She refused to accept his words. "No, that is not true; if you would have just come back to me, then none of this would have happened. This time should not have been any different than before. I need you back with me, Kaeo. I know you miss me and the things I do to you: our sex (she rubbed her body against his), our lovemaking, and the freaky places. Tell me you don't miss this."

Kaeo pushed her off him and laughed at her. "Anais, you are a piece of work. Not once did you say I love you. No, you just said you need me back, only to support you. There is nothing romantic about us. And she is not meeting kids; they are adults. It is their choice, not yours or mine."

Anais yelled, "Forget about her and give that ring to me! If you don't, you know what I will do to her. Remember the others and what I did to them? She can suffer the same fate or worse! Besides, you love me, not her so let's quit playing this game before I get angry."

Kaeo got angry and walked closer to Anais. "And remember what happened to you in the club? If you try something else, you had better have an army; she is not like the others. If I find out, trust me, it will be hell for you; I will never come back to you, Anais. Move on and move out of my way. I am not playing your games, and I do not appreciate your threats. And by the way, I don't miss you. Yanira is much better at everything, and she will give me exactly what I need and the child I have always wanted. She won't fake it and lie to me about it." Kaeo turned to open his car door.

As he was shutting the door she yelled, "I will never allow her to give you children!! No one will give you children. NEVER!! I will make sure of that, and you better think about that wedding of yours." Kaeo drove off without looking back.

Later that afternoon, as Yanira updated patient charts and filed paperwork, she received a call on her desk phone. It was Kaeo calling to check on her and see how her day was going. She told him it was fine and that she was ready to get home. She suggested they take it easy and enjoy a night out on the deck, maybe cook something light. Kaeo agreed and ended the call.

When she got home, Kaeo seemed disturbed. She immediately knew it was something about or to do with Anais and began thinking what she could have done or said this time. Kaeo rose as she walked in the door, asking, "How was your day my love? You ok?"

Yanira replied with normal answers but noticed this concerned look on his face. She sat him down and asked this time, "Babe, what is wrong?"

Kaeo opened up instantly. "I had a visit from Anais today at work; she apologized for all that she had done to me, then told me she needed me back. I refused her and then she threatened to harm you, stating she would not allow her family to be taken away from her by some woman." Kaeo seemed very worried about her, and Yanira didn't understand why.

As they talked, Kaeo explained. "We broke up a few times when we were younger, and once I began dating another girl. Anais threatened the girl, slapped her several times, and cut off all her hair. The next time I found out a girlfriend of mine had been cut in the face by Anais. I liked them both, but the girls no longer wanted anything to do with me afterward. From then on, no one in our town would talk to me or look at me. When we moved to New York, the same thing happened. Although this girl was not scared, she said it was too much drama with Anais and two kids. My reputation was that I had a dramatic life; I was a playboy with kids, and no one wanted to date me. I fear that you will do the same because there is no telling what Anais would do to you. I love you, and I am so tired of losing people over Anais. You, of all, are my world, Yanira. You are the perfect woman for me, and I don't want to lose you."

Yanira was confident that she would not try her, especially since she was beaten up in front of everyone. She knew she had the upper hand in a one-on-one, but if there were several, it could be an issue. Nonetheless, she never admitted to Kaeo, but she carried a 9 MM Magnum and was not afraid to use it. Yanira didn't have time, nor was she worried that Anais was in town. This was her city, and she was not going to play these games with Anais. She had a wedding to plan.

Yanira responded, "Baby, I love you just the same. I will never allow her craziness to come between us as long as I know you are loyal to me and our relationship. You have my word. No matter how hard it gets, I will not give up on you."

That gave Kaeo so much relief. She took his hand and led him up the stairs. She stripped him down along with herself and they climbed in the shower. Yanira rubbed his bare chest, kissing his neck, then fondling his sack with one hand. Kaeo returned her kisses, rubbing her body gently. He lifted her up and turned around to sit on the bench, sucking her neck softly, then he took his hand and inserted his dick inside her. Kaeo kept it slow, making sure she knew he was making pure love to her. It was more than just sex, or some void he needed to fill; he wanted a commitment and someone who would not give up on the love he could provide.

The hot water running on her back soothed the entry way and she swayed in and out of submission. Yanira felt his rise. Grabbing his neck and hair, she began to grip it tight, bouncing rapidly as her excitement and explosion built. Kaeo was equally excited, and both started to pant as they felt the climax coming to a head. Yanira pulled his head backwards as she released and Kaeo gripped her ass downward for his. Their mixture dripped all over the slower floor as they stood to wash.

After dinner and cleaning the kitchen, they lay in bed with no TV, just cuddling. Kaeo massaged her back, giving her the unconditional love they both needed in that moment. Yanira was the only person who could loosen his tension or cure his anger; she had his heart.

••••••••••••••••••••••••••••••••••••••••••••••

For the next two days, Kaeo called her or texted her every couple of hours throughout the day. Yanira did not understand this woman and why she was so violent and fixated on him. This worry he had was too much, but obviously he had good reason. Their wedding was happening in less than six months, and she was not about to stop planning or bow out. They had spent too much time and money.

Friday night was date night. Normally, they would go to the club, but it was Valentine's Day, so they decided on dinner and a walk through the botanical gardens. The couple dressed up from head to toe. Yanira wore a red, three-quarter sleeve, skew neck dress with a split to her thigh, some silver open-toed pumps, and a matching handbag.

Once they arrived, they saw Ryleigh and Marshall walking through the door. The four met up, ate, drank, and laughed. Marshall and Ryleigh discussed how wonderful married life had been. They were glowing and so in love. After dinner, they headed to the club to check on things since his partner was on vacation. They invited Kaeo and Yanira, but they declined, deciding instead to go and walk off their meal. The two strolled, stopping to take pictures of the different artistic features, paintings, and statues. This kept them busy for two hours. Afterward, they left to go home and have a quiet night out in the hot tub. On the ride home, Kaeo couldn't help but smile as he watched Yanira sit patiently waiting to spend more quality time with her man.

When they pulled into the driveway, she glanced over and noticed his smile; he was so handsome. Not wanting to wait or take too much time away from their night, she told him to go and grab two towels from upstairs so they could skinny dip. Without his knowledge she had previously decorated outside earlier that day, putting out some rose petals, a bottle of champagne, and chocolate-covered strawberries in the fridge. When he came back down, he walked out and noticed her standing in front of the hot tub butt-ass naked with her stilettos still on. The tray and bottle were resting on the side. He smiled brightly and mischievously; he was about to put in some work.

As he walked over to her, he began taking his shirt off. He reached her, opened her slightly parted lips further, snatched her tongue, and intertwined it with his. Grabbing fists full of breasts, he slid his hands down to her ass, pulled her up on the edge, took off her shoes, and ate his dessert right there on top of the hot tub. She let out soft cries and moans. Holding on to his head and the edge, clenching her muscles as he worked on her, she was ready to give out. Kaeo unbuckled his pants, picked her up, and held her hand as she stepped into the water. He joined her once he was naked.

As he eased in and sat, she mounted him, climbing on top of him and closing down on his manhood. "Ahh shit," he said. She felt fantastic. He stood up and held her as she rode his dick with the sounds of the waves from the water. He stayed ready around her, bending her over and fucking her from the back until she was screaming and panting for air. She took hold of his neck, whispered in his ears, then threw her ass back into him. The more she threw, the more he roared inside her walls. She finally caved and exploded; her wetness sent him into a trance. He sprayed and collapsed right with her on the edge of the hot tub.

They sat there and talked for over two hours about work, the wedding, plans, and anything else that came to mind before retreating to the shower and bed.

# **CHAPTER 6: DRAMA AT ITS FINEST**

Wednesday evening, Anais resurfaced in their lives after a long hiatus. She showed up at Kaeo's store right when he was finishing paperwork, telling him she heard about the wedding in Hawaii, and he had better call it off because she was going to ruin it. When Kaeo refused she began causing a scene, and damaging furniture in a rage. Anais used a razor to cut a couch and some leather furniture pieces, then knocking down two glass tables and a kitchen set. Kaeo tried to calm her down, but she would not listen. She was hurt that Kaeo was going through with the marriage to Yanira and not her. It was clear she had become obsessed.

Anais screamed, "If you go through with this wedding, I will hurt Yanira and you!! I will not let you leave me like this and marry someone else. You always said it would be me!"

Kaeo yelled, "Anais, what are you doing? Come on! This is going too far; this is my place of business. Stop threatening me and just move on!"

Anais went crazy; she was erratic, violent, and full of jealousy. After a brief struggle, Kaeo was able to get a hold of her to subdue her. The police arrived shortly afterward, taking Kaeo into custody, assuming he was the perpetrator or had abused Anais. The smile on her face was priceless. Kaeo was taken to the car and escorted to jail with no questions asked.

Meanwhile, Yanira was at home wondering why Kaeo was late. It was already 7:30 pm. She had called him twice, and his phone went straight to voicemail. After waiting another thirty minutes she called again, but there was still no answer. She placed their dinner in Tupperware bowls, washed the dishes and headed out, snatching her purse and keys on her way to his store. Upon arrival, she saw that the store was locked, so she looked through the window; it was a wreck and Kaeo's car was still in his parking spot.

Worry started to come over her. She called the hospital, checking with a few co-workers to see if Kaeo had been admitted into the ER or if anyone had come in with his name; the answer was no. Next, she called Ryleigh and Marshall to see if they had heard from Kaeo because she had not and informed them that his store had damage to the furniture, and several things had been knocked over.

Ryleigh was floored. She could not imagine who would want to hurt Kaeo or break into his store. Yanira began to cry, believing that something may have happened to him. While chatting, she received a phone call at 8:14 pm from Dade County. She clicked over and was told Kaeo was locked up and needed to be bailed out. She clicked back over and told Ryleigh.

Yanira raced to the jail. She could not imagine what had transpired for Kaeo to be locked up. She asked the front office clerk to assist her in finding out where to sign the proper paperwork to get someone out on bail. When she gave her the name, she was told no bail was necessary, and to wait patiently for him to be released.

While waiting for him, she called Ryleigh, letting her know where she was and that bail was not needed, but she had to wait for him to come out. After she disconnected the call, she noticed Kaeo's employee Kendall. She thought maybe he was picking Kaeo up or that they were robbed. The young man walked up to her.

"Hey Ms. Yanira. Kaeo is going to be ok. They should be releasing him soon."

"Kendall, thank you! Can you tell me what happened? Why is he locked up? What happened to the store? Is he hurt? I am sorry I am asking you a thousand questions, but they would not explain anything to me on the phone." Yanira was obviously shaken."

Kendall proceeded to tell the story. "Well, I am the one who called the cops. I was in the back and had just finished unloading my truck while Kaeo was doing paperwork when I heard arguing. I came up front and noticed it was the girl, his ex, Anais. She was going wild, yelling at him and cursing, telling him to leave you, she would hurt you, she knows all about the wedding, how she will ruin the wedding, and just talking crazy. So, I started recording it. I was going to joke with him about it later. It was petty, but I'm glad I did because all of a sudden, this chick started ripping furniture, then got out a razor or knife and started cutting furniture, knocking down tables and chairs, breaking glass, and even damaging the leather furniture.

I called the police from the office phone, but I kept recording. When she broke down a little, Kaeo grabbed her to stop her from damaging the store and tried to calm her down. He had taken hold of her and just snatched the weapon away when the police showed up. I went to lock the back door once the police arrived because I had left it open. I assumed that everything would be cool; hell, he owned the store. After I locked up, I realized I forgot my wallet in the truck, so I went back to my truck. Once I returned, the police had him in handcuffs in the back of the car and it was already taking off.

When I went to the other police officer to tell him they arrested the wrong person, he told me to shut up or I would be arrested too. He was listening to her lies and sob stories. The female police officer happened to be one of my homeboy's cousins, so I told her I needed to talk to her and show her something. Anais must have assumed he was alone, but much to her surprise, I was in the back hiding out. I began to show the video to the female officer, telling her that he was innocent, he was the owner, and he was only doing paperwork. Anais was the one who came into the store in a rage.

She must have caught wind before we finished the video. The police officer who told me to shut up or he would lock me up came over to my homeboy's cousin and asked what I was talking about. She told him the next time he sees a Black man, don't assume that person is in the wrong or has bad intentions. She asked me for my phone, then she played the video for him. He was shocked and apologized to me, but her ass was already gone. They left to go and deal with the situation with the boss at the jailhouse so I could finish closing up the store and get him."

Yanira was livid. "So, you mean to tell me these bastards locked him up in his damn store because he subdued a perpetrator? What kind of bullshit is that? Oh my gosh! Kendall, I am so glad you were there. Thank you!"

Kendall replied, "You are welcome; I am glad I was there too and was smart enough to record that shit. Like I said, I was only recording it to mess with him, but when I saw things escalate, I knew it was for his protection. You know we don't get too much help when it comes to the boys in blue. I gave my statement, but I will send you this video so if something happens, you have your proof."

"Thanks again, Kendall; I don't know what I would have done if you were not there and knew the police. We owe you one!" Yanira exclaimed as she hugged him.

"Nah, that man gave me a chance when no one else would. He helped me out when I had my kids and even gave me a few rides before I got my own. I owe him."

At that moment, Kaeo walked out, shocked to see Kendall and Yanira sitting there. He was upset, but seeing her face warmed his heart. He knew when she heard the truth, she would not be smiling any longer.

"Baby, I am so sorry you had to come. I didn't know Kendall was here until they cut me loose. Thank you for coming," he said as he hugged and kissed her sweetly. "Kendall, man, you came through in the clutch! Man, thank you for the statement. You saved my life. I owe you one." Kaeo hugged and pounded him as well. He was pleased.

Glad that he could finally return the favor, Kendall explained, "Yeah, it's no problem. I just hate that I was too late. They had already taken you before I could explain what happened. I am glad I could help."

Yanira said, "This has been a long day. It's late and I know both of you are hungry and tired. Kendall, at least let us treat you to dinner to show how much we appreciate your help."

Kendall declined. "Nah, my girl got dinner waiting on me; maybe another time."

Yanira replied, "Ok, well, how about dinner on us Friday night for you and your girl? If you can find a babysitter, we will take you both out for an adult evening; if not, bring your babies, and we will take them somewhere special."

Kendall laughed. "Now that's a bet; I will let you know tomorrow, boss, if it's two or four."

They departed the jail and went home. Once there, Yanira told Kaeo to go and shower. She would warm up dinner and have it ready when he came back down. While Kaeo showered, she called and updated Ryleigh, but that conversation did not go well.

Ryleigh said, "I hope Kaeo pressed charges on her dumb ass."

Yanira told her, "I'm sure he did not because he would not want to upset the kids. We didn't talk about it. I just let him rest in the car. Oh, and we may miss our regular dinner date-night tomorrow because I want to treat Kendall and his family to dinner."

Ryleigh countered, "If it is just adults, then they can come. We can still do the normal dinner spot and let Kendall and his girl join us in VIP since he looked out for the family."

"Ok, cool, that sounds like a plan." They ended their call.

Kaeo came down and kissed Yanira on the cheek. "Baby, it has been one hell of a day. I cannot believe Anais would come to my store and do all this foolishness. I wanted to choke her, but at this point, I am glad she attacked me and not you."

Yanira responded, "I am glad you are ok. I thought the worst, but I never imagined she would be so reckless. I'm glad Kendall was there to be your witness."

Kaeo shook his head. "Yes, me too. They handcuffed me and asked no questions. She smiled with such glory in her eyes; she felt so justified in what she had done. I wanted to beat the shit out of her, but I don't hit women. If I did, she would be the one."

Yanira said, "Yes, well, I do, and if I see her, it's a done deal; I am tired of Anais. She is nothing but trouble."

Kaeo retorted, "Yes, it is a done deal, and no, you will not do anything but call the police. Anais threatened my life and yours. I gave her a pass tonight, but we need to rethink this wedding. I feel like she will try something crazy, and I do not want it to ruin the wedding."

Yanira countered, "Damn, you didn't press charges, did you? That was your pass after she threatened our lives, Kaeo! What the fuck are you thinking? In my heart, I knew, you would not, but at this point, if she comes for me, I am putting a bullet in her head. You do what you want to."

Kaeo said, "Well, I did request a restraining order against her for you and me. She is no longer allowed within 300 feet of us, our jobs, or our homes. I felt if I pressed charges, it would hurt the kids. I do not want any drama with them because we're finally in a good place and we invited them to the wedding."

Yanira said nothing after those words. She heard him and understood why he thought that, but the kids would have to just understand why he did what he did. No one had ever threatened her life and they would not start now, no matter who they were related to. So instead of going back and forth, Yanira kept quiet; she was not mad at Kaeo, but she was not going to agree on continuing to give Anais passes for her bullshit! She deserved another ass whooping and when she finally caught her, she would definitely deliver it!

After warming up dinner, they ate, and she cleaned the dishes while he went to rest. Yanira's thoughts drifted. It had been a while since they had seen or heard from Anais, so they thought that maybe she had finally gotten the picture, and their focus had now shifted to their upcoming nuptials. It was time for the wedding invitations to go out, but Kaeo had reservations about the comments Anais made about their wedding.

The following morning, as they were lying in bed, Yanira opened her eyes, and saw Kaeo staring at the ceiling. "Baby, what's wrong? Are you thinking about last night?"

"Yes, I woke up to get ready for work, but I think we need to discuss last night." Kaeo wanted to talk about Anais, and the wedding. "So, listen, Anais knows so many people, she has so much access in Hawaii, and if we have our wedding there, I think it would be too much of a risk with her and her people. We need to keep things in order. I think we need to change and have the ceremony here in MIA where she is least expecting it. We can tell my family we made a change. I think in MIA it would be hard to find us if no one knew exactly where the wedding is. We just send an invitation with the date, but no location, for the family, that way if she found out she would not know where.

Yanira hated to uproot her wedding plans. "Kaeo, are you serious? Do you really think she would do something like that? What if we hired security?"

"Baby, you didn't see what she did to my store or the look in her eyes when I was handcuffed. Anais is not a sweet person; she has done so much that I can't even tell you about. I know this is a lot to ask, but this is best, and I want to make sure our day is perfect!"

She thought about it and agreed. If he felt that strongly about it, then she would respect his decision; it would actually be better for her to be more hands-on anyway. Another thought was, in MIA, there would be no BS. She would have security at the wedding, so, she agreed. "Ok, if you feel that strongly about it, I will make a few calls this morning and start planning!"

After a few phone calls with her mom, aunt, and a couple of people she knew in the hotel industry, the wedding location was changed, and a wedding planner would be provided for the venue. She headed to work, as she was running late after making all the calls, but luckily, she had no appointments until 9:30am.

Once Kaeo got to work, he searched the internet looking for hotels and finally booked fifteen rooms at one that would be 5 miles away from the wedding venue. He called Yanira who was in between patients.

"Hey baby, what's up?"

"Baby, I booked 15 rooms for my family and whoever else at Renaissance a few miles away from the venue."

"Great, my mother and aunt will do the catering and have their servers work the reception. The invitations have been updated and will be sent out today. The day of the wedding everyone invited and rsvp'd will receive a text link for the venue location an hour before it starts."

"Man, this is coming together beautifully."

"Yes, it is. Did you call your mom?"

"Not yet. I will call her during lunchtime. Do you think you can join around that time? That way she will know you are ok with all the changes."

"Sure, let's do about 12:30 pm."

"Ok I will call you then. I love you, Yani!"

Once that business was handled, Kaeo left out of the office to start cleaning up, and saw that Kendall was already there. He had come in early to help. Together they spent the next hour cleaning up the mess and preparing to discard the furniture that Anais damaged.

"Hey, I already asked the repairman to come and fix the broken items," he stated.

Kaeo told him, "I appreciate you, but I plan on trashing them unless you want to take any of those items home. I want them out of the store. They are just a bad omen for me; I can't sell them to anyone else."

Kendall countered, "It's not that bad. The repairman can fix it; but I mean if you plan on trashing it, I really could use the furniture."

Kaeo felt him on that. He said, "Well, let's load it on the truck. You can take it home and have the repairman fix it at your place and bring the replacement glass and all. All expenses charged to the company."

They loaded the leather couch set, kitchen table and the end tables with the broken legs onto his truck, then trashed the broken glass and other items in the store. Kendall left to take his new furniture home and meet the repairman who was already in route.

After Kendall left, Yanira called, just as she said she would, at 12:30 pm. Kaeo called his mother, explained the incident that occurred and let her know they were changing the wedding location. He advised her that the wedding would now be in MIA, and he would fly them out and cover the expenses and had secured rooms for her and his father, siblings, aunt and uncles, and his business partner Pratt. The ceremony would take place on the same date, Saturday, September 18th, and the reception would follow. Yanira and Ryleigh's mother's catering service would cater for the event.

Yanira chimed in and asked Kaeo's mother to assist with cooking some homemade dishes for Kaeo and the rest of her family as a special gift to the family. She was delighted. Everything did seem to work in their favor; the guest list would include 100 people, from family to friends, co-workers, and associates, now that it was in Miami. The plan was all coming together, and their hopes for a beautiful wedding would prevail.

*************************************************

Friday night around 8 pm, Kaeo, Kendall, Marshall, and their ladies met up at Swanz, an upscale restaurant. Kaeo was paying for their night as a treat to Kendall and Marshall for allowing them to all go in VIP and get free drinks. Kendall's girlfriend, Kishida, was beautiful, just like Ryleigh and Yanira, with a great body. She seemed to be from the hood but was well poised. As the couples talked over dinner, they found out that Kendall and Kishida had two children together and had been dating on and off for the last seven years. Their relationship had gotten stronger over the last two years; mainly because Kendall had changed his life since working with Kaeo.

Kishida worked in home health care but had crazy hours, so she was looking to change positions and get a job in administration once something came up. Ryleigh asked for her resume, and she sent it while waiting for dinner. Within ten minutes, after thoroughly looking over her resume, Ryleigh had unofficially offered her a job as an administrative assistant, Monday through Friday, 8 am to 5 pm, making 10k more than she was making. The group got along so well, and it was a great coincidence. The couple now had a real reason to celebrate and dance.

After dinner, all three couples headed to the club, parked in valet, and went straight to VIP. Kendall and Kishida said they have been to the club before but not as special guests of the owners. The first shots of Hennessy went around within five minutes to celebrate their night. Many more shots were poured, and the group turned up in VIP. Kaeo and Yanira went to the Latin club on the second level to dance it up. The floor was their canvas, and they painted all over it for an hour straight —no issues or drama, and especially no Anais. They had a blast.

Ryleigh and Marshall walked up with Kendall and Kishida just as they returned to VIP to grab a drink and cool down. Kendall was amazed as he had never been to the second floor of the club. They sat and enjoyed a few drinks there and decided to head home at 2:30 am. Yanira and Kaeo followed them out. As they walked, Kishida said, "Oh and thank you so much for the new furniture; my house feels like a real home now. We needed something new, but it was not in the cards since I am going to school."

Kaeo smiled. "You are welcome. Your man there deserved it. Big things are coming to him in due time, thank you for letting him stay to help me the other night."

As they parted, Yanira asked Kaeo what he meant by big things in due time. Kaeo told her he planned to make Kendall a manager at either the current store or the new store, explaining that Kendall had been a great employee, always staying late and showing up early. Although there were times when he left, it was always because of his kids and Kishida, which he understood. Wednesday night showed his loyalty and support, so he wanted to do something good for him.

# CHAPTER 7: ACCIDENTS HAPPEN

The next few weeks went well. Kishida started working for Ryleigh in the corporate office as her Project Coordinator. On the flip side, the wedding plans and work were coming along for both Yanira and Kaeo. Yanira had secured security for the wedding and reception, the DJ, and the photographer, all from Marshall's club. With all the in-house support, there was no way Anais could slide through.

Friday, the couple decided on a low-key dinner and bowling date versus their normal dinner and the club scene. When Yanira called to inform Ryleigh, she had the same thoughts and agreed to make it a quiet night as well. As they continued to talk, Ryleigh filled her in on how great things were going with Kishida, advising that she was really smart and could possibly get promoted once she graduated school within the next year. Her plan was to make sure before she made any moves for herself to get Kishida straight! The incident was a disaster for Kaeo, but a blessing for everyone else.

*******************************************

Monday after work, Kaeo and Yanira met for the cake tasting and dinner. After six cake tastings they had finally decided on a three-tiered cake, with the left side red velvet and the right side yellow on all three layers. Satisfied with their selection, they left out hand in hand, walking towards the cars smiling at one another, until they got close enough to discover the flat tire on Yanira's car. Kaeo took off his business jacket, threw it in the car and immediately began changing Yanira's tire so that she could go home.

After jacking up the car he noticed that all four were rapidly deflating. Anais had flattened all four tires, not just the front two. She even did the same to his truck. Kaeo was livid! Yanira could see the frustration in his eyes. She went to his side, kissed him, and told him, "Kaeo, just stop. I'll call the mechanic and have the cars towed. We will get new tires for both vehicles."

Kaeo felt defeated and leaned against the car wanting to kill Anais. Yanira called her mechanic, asking him to send two tow trucks and bill her for eight tires, but to make sure the tow truck was there asap, if possible. She needed to get home. Kaeo opened her door, and she sat in her car, pondering over the ordeal.

After forty-five minutes of waiting, the tow trucks arrived. While they loaded both cars, Kaeo called Uber. Neither of them said anything on the ride home because they already knew it was Anais. She must have been following Kaeo, but this time they had no proof. Kaeo guided the driver through the back way to Yanira's house, continuing to watch behind them to make sure they were not followed. The driver was reckless; he drove through several yellow lights which ensured they were not followed. Ordinarily he would have checked him about his driving with Yanira in the car, but this time he was happy that his driving skills were fast and furious.

Once home, they ordered Chinese and jumped in the shower together. Kaeo could tell Yanira was getting fed up; it was all over her face. He kissed her neck and back as he rubbed her breasts. Yanira told him softly,

"Kaeo, not tonight. I'm sorry, but I'm not in the mood."

Kaeo sighed, "It's ok! I can see that you are stressed and tired of this all and I only wanted to please you. I realize this is not easy and continues to cost us time and money. I apologize to you, my love. I mean, especially after participating in our wedding planning. I just need you to understand that I am worth it."

Before he could utter another word Yanira turned around. She spoke in an even quieter, yet broken voice. "Baby, you are worth it, but this drama is too much. I just don't understand why we keep going through the same shit with this woman. Right now, I feel burnt out, and I don't even know how she found us. Who is to say she will not try to ruin our wedding, regardless of where it is? I feel we should have just eloped, maybe that would make her stop."

Kaeo yelled, "Hell No! You deserve a beautiful ceremony. We are not going to let Anais ruin anything! I know it's hard to deal with all of her stupid behavior and all the added stress but promise me you will not give up on us. Once we are married, she will stop. Right now, she thinks this will stop us, but it won't. However, you were right; I should have pressed charges the first time. If something else happens and we can get proof, I am pressing charges for everything, ok?"

Yanira nodded as Kaeo picked up where he had left off, grabbing her legs, and feeding himself with her body and inner thighs. She squealed and squirmed. Kaeo had the best tongue in the world. He licked in and out, flickering his tongue and eating her like she was steak and potatoes. As Yanira was starting to shake and lose control, Kaeo sucked and nibbled more aggressively until she erupted. They washed and exited the shower.

Dinner arrived just as they walked into the kitchen to get her a glass of wine and Kaeo a glass of Hennessy. They sat at the kitchen table, enjoying their takeout, and sipping in silence. After fifteen minutes, Kaeo told her, "I set up Ubers to come and pick us up for work, and I will make sure to get both of the cars."

The following day seemed to go by quickly. Yanira hadn't noticed the time until her phone rang with a call from the mechanic around 2:50 pm. "Hey Yani, not sure who y'all pissed off but all tires have been replaced on both cars. I put run flats on them so even if someone does this again, you will still be able to drive them home or here. You guys can pick them up, I can get yours delivered to your place of business and you can bring Kaeo to get his, or I guess I can even drop his off as well if you give me an address."

Trying to keep her business her business, she told him, "Listen, thanks. I appreciate you very much. Let me speak with Kaeo and I will text you back within the next few minutes."

She called Kaeo, asking him how he wanted to handle picking up the cars since they were ready, stating the mechanic was willing to drop hers off, if need be, or they could Uber there and pick them up. Kaeo told her to sit tight, he would handle getting the cars, and he would be there at 5:10 pm when she finished her paperwork.

As promised, Kaeo knocked on her office door at 5:10 pm with a dozen roses, chocolates, and the keys to her car. Once they exited, she saw his truck and her car; she asked no questions. When Kaeo said he would do something, he always did, and he was always on time. She loved that about him. Kaeo told her to meet him at their favorite Italian place; he was treating her to dinner.

When they arrived, Kaeo made sure to park in the front and signaled her to do the same, requesting a seat near the front so he could watch their cars and the cars incoming to the parking lot. Yanira didn't care. She was happy with her flowers and unexpected dinner date. He was trying, and that was all she could ask for.

When they left the restaurant, Kaeo watched her leave, made sure no cars followed her, then pulled out after watching the traffic behind him. They arrived home, and as Yanira went to shower, Kaeo checked all the doors and set the alarm; once she came out of the shower, he went in. When he walked into the bedroom, he saw Yanira on the bed naked with an enormous smile on her face. She had him for dessert, sucking him washing machine style, getting it wet, slurping, shaking it up, whirling it around, and drying it by swallowing his release.

Kaeo entered her gently, kissing her as he inched into her tunnel. Yanira arched her back, opened her legs wider, and let her man dig deeper. Kaeo hummed; Yanira was wet and slushy, making him strengthen the power of his stroke. He grabbed her ass, thrusting into it, slowly circling, and drifting around in her puddle of love. Yanira yelled out as she came on his dick. Kaeo smiled at his work; he had held out so she could receive hers. He became excited and dug way deeper than before, pressing, pounding, grinding; Yanira couldn't take it. "Baby, baby," she screamed out. Kaeo kept going. He was feeling the deep end of her jaws of life and didn't want to stop. She made his dick hard. Pushing through and barely holding on, he felt her squirt. He came hard, and Yanira gushed out right with him.

\*\*\*\*\*\*\*\*\*\*\*\*\*\*\*\*\*\*\*\*\*\*\*\*\*\*\*\*\*\*\*\*\*\*\*\*\*\*\*\*\*\*\*\*\*\*\*\*

Friday's date night with Marshall and Ryleigh this month was at their house. Marshall had family in town, and they were having a Caribbean feast with oxtails, jerk chicken, curry goat, rice and peas, shrimp, plantains, Crayfish soup, and cabbage. Yanira and Kaeo brought two half gallon bottles of Hennessy to the dinner. The family had a terrific time; everyone was tipsy off of rum punch and Bob

Marley's. Marshall's family was tight knit and loved to enjoy life and laughter. They sat outside by the pool, smoking and drinking, reminiscing about old stories from Jamaica. Ryleigh insisted that Yanira and Kaeo stay the night because they had plenty of room. She didn't want them to leave early, so they stayed and drank and ate until 3 am, then went to their room to sleep for the night.

The next morning, Ryleigh and Yanira woke up at the same time, around 10 am. Ryleigh gave her cousin fresh clothes, brand-new undies, and toothbrushes for her and Kaeo. Yanira showered and then headed to the kitchen to start breakfast/brunch. Ryleigh came down to assist.

"I should have known this is where I would find you," Ryleigh smirked.

Yanira replied, "You know I have to; it's what we do."

Ryleigh nodded; it was indeed how they were raised: never wear out your welcome and always earn your keep. The two made every breakfast food you could think of, along with a few brunch dishes and mimosas. Everyone began to trickle down just as the food was being placed on the table.

Marshall said to Yanira, "Yani, I should have known you would be down here cooking in this kitchen. You can't help it, right? We can't treat you at all."

Ryleigh chimed in, "Right babe, she beat me to the kitchen; I became her assistant in my own kitchen."

Marshall hugged Yanira and kissed her on the cheek. They were not blood, but their relationship couldn't get any closer. He was a wonderful man, and she loved him unconditionally for her cousin.

The family agreed to have a BBQ at the house around 4 pm. They did not want to go out to eat; enjoying family in their own space was their thing. Ryleigh told Yanira to come back a little before 4 pm if she could; she would need her help setting up. Marshall's sisters interrupted her, "No, she doesn't, because she will not be helping. We are doing everything. Show up at 4 pm, please, and we love you, dear."

Both ladies laughed. They were not surprised; Marshall's family loved Ryleigh and would do anything for her as if she was already one of them. They were happy that their little brother had found true love with a woman who already had what she needed but appreciated a real man. He needed one who could tame him, and that was Ryleigh. Kaeo and Yanira left to rest a little before returning to the BBQ.

*********************************************

The wedding was fast approaching. They had two more weeks, and she would be the one and only Mrs. Yanira Catori Iosua. Yanira and Kaeo decided to change date night this weekend to Saturday; they wanted to do something different and go mini golfing. Kishida and Kendall also joined along with Marshall and Ryleigh. They played 18 holes. After golfing, they all went to the Collar Gin lounge to eat and drink. An hour later, everyone else went to the club while Yanira and Kaeo finished their drinks and went home to rest.

Sunday afternoon arrived; they went to a matinee, then went to the grocery store by Kaeo's old place since it was close to the theater. Kaeo and Yanira walked through the grocery store talking and grabbing things off the shelf. As they were turning on aisle number 8, Anais purposely ran into their buggy. Yanira didn't notice initially as she had stepped back to grab an item off the shelf. Anais sprayed pepper spray on Kaeo and tried to get Yanira but missed as she was too far away. She screamed to Kaeo, "You better cancel the wedding, or there will be more damage to you, her, and your store!"

Yanira turned around and smacked fire from Anais. Anais acted as if she was going to hit her again and Yanira smacked her several more times, then punched her in the face and kicked her as she fell to the ground. Bystanders stood watching the commotion.

Kaeo yelled, "My eyes! My eyes! Yani I can't see. What the fuck did you do Anais!"

She heard Kaeo yell again, and one of the clerks came to give Kaeo some water to flush his eyes. Yanira ran to help Kaeo, and as she bent down, Anais pulled her by her hair and moved her away from him, dragging her across the floor. Pulling herself up with her legs, Yanira was able to fall into Anais and elbow her right in the stomach. This caused her to bend over and release her hair. Yanira turned around and began punching Anais repeatedly.

She yelled, "Bitch, I told you I would whoop your ass! You better stay the fuck away from us before you see motherfucking damages, stupid bitch!!" She continued to throw connecting blows, all of which landed on Anais' face. Security pulled Yanira off of Anais, but she was overpowering him, so another joined in to assist. Slowly she was losing her grip on Anais, yet she continued kicking at her until they managed to pull her five feet away. They held her as the police were rushing down the hallway.

A once again bloody Anais screamed, "Arrest her! She attacked me; arrest her now!" The officers came towards

Yanira with handcuffs out, ready to place her under arrest. The shoppers began to yell, "No! No! No! It was the other one; she should be arrested. She sprayed that man and hit that woman first. She is the one who needs to go to jail."

"I got it on camera," one girl yelled.

The officer looked at the evidence and could see the ending of Anais pepper spraying Kaeo and attempting to pepper spray Yanira, but her back was turned. He shook his head after watching, then released Yanira's arm. Yanira went back to where Kaeo was. He was ok, but his eyes were red. Security signaled them to go to the office with the clerk who had called the police. Yanira tended to Kaeo, continuing to flush his eyes out with milk.

The police talked to several other shoppers and watched the store video to see the beginning. They spoke with Kaeo and Yanira and were getting ready to arrest Yanira because she had assaulted Anais, and the rules were that they arrest both. Kaeo was angry as he yelled, "Why would you arrest my fiancé for defending herself against someone we have a restraining order against? You should not be hauling a woman to jail who assaulted someone in self-defense. I have a photo of the restraining order right here." Kaeo pulled out his phone and showed it to the officer. He signaled to the other officer to uncuff Yanira. The anger in her face said it all. Kaeo just hugged her; this was the last straw.

After the police officer called it in and confirmed, they cuffed Anais and told her she was violating her restraining order and was the cause of this altercation due to her pepper spraying Kaeo. After apologizing for the incident, the clerk checked out the groceries in their buggy and placed them in a bag for free. They just wanted them out of the store.

As they exited the building, Anais yelled, "Kaeo, why are you doing this to me? Honey, please!" She paused as they kept tugging at her, while Kaeo kept walking in the other direction holding Yanira. "Fine, Kaeo! You and that bitch will both pay for this; I promise you!"

On the car ride home, Kaeo's mother called out of the blue. She could hear the frustration in his voice and asked him what was going on, telling him that she felt she needed to call him. It was then Kaeo explained the entire situation to his mother. She was appalled.

Mrs. Iosua said, "Kaeo, this is too much. What is going on with Anais? I am contacting her mother before someone gets seriously hurt. I am not happy with her. Are you ok? How about Yani, how is she?"

Kaeo replied, "We are both fine. The clerk and Yanira took care of me. I just need to go home, shower and rinse my eyes a little more."

His mother told Yanira, snickering, "My daughter, keep kicking her ass! Let no one take advantage of you and Kaeo. You do what you need to do. You have a weapon, so use it if you need to."

Kaeo shook his head because he knew she was serious. Yanira was surprised but laughed. "Yes, ma'am, will do." They disconnected the call.

*************************************************

Arriving home, Kaeo showered, and Yanira put up the groceries then ordered pizza and wings for dinner; she was no longer in the mood to cook. When Kaeo came back downstairs he was angry, spilling out, "I am sick of her! I am glad she is in jail. I hope she stays there until after the wedding. She has really lost her mind. Baby, I am sorry. I promise you I will be pressing charges this time. No more Mr. Nice Guy to her; this was the last straw. She fucking pepper-sprayed me! Can you believe it?" His anger was not funny, but his tone when he stated she pepper sprayed him gave her a chuckle.

She walked over to him, sweetly rubbing his hair and face. "My love, calm down. Anais is in jail, and now we will be fine to marry one another in peace. Surely no one will bail her out."

Yanira was not angry because there was proof and witnesses this time. She had every intention of picking up the police report on Wednesday and adding it to the pile of incidents they already had. They rested for the remainder of the evening; both were exhausted, yet happy Anais was out of their hair.

On Wednesday, just as she planned, Yanira left the office to take a breather, pick up the police report, then grab a bite to eat. Kaeo must have had the same thought because he was there too. Both were trying to save the other from the grief of having to go. They took the report and went to lunch at a sandwich shop around the corner. Neither had a lot of time left for their break.

\*\*\*\*\*\*\*\*\*\*\*\*\*\*\*\*\*\*\*\*\*\*\*\*\*\*\*\*\*\*\*\*\*\*\*\*\*\*\*\*\*\*\*\*\*\*

Thursday afternoon, Clariana called, saying she had made it home and was at the airport. Since Yanira didn't have any appointments for another hour, she left to go get her, and they grabbed a quick bite to eat on the way back. When they arrived at the office, Yanira's staff and physicians wanted to introduce themselves as they were the ones chipping in on her education; even her CMO stopped by. Clariana felt like a celebrity. She performed rounds with

Yanira, who allowed the patients to provide Clariana with all her symptoms and issues; they were able to tag-team and treat them with no problems.

When the ladies arrived home, Kaeo was there waiting. He had already started dinner, making his famous empanadas. Clariana couldn't wait to tell him how she treated her first patient today and was able to translate.

"Dad, you would not believe my day, omg! I was a real nurse. I treated patients with Yanira, and I even translated. It was amazing!"

Kaeo smiled as he hugged her, saying how proud he was while simultaneously mouthing the words 'Thank you' to Yanira. As the family trio ate dinner, they discussed how things were going with school, and chatted about her personal life with friends. She told them she had not spoken with her mom in a week or so. Kaeo looked at her and told her he had some things to discuss with her.

Clariana said, "Oh no, is she ok? What did she do now?"

Kaeo divulged that her mother was in jail. He explained that she had attacked him at his store and got him arrested, but he let it go, and did not press charges. However, over the weekend, she followed him and Yanira to a grocery store, pepper-sprayed him, and tried to fight Yanira. The police were called by the shoppers and store employees, and this time she went to jail. Kaeo apologized for having to be the one to tell her, but she endangered his life twice, along with Yanira and several others in the store.

Clariana could not believe her ears. She was hurt that her mother was locked up and her father pressed charges, but at the same time, she knew he had to do something about her mother. She seemed relentless and Clariana couldn't understand why she was doing this when she too was dating. Knowing a person can only take so much, she couldn't be angry with either of them.

"Dad, when will she get out? I would like to see her so I can talk to her and tell her to stop all this. You guys are doing so much for me, and she continues to try and tear you apart. For that, I am sorry."

Yanira chimed in, "Hey, let's not ruin this time we have here; you are here for a break and a wedding. You had a fabulous day as a nurse. Let's talk about you joining me again tomorrow, assisting me with my patients, and maybe even making rounds in the ED tomorrow with a few physicians."

Clariana advised, "I would love that!"

Yanira cleaned up the kitchen while Kaeo and Clariana talked. After she finished, she gave Clariana a new pair of scrubs to wear for work tomorrow. The excitement on her face warmed Yanira's heart, but it also tampered with her mentally because she knew the news of her mother was a blow and not something she expected to hear.

Yanira did her morning run the following day, came back to make quick omelets for all three of them, then woke up Clariana and Kaeo to eat. After breakfast, they all showered and went on their way. Clariana let Kaeo know she would be hanging out with her friends later that night and coming back on Saturday or Sunday, but she would confirm with her friends and call him or Yanira. He hugged his daughter and told her he loved her.

Their weekend went as planned. Friday night, Kaeo and Yanira dined with Ryleigh and Marshall as usual, then Saturday they cleaned the house and finished last-minute preparations for their wedding the following Saturday. It was finally time for her to become his true queen. While they were working out the wedding details, Clariana returned home on Sunday so she could go to work with Yanira the next day; she had a shadowing session with one of the physicians.

On Monday, Yanira had four surgery anesthesia preps, while Clariana made rounds with her CMO, walking through the hospital, learning about patient flow, nurse education, and protective equipment. After her rounds, Yanira texted Clariana and told her to take some cash from her purse and go grab some lunch from any place of her choice, advising that when she returned, they would meet in her office and eat around 12:15 pm. Clariana was excited. She loved driving Yanira's Jaguar; she felt like a queen and posted it to her friends on social media.

Yanira got worried when Clariana was not back by 1 pm, wondering what had happened to her. She tried to call her multiple times, but she received no answer. Yanira called Kaeo to see if he had heard from her as she was late returning from picking up food. Kaeo told her to hold while he called Clariana multiple times, and he, too, received no answer. Yanira began to worry; Kaeo told her to give it a minute. She probably stopped to chat or was showing off in the car.

At 1:05 pm, Kaeo received a text with a smiley face, but no words. Kaeo could not think of whose number it was nor what the message was for. Now was not the time to try and play games with someone who had the wrong number. Kaeo quickly called Yanira to ask if she was ok and asked if Clariana had made it back. Yanira explained she was caring for patients and that she was ok, but Clariana was still gone. Just as she answered him, there was a knock at her office door,

"This may be her baby; hang tight. Come in," Yanira answered at the door.

"Dr. White, we need you in the ER! It's your stepdaughter; she has been hurt."

Yanira yelled into the phone, "Kaeo get here now! Clariana has been hurt."

Yanira ran to the skywalk then descended down three flights of stairs; she refused to wait on the elevator. Her CMO was there waiting for her when she made it through the stairwell door. Looking in her eyes, she said,

"Calm down. I know emotions are high, but you have to remember she will be fine, and we will do our best for her. She is family, ok."

Yanira nodded and took deep breaths, then her CMO escorted her to the door of room ten, where she looked in and saw Clariana. As she entered the surgery unit, she looked through the surgery window; Clariana lay there unconscious with bruises on her face and legs. The team was working to stabilize her. Tears fell from Yanira's eyes. Who would have done this? Why would someone want to hurt this little girl? It couldn't have been an accident. This should have been her. Why a freak accident now, right before her wedding? She needed answers. Nevertheless, whoever it was thought she was in the car and not Clariana.

Yanira stayed there until the team finished tending to Clariana. Thirty minutes later, the physician came out of the room to speak to her. "Dr. White, your daughter is fine; they are taking her to an ICU room. We need to monitor her for a while. She suffered a concussion, had some minor bruising on her face, and lacerations on both arms, legs, and hands. Her arm is broken; however, there are no other broken bones. She is still unconscious, but we hope she will wake up soon. She was lucky that she was so close to the hospital. The EMT team was just leaving, and apparently witnessed a car run your daughter off the road into the guard rail and into some trees. They were able to get to her and provide her with care quickly, enough to stabilize her until she reached here. She hit her head on the steering wheel, window, or some other component that knocked her out. Once we place her in an ICU room, you can see her; she will be fine. You know I will care for her as if she were my own."

Kaeo arrived and ran to Yanira. "Baby, what happened? Where is she? Where is Clariana?"

She said, "They took her to ICU, Baby!"

"Wait, what happened?" He was scared and nervous, not knowing her condition.

Yanira explained, "Someone ran her off the road into a guard rail, then into some trees. She has a broken arm, bruises, and a concussion, but she will be fine; her vitals are good, and she should wake up in a couple of hours. They are taking her to a room, and we can go in shortly. She has been here since 12:30 pm. The attending physician had not met her and did not know she was my stepdaughter. My CMO was called in because they could not locate her property, and with her looking so young, she wanted to check on her. That's when she noticed it was Clariana. Baby, I am so sorry. I never should have let her drive. I don't know who would do this. With Anais in jail, who would want to hurt her? It had to be a drunk driver or something. I mean Clariana is such a sweet and bright girl. I am so sorry."

Kaeo was hurt. "Baby, it's not your fault; you didn't do this. We need to find out who did. I need to call her brother and let him know what is happening. I know Anais is still locked up, but someone has to know. I can see if he can fly in a little early. Is it ok if he stays at the house until it is time for him to check in at the hotel?"

"Of course, they are welcome to come to the house. We will make sure the bill is paid for as well. It was me who asked her about lunch. Anyway, by the time you finish your call, she will be in a room, and we can walk up."

Ring, Ring, Ring, Kaeo was anxious. "Cordero? Hey son, it's me, Dad; um, I need to talk to you. I am calling because your mother is in jail, but something happened to Clariana. She was working with Yanira, getting a little experience. She left to get lunch and never returned. Yanira was worried, and we found out that she was involved in a hit-and-run accident. Someone ran her off the road. She is unconscious but stable, nothing too major, but with your mom locked up, I figured we need to get you here asap."

Cordero replied, "Wait, what, mom in jail? Why? Damn, is Clare good? I mean, is anything broken, Pops? I mean, like, can I talk to her?"

Kaeo responded, "Yanira and I are about to head upstairs now. She suffered a mild concussion, a broken arm, lacerations, and some bruising on her face and legs. I can Facetime you whenever we get to her. I am not sure if she will be awake yet, but I would like to get you on a plane here today if you want, or if you trust me to take care of her until you can come, that is cool too. Whatever you want, son."

"You are her dad; I trust you with her more than anyone else. Yanira too. She is a doctor. Y'all can do more than I can. I planned on coming for the wedding and leaving later in the week, but I will see about getting off and coming sooner. When did my mom go to jail? What happened?" Cordero questioned.

"I know I am giving you a lot of bad news at once, son, but her being in jail is my fault. I put her there."

"What do you mean?"

"Cordero, recently your mom attacked me at my job, damaged things in my store, got me locked up, and I let her go. Then over the weekend, Yanira and I were shopping at a grocery store, and she attacked me, spraying pepper spray in my face and attacking and fighting Yanira. The police were called, and I decided to have her locked up. I know it sounds cruel, but she attacked me too many times, and I can't keep going through this with her and putting Yanira through this, it's unfair. I am sorry, son," Kaeo conceded.

"Dad, it's ok. Frankly, her ass needs to slow down. She called me and told me that you were locked up, but of course, she never told me she attacked you at the store or at your job. She is wilding out. There were so many signs when we were kids, but I was too young to see them. Now I see her for who she is, a damn lunatic; I mean, that is my mom, but fuck, that is too much. I see why you locked her ass up. Let me talk to my boss. I will call you back soon." Cordero was so disappointed in his words with his dad. He, too, knew Anais was on the edge.

Yanira and Kaeo arrived in the room with Clariana; she was still unconscious. Kaeo was weak; tears rolled down his face seeing his daughter lay up in a hospital bed because of someone's ignorance. Yanira felt responsible. Whoever did this meant it for her. Who would want to harm her? She had no enemies, bad patients, or broken relationships; this was too difficult for her to handle. She needed answers but had none.

The two sat patiently with Clariana, both staying in the room and taking turns going to the restroom. Neither had left to grab a bite to eat. Eventually, they both fell asleep on the couch in her room. Kaeo's phone rang around 6 am.

Cordero said, "Dad, I changed my flight, so I will be there at 2 pm your time. Can you pick me up from the airport? If not, I can rent something."

Kaeo countered, "No, you can stay with us until it is time to check-in. There's no need to rent a car; you can use my truck. I will reimburse you for the changes to the flight, too. See you at 2 pm."

Yanira woke up to Kaeo's voice. She thought Clariana was awake, but she was not. Kaeo told her his son was on the way and would be there today at 2 pm. He would need to leave and pick him up around 1:30 pm. Yanira advised that he should leave, take a shower, get some rest, and grab something to eat also. She would stay with Clariana because she felt responsible. Kaeo insisted that she was not responsible; it was an accident that he wished never would have happened. They slept there a little longer, hoping and waiting for Clariana to wake up.

Around 8:30 am, Resha came in with steak biscuits and orange juice for breakfast. She knew Yanira would not leave, so she brought breakfast for her and Kaeo.

"Thank you! What would I do without you? I appreciate you so much," Yanira said to Resha.

"No worries. You were not scheduled for anything this morning. I had your calendar blocked off for paperwork today and Wednesday, throughout the next week you are off. Would you like me to do anything else for you?" Resha inquired.

"No, ma'am, this was more than enough. Thanks again. I would hug you, but I smell like yesterday." Resha laughed at Yanira's comment.

"Ok, well, whenever you are ready, we will bring you some fresh clothes and undergarments. Here are the tennis shoes from your office; I wanted to drop them off first. If you need anything else, just buzz me."

Yanira and Kaeo ate breakfast, taking turns talking to Clariana at her bedside, just hoping for a sign that she was waking up and ok. Yanira went to shower at about 11 am because Kaeo would need to go home and get dressed, then pick up Cordero. After fifty minutes, Yanira returned from showering and checking in with the attending physician and nursing staff. It was time for Kaeo to go home and take care of himself. He kissed Clariana one more time, kissed his fiancé, and left to handle his business.

Around 12:28 pm, Clariana showed brain activity as if she was awake, but her eyes were still closed. The machines started beeping, so the nurse came in, and together they watched Clariana; her eyes opened at 12:52 pm.

"Clariana!" Yanira teared up. "Oh, my love. Baby, I am so glad you are awake. Lord, thank you. I am so happy to see you awake."

The nurse checked her vitals and took out the mouth guard. They concluded that she awoke from her coma but stayed asleep for a couple of hours. It appeared something in her sleep was startling her so she became alert. The nurse advised that Dr. Dowe would be in shortly. She made some adjustments with the help of Yanira and then left the room. After a few minutes, Yanira called Kaeo.

He answered, "Baby, everything ok?"

"Yes, baby. She is awake! She is awake! Please Facetime." Yanira wanted her to see the people who loved and cared for her to lift her spirits.

Kaeo Facetimed so he could look at her face. "Baby girl, I am so happy you are awake. I am returning there shortly, ok?" Clariana nodded.

Dr. Dowe entered the room at that moment. "I see you are awake, my dear; you gave your mom here a big scare. I'm going to check your vitals, Clariana, but before I do so I have a few questions. If you can answer them, please do; if not, it's ok. I have three questions: Do you remember what happened to you? Do you know where you are? Who is this woman in front of you?"

Clariana nodded, but her lips were sticking together. Yanira gave her a little water as her mouth was dry, and she could not talk.

Dr. Dowe asked, "Is your throat sore or just dry? Do you feel any pain or discomfort trying to talk?"

Murmuring, "No sir, I can talk; my throat was just a little dry," Clariana explained.

Dr. Dowe then asked, "Can you describe what you can remember about why you are here?"

"Yes, sir. I remember driving, and a car like my mom's came into my lane to hit me. I hit the rail and trees, and I do not remember anything else. I know I am in the hospital from the looks of it. and that lady in front of you is my stepmom. Yanira, I wrecked your car. I am so sorry." She began to cry.

Yanira walked closer, "Honey, no, no, I am not worried about that car. It is replaceable. You are not. We can always get another car; it's ok."

Clariana continued to weep as Yanira hugged her. "Trust me, you, and your health mean more to me and are way more important than any possession I own. Please don't cry, ok?"

Clariana nodded, "It just happened so fast. I didn't see the person, but it looked..."

Yanira stopped her. "Honey, it's ok. Just relax and don't worry. Let's keep your blood pressure down, ok?"

Dr. Dowe spoke again after checking Clariana. "Alright, so your vitals look great, but I want to monitor you a little more. You may be in a little pain due to the soreness in your bones from the bruises and the broken arm, so we have placed something in your IV, but it can only be released every 4 hours. Let us monitor you for a couple more hours; if all is ok, we can talk about releasing you shortly after some tests are run, being that you have a doctor at home. Sound, ok?"

"Yes, thank you," Clariana said.

Yanira's mind raced. Clariana kept talking.

"Are you hungry, Clariana? Do you want something to eat?" At that moment, Resha came in with chicken noodle soup, tea, and chicken tenders for Clariana and other food for Yanira.

Resha asked, "How is she? Everything ok?"

Yanira retorted, "I was just about to get her something to eat. You are a mind reader. My tab keeps on building, doesn't it? Thank you for all that you have done."

Resha told her, "After all you have done for me, it's no problem. I still owe you for all the favors and for looking out for me. If we were keeping tabs, I would need 10 lifetimes to repay you." They chatted in small talk then Yanira gave her the paperwork she had completed to take back to the office. Kaeo and Cordero arrived. Resha turned to the exit and told Yanira she would check in before leaving work.

Kaeo and Cordero rushed to hug and kiss Clariana; both were excited to see her awake and asked her a thousand questions. As she began to talk, Yanira closed the door. She wanted privacy and only for those in the room to hear what Clariana had to say.

"Guys, I am ok. I was worried about Yanira being mad at me for totaling her car, but she said she cared about me more than anything else. I still feel bad though." They all looked at Yanira; she fanned her hands like there was no way she was angry.

Kaeo said, "Baby girl, you know Yanira is not worried about the car; we will get her a new one. You just focus on getting better. Do you remember what happened? Did you see anything?"

Yanira walked up to grab Kaeo's arm.

Clariana answered, "Dad, I just remember driving because Yanira told me to take her keys, grab some cash, and get us lunch after the rounds. I was driving, and suddenly, a car came to the side of me and hit me; it was intentional. I did not see the person inside the car. It all happened so fast. I'm sorry I can't remember more."

Cordero said, "Hell Naw! They hit you; why are you sorry? They should be finding that car. Sis, we are just glad you are ok, and Yanira got pull up in here. I got a major question, though."

Clariana looked closely at her brother. Cordero spoke with a serious face. "So, you were out here ballin in a brand-new Jaguar and didn't even let your bro ride? That's messed up."

Everyone laughed, including Clariana. Her brother was always the best at making light of a situation to make her feel good. He was a terrific brother, and he loved his sister very much. Kaeo, on the other hand, looked at Yanira. He was alarmed when she said it was intentional. He would do his best to find out who it was because they were going to pay for scaring his daughter.

After a little more talking and eating, Clariana dozed off. Kaeo, Yanira, and Cordero began to talk.

Cordero said, "Dad, did you hear that? She has a description. Have we got the police involved to try and track down the car? I mean, this is crazy."

Kaeo replied, "I agree it is crazy. Yes, the police came by last night, but Clariana was not awake and could not give a statement. I expect they will be here today. Your mom is still in jail, so it can't be her, but when she gets out, let her know. She definitely should know what has happened."

Cordero spoke quickly, "No, she is not; I talked to her. I thought about it after you called me. I wasn't thinking when we had talked, but Kamryn reminded me she called a few days ago. She was mad at you, rambling on and on telling us she was done with you. It was late and I was tired. This was within the last five days. She was not in jail; I thought this was something new. Let me call her."

The phone rang, but there was no answer.

"Well, maybe she is locked up. I'm not sure how she called; maybe someone had a phone. Who knows? "

Thirty minutes later, Cordero's phone rang. "Mom, hey, where are you? I am in town. (Anais talking) Mom, I didn't come to see you because Clariana is in the hospital. Can you get here? (Anais talking) Mom, I don't have a rental car. Just take an Uber or something. (Anais talking) Well, I am just letting you know. (Anais talking) No, she is sleeping right now. (Anais talking) Man mom, her ass has been unconscious, but she woke up a little while ago Yanira said. (Anais talking) Mom, I don't have time for that. Your daughter could have died, and you are being petty. (Anais talking) Yes, it was that serious. (Anais talking) Yes, where are you? Ok, well, get here when you can. Bye!"

Anais arrived within an hour and ten minutes and immediately started crying as she saw the IV and other needles in Clariana's arm. She began yelling,

"What happened? What happened to my baby? Who would do this? Where were you Kaeo? She was with you, so how could you let this happen? I told you! This bitch has clouded your brain. I am over you!" Anais tried to lunge for Yanira, but Kaeo and Cordero caught her.

Kaeo looked sad, "Anais, I am sorry. Really. I was not around; I was working. She is going to be ok. Clariana was…" At that moment, Clariana opened her eyes and started moving, so he did not finish. The commotion must have awakened her.

Clariana tried to speak loudly but couldn't speak clearly. She mumbled, "Mom, calm down. Why are you yelling? I am ok." She began to cry as she looked at her mom.

Anais cried as well; she wept over her daughter's body. "Baby girl, what happened to you? Please tell me. Why would someone hurt my baby?"

The police walked in with security. "Dr. White, we have the investigating officer here. Do you think your daughter is up for questioning?"

Yanira signaled him in, and the security guard began to walk away.

Anais screamed, "That bitch is not her mother. I am her mother. Officer, she is not family, so she should not be here. I am the mother, he is her father, and this is her brother from California. We are her family. This woman is a homewrecker. You must talk with her and find out who would be so stupid to hurt my baby."

Kaeo spoke up, "Officer, I am her father, but this is my fiancé, the same person who has not been home and has been sitting with us since this incident and the first one on the scene here at the hospital after the accident occurred. She has just as much right to be here as I do or anyone else. My daughter is comfortable with her around."

Anais scolded Kaeo. "No, she does not! My daughter will talk when I tell her; she is nothing to her. You are upsetting her and me both with this foolishness. Officer, please, I am her mother. I would like to know what you are going to do about the person who hurt my daughter?"

"Ok, let's all calm down. I am Detective Bronson, and we need to relax a bit. I can tell there are some hostilities, so first things first. Clariana, is it? How old are you, my dear?"

Clariana said calmly, "I am 19."

"Ok, since you are of legal age, I would prefer to speak with you alone. It may help you recall things a bit more clearly without all of the confusion going on in the room. The choice is yours."

"No, sir, it's ok. Everyone can stay. They can just quietly stand in the back or leave if they choose. I do not think I will be much help, but I will tell you what I remember."

"Ok, that sounds good. Your voice is faint so I will come and sit a little closer. Now, let's start from the top with how your morning started leading up to the accident and what you remember," Detective Bronson instructed.

"Ok. Well, I woke up, and Yanira made us all breakfast, then she and I rode to the hospital. She is a Doctor and Anesthesiologist here. The people here gave me money for a scholarship, so I have been doing rounds with the CMO this week. Yanira told me, once my rounds were over, to go to her office, grab some cash from her purse and keys, then head to get us lunch."

Detective Bronson interrupted. "And just for the record, this all happened yesterday, correct?"

"I don't know, sir. I believe so. I have been sleeping for a while," Clariana answered, troubled.

Kaeo spoke up, "Yes, sir, this happened yesterday."

"Ok, Clariana, continue, please," Detective Bronson encouraged her.

"So, I went to grab her keys and money around noon. I went to the car, and I took a few pictures. I just wanted to show my friends I was about to drive the Jaguar. I took a few pictures once I got in the car. After that, I put my phone down because Yanira doesn't like it when my phone is within reach of me when I drive."

The detective said, "Well, I like this rule; she makes my job a little easier. So, to confirm, you were not on the phone when all this took place."

"No, sir, I was not on the phone." Clariana wanted to make it noticeably clear.

He looked back and smiled at Yanira. "Ok, go on," he instructed again.

"Well, after I put my phone down, I was driving, and suddenly, a car came out of nowhere. I looked over to turn right and all of a sudden BOOM. I don't know what happened. The next thing I know, I woke up here with Yanira today."

Anais turned pale as she listened to her daughter relive this moment. It was heartbreaking for her. She ran to the trash can and began vomiting and crying. Everyone was in shock; they did not know what to think, but they knew she was not pregnant.

The detective turned and said, "Is mom ok? Do we need a minute? Anything Ms. Yanira or the nursing staff can get her?"

Cordero walked over to his mother, "Mom, you good?"

Anais replied, "No, this is just hard. This is my baby girl, that's all. I am just sad and emotional. It's ok. I just need a minute." Anais walked out. "Shit, oh my gosh, no! Oh no, please, just watch over her. Just breathe." Anais was torn; she couldn't believe this happened to Clariana.

Back in the room, Dr. Detective Bronson signaled Clariana to continue. "Sorry, umm, that is really it; I don't remember much."

"So, can you give me a description of the car that hit you? Could you see the car make or model?"

"I can't remember; I just saw a flash of grey. I could not see a driver or whatever hit me." Clariana began to cry. She was trying to remember, but it was all too much.

Kaeo went to her, rubbing her hair and gripping her hand, "Hey, baby girl, it's ok. Relax; this is not your fault. You are the victim here. Detective Bronson understands this. There is no pressure; he just needs to know what you remember."

The detective spoke up, "Yes, your dad is right. This is not your fault. I think I have asked you enough questions for now. I'll borrow your dad and your brother for a short while, and you sit here with Ms. Yanira, but if you remember anything, I will leave my number for you, deal?"

Clariana nodded, and Yanira walked to her bedside. Yanira stood holding her hand.

The gentlemen exited the room and talked with Detective Bronson for about 10 to 12 minutes before returning. Yanira consoled her as they waited patiently.

When the gentlemen returned, and the officer was gone, Anais returned too. Walking up to Clariana, she stood beside the bed and broke down again. "Baby, Mommy is so sorry this happened to you. I am so sorry. You are my sweet girl; this is so bad. I am so sorry, baby, I am."

The room felt sorry for Anais; she was finally showing compassion, hurt, and sadness for her daughter. Anais told Kaeo that he could leave; she would take over for the night, giving him a break. She needed to be close to her daughter to make sure she was safe.

Kaeo and Cordero agreed; they both felt they needed some rest. Yanira had previously refused to leave, but with Anais there, she knew it would be a bloodbath if she stayed. Kaeo went and kissed Clariana.

"Are you ok? Do you want me to stay here?"

"Yes, Dad, I will be ok; you and Yanira get some rest. Yanira could use some sleep and a bathroom break. She hasn't left my side since I have been here. It's ok. Mom can take care of me until I get out and come home tomorrow. Ok?" Clariana pleaded.

Clariana held her hand out for Yanira. Anais stood and shouted, "No, you are not her mother! You need to leave. This is your fault. You should have been driving that car, not Clariana! She doesn't need you. She needs me. It's your fault; you remember that!"

Yanira looked at Anais. A part of her wanted to beat the hell out of her; however, she was right. She should have been in the car driving, not Clariana. Her wedding was in days, and the little girl she now loved was hurting. Anais was hurting as well, and she needed to respect her decision and give her the time she needed with her daughter.

Clariana yelled, "Mom, stop! It is not her fault. Yanira has been there for me; she has been here all night. Where were you? You just got here. She searched for me when I didn't come right back; you didn't even return my calls when I called to let you know I was here. So, stop it, please. I need to hug her, to thank her. If you don't want to stay with me, then fine, but don't be mean to her. She doesn't deserve this. Please, Mom."

Anais was hurt. "You are protecting her! She has turned you against me. They locked me up; that's why I did not call you. I bet they didn't tell you that! I had to spend nights in that place. Oh, how I hate you! Woman, you are evil. Clariana, if you want her to stay, I will leave. You are choosing another woman over your mother. I just need to be near you; let me have this moment."

"Mom, it is not her fault. Why do you keep saying that? I just wanted to hug her. If you have a problem with that, then I don't know what to tell you. I do want you to stay. You are my mother, but I care for Yanira, and she cared for me in your absence. Can you not understand that?"

Yanira spoke up, "Clariana, it is ok; your mother is right. She should be here, not me. I understand her pain and frustration. A mother's love is a mother's love. I love you enough to never make you choose anyone or feel uncomfortable."

"No, Yani, please give me a hug. I am sorry I wrecked your car, and I just feel bad!"

Looking at Anais, Yanira said, "I am going to hug your daughter and I will leave."

She hugged Clariana. "Listen, I told you to forget about the car; you are important to me. I will be back first thing in the morning, just call us if you guys need anything or want something; I will get someone to help you or your mother, no matter the time, so don't worry."

Cordero walked up behind Yanira, tapping her on the shoulder. He bent down to kiss his sister. "Hey, Yanira and Dad are helping to find out why you are here and who did this to you. Just rest with Mom, but if you need me to, I can stay here with you."

Clariana nodded, "It's ok, get some rest. I need a woman here to help me use the restroom. I appreciate you. Hey! Don't sleep in my bed Dero." She laughed.

"Whatever… if it's comfortable I just might!" he teased and smiled at Clariana. He turned and looked at his mom, advising, "Mom, this is not Yanira's fault. It is whoever did this to your daughter; whoever drove that car and hit her. It's their fault. So, chill. Yanira is just trying to help; she means no harm so be nice. Just stay with your daughter, and I will see you tomorrow."

Anais began to cry profusely as Cordero spoke his words. Cordero held his mother, rubbing her back as if she was the child and he was the parent consoling her. He could feel something was terrorizing his mother, but he just didn't know what. Maybe it was seeing Clariana in pain or guilt for not being there when her daughter needed her. The more he spoke, the more tears she shed on her son's shirt from the loud cries she projected.

Kaeo watched in silence. He did not understand the tears. He had not seen Anais cry in years, only when her crazy and abusive father passed away. He felt sad for her. Her pain was unbelievable, and he couldn't understand why her cries were so abundant. It didn't make sense to him, considering her daughter was alive and well.

Yanira stood in silence as she watched her fiancé watching his ex. There was a look on his face that she couldn't read or relate to. It was hurtful for her to see his glare at Anais; she didn't know if he was still in love with her and questioning their wedding. The look was very intense.

Yanira stepped out of the room without saying a word; she called herself an uber, requesting two stops. Today had proven to be way too much with all the drama, the emotions, and not to mention her now bruised heart and ego. She reached her office, grabbed her items, got in the uber, and headed to the store to get groceries and dinner for herself, Kaeo, and Cordero.

Yanira arrived home, turned on some light music, and began cooking fried chicken, asparagus, mashed potatoes, and brownies. Cooking was her form of relief from her thoughts, emotions, and anything that caused her pain and frustration. Listening to music as she worked her way around the kitchen, her mind had traveled to a place of happiness. Just as she dropped the pieces of chicken, the gentlemen walked in. Kaeo came over to hug and kiss her as normal, but she gave a fake smile.

"Welcome, Cordero, make yourself at home (genuinely hugging him). You can take whichever room you would like. The room upstairs has a bigger bed while the office has a gaming system in it, or you can take Clariana's room, but don't tell her I offered it to you."

Laughing at her words, Cordero smiled. "I will definitely take the room downstairs. The game might help me relax, so I might take part in a game or two. The food smells good, though. I am looking forward to some homemade fried chicken; it has been a while."

Yanira smiled. Knowing she was doing something right made her feel slightly more relaxed. Kaeo took him on a tour of the home, then took him to get settled in the office room and told him to freshen up. When they both returned to the kitchen, Yanira had everything laid out perfectly on the table.

Cordero told Yanira, "I love the home and appreciate you guys for allowing me to stay."

She smiled and turned to him, "I wouldn't have it any other way. You are family, and you don't need an invitation."

Cordero then asked, "So, with all this excitement about Clariana, you only have a few more days until your wedding. Are you ready?"

Yanira responded, "Honestly, I was thinking about calling it off. I mean, we need to care for Clariana, and your father needs some time. I mean, it's a lot going on."

Kaeo looked up. "Hell No! We are not canceling our wedding; there is no reason to. Clariana will be home tomorrow or Thursday, and my parents and siblings will be here on Thursday. Cordero is going to stay here, and her mother is around. I see no need to cancel everything after we have worked so hard. I love you, babe, more now than ever; I am ready without any hesitation about marrying you."

Yanira was shocked to see his facial expression and to hear those words. She must have read him wrong in the hospital. It had to be the emotions of getting married and the uncertainty of what happened to Clariana. Yanira perked up a bit. Knowing that Kaeo still wanted to go through with the wedding warmed her heart.

They were chatting briefly about random things while eating dinner and out of nowhere Cordero inquired, "Dad, I have to ask, what is up with Mom? Why is she so distraught about this accident? I mean, I know you called me because she was unconscious; that made sense then; once I saw her, I was cool, but all the crying and agony from Mom after seeing her seems weird, don't you think?"

Kaeo side-eyed him. "Honestly, son, I was thinking the same thing. I glared at her when you held her and tried to console her. I do not understand why she is taking it so hard when Clariana seems to be doing so well so quickly. Her blaming Yanira was expected…anything to take her frustrations about our relationship out on her, but the dramatics of it all didn't sit well with me.

Cordero replied, "Yeah, I think maybe she is going through some things, and she realizes she needs to get her life together, if not for her, for her kids. I mean, we are grown, but we still need you guys, you know?"

Kaeo smiled brightly, "Yeah, son, I know, and make no mistake, Yanira and I will always be here for you both." He held out his hands to intertwine them with Yanira's. He then kissed her hand sweetly and ever so gently. The chat ended after that consensus. Everyone agreed to wake up and go to the hospital first thing in the morning.

\*\*\*\*\*\*\*\*\*\*\*\*\*\*\*\*\*\*\*\*\*\*\*\*\*\*\*\*\*\*\*\*\*\*\*\*\*\*\*\*\*\*\*\*\*\*\*

In the bedroom Kaeo asked Yanira, "Baby, what's up? Why did you think I needed more time for our wedding? Or why would you want to cancel it? Do you have second thoughts, or are you not ready? I am more than ready, but I don't want to push you if you are not ready; I will try my best to understand."

Yanira was taken back by his questions and his confidence in how certain he was about their marriage. "Babe, I just thought maybe you would want to make sure that Clariana was ok. She is our priority, and our wedding can be postponed, but her care cannot. I thought maybe we just needed to hang tight, but I want to marry you just as much as you want to marry me."

Kaeo rose to approach her, "Medically, do you think she is not ok? Is there something you are not telling me?"

"No, medically she is fine. Her bumps and bruises are minor. I was worried about the concussion, but if she has no issues overnight, and if her test results come back normal, I see no reason for any concern," Yanira exclaimed.

Kaeo retorted, "Ok then, why would we postpone our wedding? I mean, if she is medically ok."

Yanira lowered her head. "I need to be honest with you, Kaeo. I saw how you were looking at Anais. I read you wrong and jealousy slipped in. I thought maybe you were reconsidering your choice. That maybe you were still in love with her, and with her vulnerability, maybe you were having second thoughts."

"Baby, there is no way in Hell I would reconsider anything with Anais! To be honest with you, I couldn't say this to Cordero, but it crossed my mind, with all the crying and dramatics, saying it should have been you. It doesn't sit

121

well with me. I know why she said it, but it was how she said it. I get a strange feeling about Anais; I have seen her threaten us but this hard on for you is taking a toll on her. I could be wrong, and I am sure that I am, but it was on my mind."

Yanira couldn't believe Kaeo was saying this; hell, she thought the same thing but was afraid to tell him. It was only a suspicion, nothing factual. She responded, "Well, dear, I know Anais hates me, but her trying to kill me is a little far-fetched. She is all talk. I think we should get some rest and head to the hospital in the morning."

Kaeo agreed as he picked her up and escorted her to the bathroom. He sat her on the counter, caressing her neck with his lips and tongue, wrapping his arms around her, softly massaging her breasts with his big hands. Taking off her sweater, shirt, and bra, he felt her silky-smooth skin on his fingertips, and began using his mouth to suck on her breasts as he rubbed her back. Yanira pulled down his sweatpants. Manipulating her body with his love, Kaeo picked her up, flipped her, and then bent her over the counter. She made a squirming sound as he began to push gradually into her walls.

He took a deep breath, stroking Yanira tenderly while he reached around and played with her pussy lips with his fingers. He entered in and out, while his other hand cupped her breasts. Yanira became louder and more breathless as he worked her body. He was already hidden inside, yet he bent her over a little farther down and drove in a little more. Yanira screamed, and her walls collapsed, filling his dick with her creamy sauce. Kaeo couldn't help but relieve himself too.

The next morning around 8 am, Yanira woke up, cooked breakfast, then they headed to the hospital. Clariana was still sleeping; however, Anais was sitting next to her, wide awake as if she had not been to sleep the entire night.

Kaeo asked, "How was she last night? Any changes or anything we should know about?"

"No, nothing; she slept all night. She is ok. They said the doctor should be coming back soon," Anais stated dryly.

"Mom, what's wrong? Did you not get any sleep? You should be happy. You seem so sad, like you've been crying. I thought you would be happy to see her for yourself, knowing she is ok." Cordero hinted at his mother.

Anais looked at him and said, "I am glad she is ok, but she should not have been in the car in the first place. The more I think about this, the madder I get; it should have been that bitch in the car and not my daughter. She should have run off the road into a ditch. The ambulance should have escorted her here, but instead, they sat there and pulled my baby from that car."

Cordero was about to reply, but Clariana woke up. "Hey, guys, how are you? Did you bring breakfast?" Clariana asked.

Yanira walked up, "Yes, here, baby girl; we stopped and got you both something to eat."

Cordero corrected her, "No, Yanira insisted we get you both something to eat. The same woman who mom keeps calling a bitch bought her breakfast."

Cordero held his hand out to receive the bag from Yanira and passed out biscuits to his sister and mother. Anais just looked at him, but she took the biscuit. She may not like Yanira, but she will eat the bitch's groceries. Clariana got up by herself and went to the restroom; the doctor was walking in when she returned.

Dr. Dowe cheerfully exclaimed, "Good morning, family; how is everyone doing this morning? Dr. White, I should have known you would be here instead of preparing for that wedding of yours. Well, let me check on my beautiful patient and rounding partner. If all looks well, then I would say she can go home with you within the next hour or so. Sound, ok?" Everyone nodded their heads.

Anais asked, "Do you not think it is too soon? She needs to rest. And what about her head? Do we not need to do anything more about that? She was not awake for a long time."

Dr. Dowe advised the room, "Well, no ma'am. We see no need for concern. I ran more tests late yesterday evening to ensure the swelling from her head was gone, and there was nothing to be alarmed about. All test results came back normal and within range. So, if all is well now and there are no reservations, we will begin the discharge process."

"Sounds great," Cordero blurted. "Thank you for caring for my sister, sir. I can't live without her." Everyone smiled, and Dr. Dowe chuckled.

"You are a big brother. She said you antagonize her and protect her."

Cordero laughed and nodded, as he knew the doctor spoke the truth.

Dr. Dowe checked her vitals as she sat up in the bed, allowing him to poke at her because she would soon be going home and attending the wedding. More importantly, she wanted to get away from her mother. She did not want to spend another night, much less a moment alone with her or be in her presence at all. Clariana had enough.

Dr. Dowe said, "Alright everyone. Everything looks great. Her vitals have been consistent, and she had a bowel movement, so we are good. I am ready to release you into the hands of Dr. White. You must continue to take the medications that will be provided as needed for the pain and swelling. In addition, care for that arm and follow up with your physician in 6 weeks to have the cast from your arm removed. The medication may make you drowsy, so I suggest not trying to drive or operate any moving objects. Do you have any questions, Clariana?"

"No sir, thank you, Dr. Dowe," Clariana replied gleefully.

"I have questions. Why is she being released in the care of Dr. White? She is not her mother. I am her mother, and she has no right to care for my child. I do. I want her released into my care," Anais scolded Dr. Dowe.

Dr. Dowe retorted, "Respectfully, ma'am, she decided to leave and be in the care of Dr. White. Frankly, she is 19 years of age and free to leave with whomever she elects, that's if she chooses to leave with anyone. I am merely respecting the wishes of my patient. However, I will leave you all to decide. Clariana, if there is anything else I can do, please let me know. I believe you have my information should you need anything. Dr. White best wishes to you and your family. If there is anything I can do, you know how to reach me."

Yanira nodded shamefully. Anais had embarrassed her in front of her peers yet again. The entire hospital staff was now informed of all her dirty laundry with this woman. She felt she was the laughingstock and center of attention. Anais was such a horrible person, and she wanted nothing more than to rid her of her life, but it was not possible. She was marrying Kaeo, and as long as she had him in her life, she would have to deal with Anais. The children belonged to her and him; they would always be in their lives. If her love for him were not so strong, she would not have allowed any of this to go on, but she loved Kaeo. He made her happy; he was caring, attentive, affectionate, and had devout love for her.

Kaeo told Clariana, "Baby girl, we will let you get dressed while we pick up your medication from the pharmacy. Think you will be ready when we get back? Maybe thirty minutes to an hour?"

"Yes, Dad. I will be ready," she replied.

Anais yelled, "No! What makes you think she is going home with you? Why is no one asking me what I want? She needs her mother. I need to be the one who takes care of her. Not some bitch who thinks she knows everything because she went to school. Don't force your girlfriend on my children."

Kaeo looked at her intensely. "Anais, I am not going to tell you again to address my wife with respect. Clariana is free to go where she wants, but she has chosen to come with me and Dr. White, and for the record she is soon to be Dr. White-Iosua; now, if you don't like it, that is your problem. She has done nothing but be good to the children and you, even though you don't deserve shit. We are leaving, and we will be back. Clariana, let us know what you decide. Cordero, are you ready?"

"Yeah, Dad, I'm right behind you." (he turned to look at his mother) "Mom, you are wrong. Why do you keep provoking this woman? If it were not for her, Clariana might not even be here. Who the hell do you think is paying these hospital bills? Who do you think sends your daughter money to live off of every month? You are wrong on so many levels." Cordero was filled with frustration as he released his words.

"No, it is her fault that Clariana is here; she did not save her. She should have been in that car, and that would have saved my baby. I blame her for not being in that car!" Anais yelled.

Cordero looked at her, rubbing his face in anger and dismay. "Mom, you keep saying that. She wasn't in the car; it was an accident. Nothing was planned. It was simply an accident; stop blaming her. Clare, I will be back, ok."

"No, can you just stay?" (Cordero looked at her with a bewildered look on his face) She was quick, "Ah, just in case I fall or something, you can help Mom. You, because Dad and Mom won't get along. Please Dero!" Clariana pleaded.

Cordero saw a look in his sister's eyes and knew something was wrong. He damn sure didn't like it; it was fear. He taught her to fear no one, but now was not the time to discuss it. "Ok, Clare, sure. I will wait here while you go shower. Just yell if you need me, ok? Yanira, do you think you can get a nurse to come help her? I will stay, but I'd rather not be the one to go in the bathroom with my little sister, you know what I mean?"

Yanira smiled, "Yes, I understand. I will get someone, and we will be back shortly."

When they returned, the nurse was walking in with the paperwork, and Clariana was officially being discharged. She was ready, exiting the hospital with only a cast. The family walked her out together. Anais refused to walk with them as she wanted Clariana with her, and Clariana would not budge; her brother was there. She also told her she did not want to go to her boyfriend's house because she was not familiar with him. Anais had become more upset than when she entered the hospital—knowing now that she would have to end Yanira and ruin their wedding once and for all.

## CHAPTER 8: CORDERO HOLDS NO PUNCHES

Clariana settled in nicely upon their arrival at home. Cordero walked up calmly, searching her eyes and body language in anticipation for the answer he was expecting to receive. He asked, "Clare, you good? Anything you wanted to talk with me about. You've been off all day. I feel like you got something on your chest."

Clariana played it off. "No, I'm ok. Just a little tired, and realizing I had an accident you know. Glad to be alive, but I am cool now that I am back at home." She reached out for a hug. Clariana held Cordero for a brief time, but longer than normal. In that instant he knew something was wrong, but maybe it was just her anxiety from the accident making her rethink life. However, if it was not, he would soon find out.

Kaeo and Cordero went out for dinner, while Yanira caught up with her wedding planner, who had to take over because she was tied up with Clariana. She refused to allow Kaeo to handle things on his own because he had too much to worry about with Clariana, and he needed to spend time with Cordero. Yanira couldn't help but continue to think of what they had been through the last couple of days, and Anais was right about one thing; it was her car Clariana was driving, and she was responsible for her. Had she just waited and went on her own, Clariana would have been safe, she thought. Reality was, even though it was an accident, and regardless of how terrible she felt, Anais did not help the situation by constantly blaming her for the issue at hand.

Thursday afternoon, Kaeo's family arrived, as well as Cordero's wife and child. Kaeo had the hotel concierge pick everyone up from the airport and bring them to the hotel; he and Cordero waited for them there. His mother was so happy to see them all, including Cordero; he was her grandchild, and she loved him still, even considering what happened to Kaeo. It was Anais she could not forgive for lying and convincing the kids to lie and deceive people; it was not how she was raised. Cordero was just an innocent child following the direction of his mother.

After the meet and greet, everyone seemed to settle in nicely. They dined in a buffet style restaurant and chatted about their flight, the upcoming wedding, things left for Yanira and Kaeo to do and how they all were excited. Kaeo was pleased to see how the two families were coming together; it was as if they had known each other all their lives.

Yanira's father and uncle sat close to Mr. Iosua and the men discussed life in the old days, true love, religion, marriage, and fishing, all while the mothers discussed the wedding facility, decorations, food, and desserts. Each one trying to put in last-minute desserts and food items while the wedding party would be taking pictures.

Ryleigh brought up the idea to have one of those new 360 photo booths for the guests while they were all taking official photos. Yanira and Kaeo loved the idea, so as usual, Marshall made one call and two 360 booths would be at the wedding reception along with the photographers and videographers. This would be a great addition to the entertainment and help catch special moments the photographers would miss since they would be occupied with the family. After two hours and forty-five minutes the family left the restaurant and headed to the hotel and their homes, even more thrilled for the soon to be union of Kaeo and Yanira.

Anais called Cordero and Clariana the day before the wedding, asking them to meet with her for lunch. Cordero agreed, but Clariana convinced him she was not well enough to get out and wanted to save her energy for the wedding. Cordero thought it was a little off, but he did not pressure her. Cordero knew his sister, and even more so, he knew when something was wrong; he just didn't know what and nothing he thought of made sense. Their mother was awful for sure, but Clariana never missed the opportunity to spend time with her hoping she would come around.

Despite his suspicions, Cordero left and met with his mother. When he arrived, Anais kept looking past him to see if Clariana was behind him, but she wasn't. Puzzled about Clariana's whereabouts, she interrogated him before he could even sit down. "Where is Clare? Why did she not come? I can care for her if she is not well."

Cordero made up an excuse and said, "She is still taking the medication; it makes her drowsy." Although Clariana had given him that reason, he knew she just did not want to be around their mom.

After a little small talk and chit chat, Cordero couldn't help but ask, "So, Mom, why do you keep coming for Yanira? You need to relax with all the issues with her; she has only been trying to help. There is no need for all the drama."

"I will never relax; she should not be in this position. It should be me."

"Mom, you have already moved on a couple of times. Why can't you allow Dad to do the same?"

Anais told him boldly, "Kaeo would not be the same with her. He promised to be with me always, and I still love him. I will not allow him to leave me for another woman; we have too much history. She does not need his love, I do. She simply cannot win."

"Mom, if that is the case, why did you do all that shit you did? I mean, it's me. Let's just be honest. What is this all about? You can be happy, but no one else can? That's some narcissistic type of shit; you're better than that."

Anais became aggressive and argumentative. "Where do you get off protecting some stranger? I raised you, not her. You don't ever go against your mother; you hate who I hate. You need to understand that Kaeo made promises to me, and he needs to keep them. No other man has kept his word with me but him and I deserve him. No matter what I have done, he belongs to me! So, you just protect your mother and stop acting like an ungrateful child."

"Mom, me ungrateful? Really! And it's not about me protecting someone over you. It just seems like you fucked up and you want your cake and you want to eat it too. It's not right. She helped your daughter get into college; you didn't. I told you she takes care of your daughter in college and sends her money faithfully. You aren't doing any of that, so why can't you be nice for those reasons? Her presence is benefiting your daughter and what is between you and dad was before her time."

"Cordero, who the fuck are you? So, you are judging me because I am not a doctor and can't get friends to help? Or afford to help Clare with school? Does that make me a bad mother? I sacrificed for you both, but now you want to make me feel bad because I am poor. You do not get to tell me who to be nice to, or who deserves what! You are an ingrate; this woman is poisoning my own children against me. Don't you hear yourself? Now you love her more than me? The woman who gave your life!"

Cordero was no longer in the mood to eat or be in the presence of his mother. He quipped, "You know what, it has nothing to do with any of what you said, but here, let me pay you back a little. Lunch is on me. I gotta go." He kissed her forehead and turned his back, saying, "I will see you after the wedding."

Anais was now even more enraged to know that Cordero was also going to the wedding. She thought he was only there for Clariana. She blurted, "Why would you betray me by condoning that wedding? You have no business being on the side of a traitor, especially one who wanted to ruin our family. You better not go or else!"

Cordero looked over his shoulder and replied, "Nah, remember you were the liar and traitor, not Dad. We were just pawns. I'm going!" He left without turning back.

Anais was enraged. She threw everything off the table, then began yelling at the patrons, "What are you looking at? Mind your business." She got up, leaving all the food and dishes on the floor where she slung them.

When Cordero arrived at the house, he was pretty upset. He told his dad all about the lunch. Kaeo was outraged. He felt sorry for the kids because she was making them choose. Apologetically he stated, "Cordero, I am sorry that you and Clare are getting stuck in the middle of the drama with your mother and me."

Cordero interjected, "Dad, it's not on you. It's on her. She is the problem. To be honest, I don't know what is off with Mom. What I do know is that I am proud to have a stepmother like Yanira. Mom tried to ruin your relationship, and there was no way I would ever betray you again after all you have done for me and Clare over the years."

"Thank you, son. This means more than you know." Kaeo was overwhelmed by his maturity.

133

"Dad, one more thing. I've got a bad feeling. Since Clariana stayed at the hospital with Mom, she has not wanted to see her or talk to her. I can't help but think that maybe she said or did something to Clariana, but she does not want to say."

Kaeo sighed. "Son, I got that same strange feeling too, but Clariana will eventually tell you. I am sure it is just the pressure of the wedding and wanting her to choose her or us. It should not be that way, but we will focus on the wedding, and hopefully, we can get back to normal afterward. Clare will return to school and put all this behind her."

Later that afternoon they had rehearsal dinner, and this seemed to cheer them all up. Both sides of the family were able to laugh, talk, and make the last-minute touches to the wedding event; everything went as planned. After rehearsal, Ryleigh and Marshall took Yanira to their house so she could stay with them overnight and head to the penthouse suite the next morning for hair, nails, makeup, and to get dressed. Ryleigh was excited to have her there.

She and Marshall planned a Jamaican BBQ in their backyard with all of the wedding party, promising to close everything down by 2 am and make sure Kaeo had a driver to take him, Cordero, and Kamryn home to pick up Diego. Clariana would stay with the baby during the party. Kaeo ordered her a large pizza, Sunkist orange drink and a brownie for her dinner.

Anais called Clariana six times that evening while she tended to the baby. She continued to call, leaving message after message, but Clariana refused to answer her mother. Instead, she and Kaleyla traded holding Baby Diego and cuddling with him until he fell asleep. He was extremely sweet and low maintenance.

Kaleyla finally asked, "What's up with your mom? Is it true she had been threatening Yanira and fighting her?"

Clariana shook her head. "Yeah, girl. She has changed so much. She wants me to hate the very person who raised me and the only person who has put me in a position to succeed. She had me hating Yanira, thinking she cheated with my dad, but come to find out, Mom was the one cheating, lying, leaving us overnight to be with other men, taking Dad's car so he would not leave, leaving him at work, and so many other things I could tell you. She also beat him with a metal pipe. My brother told me all about it. Recently, she has done something to me that I just can't wrap my head around why she would be so careless. It hurts so bad."

Clariana began to cry, unable to control her tears. The pain residing in her heart was rising to her stomach and throat. She ran to the bathroom to throw up. It was making her sick, but if she told anyone a secret, it would be Kaleyla. At one point, they had been the best of friends growing up.

Kaleyla came into the bathroom, held Clariana's hair while she vomited, and then gave her a wet towel to wash her face. The two began to talk, and Clariana told her the whole dirty evil truth.

"While I was in the hospital, my mom was extremely rude to Yanira and Dad. She kept saying the accident was all Yanira's fault and that it should have been her in the car. I couldn't understand why she kept saying that because she had said it one too many times. She stayed with me Tuesday night, so Dad and Yanira could go home and rest. At one point in the night, I must have dozed off, but I woke up to my mom saying she didn't mean to hurt me. Yanira was supposed to be the one driving. She only wanted to ruin their wedding day, so my dad could rethink his decision. She told me she still wanted to be with him and would never let him go. It wasn't meant for me to be the driver. She couldn't see who was in the car when she ran into it. She was so sorry, and then she cried so hard. I faked sleep until Dad and Cordero came back. I am scared of her now."

Kaleyla couldn't believe her ears. "So, you mean to tell me your mom is the one who hit you and did this to you? Oh my gosh, like she hates Yanira that much? Man, have you told your dad or Cordero? I don't know what my brother will do; he will be so angry. Cordero will, too; he is so protective of you. What will you do?"

Clariana lowered her head and said softly, "I am not sure, but I can't tell them now; it will ruin the wedding. Please promise we will keep this as our little secret. We can't tell them anything. I don't want the drama, and I honestly just want to forget. Promise me, OK?"

Kaleyla responded, "I promise, but if she does something else, you have to tell. Someone else could get hurt, Clariana. I know that is your mom, but that is nuts; you could have died. They say if you had rolled two more feet past the guard rail you would have gone off the highway into ongoing traffic."

"Yes, I know. I am afraid of telling. She is losing her mind about this, but I can't blame anyone but her. It is all her fault. If she were loyal to my dad like he was to her, she would not be living with someone she didn't love. She would be happy. On the other hand, I am glad she did because Yanira is perfect for him; she loves him, and it shows. Not to mention I am getting the opportunity of a lifetime. She has been such a blessing to me, helping me follow my dreams. We were all happy until my mom came back."

After the conversation and tears, the girls binged on snacks and Tahitian treats until they fell asleep in the living room around 12:30 am. Cordero and Kamryn came in shortly after, around 1 am. They had never left Diego alone with anyone other than her mom, and since Clariana was not answering her phone, they decided to leave the wedding party early. When they came through the garage door to the living room, they got a full view of baby Diego bundled with a blanket and pillows on the opposite side of him so he would not roll. Kamryn smiled; Clariana and Kaleyla had taken good care of her baby. Usually, he would wake up around this time, but he seemed like he was fast asleep.

Cordero picked up Clariana's phone. It was powered off, so he powered it on. Clariana's phone began buzzing immediately, and Cordero picked it up. "Mom, she is sleeping right now. What's wrong? (Anais spoke on the line) Well, why have you called her so many times? (Anais talking) Well, Mom, she has been with Kaleyla, and they had Diego. She was just busy. What's up? (Anais talking privately to Cordero) I will have her call you after the wedding, ok? (Anais guilt trips Cordero about the wedding) Mom, we are going. There is no way you can stop us. We are adults. I told you, you fucked up, not him nor us. We want to see him happy, and she makes him happy, end of story. (Anais continues to yell into the phone) Mom, you have moved on. Let him do the same."

Cordero was talking so loudly that it woke up Diego, Clariana, and Kaleyla. Kamryn picked up Diego, took him to the room Cordero was sleeping in and rocked him back to sleep with a little rubbing and patting on the back.

Cordero questioned Clariana, "What's going on between you and Mom? Why haven't you answered her all day, and why did you not want to be alone with her at the hospital? Don't lie to me," he demanded.

Clariana looked at him and then at Kaleyla. "I just wanted to catch up with Kaleyla; we haven't spent any time together, and Mom just kept calling. Plus, I had Diego, and she would have tried to weasel her way here to see me or him. I did not want that. You know how mom can be."

Cordero thought hard about her answer, then said, "Yeah, I get it, and I understand that, but what about the hospital? Why did you not want to be alone with her? If there's something you are not saying Clare, I want to know."

Clariana became nervous, "Bro, I promise we will talk after the wedding; my meds have me a little sleepy. I took them after Diego went to sleep, and I am tired."

Cordero looked at her mistrustingly, then replied, "Yeah, ok, but after the wedding, we will talk, meds or no meds, understand?"

She lowered her head, knowing he meant exactly what he said. She could not use any more excuses and would have to tell him the truth soon. "Yeah, I understand. Good night," Clariana said as she quickly walked into her room. Kaleyla followed her with their blankets.

When they got to the room, Kaleyla told her, "Sis, that was close. You know Cordero can always tell when either of us is lying, just like when we were kids; he has done it all. You know you are going to have to tell him eventually. "

Clariana was sad. "Yes, I know; I just need to wait until the wedding is over."

"Anyway, how many times did she call?"

"She has called and texted a total of 28 times throughout the day. It is obnoxious, and I just don't feel safe with her. I know it's my mom, but how could she be so reckless to want to hurt Yanira that much? I mean that could have been murder if the car would have gone further and she acts like nothing is wrong."

"Yeah, what bothers me is that she still looks at you and expects you to be ok with what she has done. I know she doesn't know you know what happened because you were asleep, but dang, I mean I can't imagine my mom doing anything like this."

"Who are you telling! Momma Iosua is too good to make these types of mistakes. Only my mother would do something like this. Anyway, I don't want to think about it anymore. And yes, after the wedding, I need to tell Cordero so he can talk with her."

"Yeah, but that scares me too, Clare. I mean, can you imagine what he will do to her when he finds out this was her fault? He is going to go ballistic. I can't even imagine."

"That's why I can't tell him now. He may end up in jail and it shouldn't be him, it should be her. Then dad is going to feel bad, and Yanira already thinks it's her fault. It's all just too much, and I am at a loss."

The girls went to bed, wanting nothing more than to pretend everything would be ok.

• • • • • • • • • • • • • • • • • • • • • • • • • • • • • • • • • • • • • • • • • •

# **CHAPTER 9: WEDDING BLISS OR MAYHEM**

The wedding day had finally arrived. Yanira woke up to a message from Kaeo.

"Good morning, My Love! The party was great; celebrating our love and union means the world to me. I am extremely excited to make you Mrs. Yanira Catori White-Iosua. I love you more than life itself, and I cannot wait to see you walking down the aisle to say yes. Always and forever, Us. Until 4 pm!"

Yanira smiled at the thoughtfulness of her soon-to-be husband. She couldn't believe how lucky she was and was just about to pinch herself to make sure she wasn't dreaming when at that precise moment Ryleigh and Kalia walked in the door. She smiled.

"Knock, knock, you up?" they said in unison.

"Is this real, you guys? Like am I really walking down the aisle to marry the man of my dreams? I was just thinking of pinching myself to see if it is real."

"Girl, it is definitely real, and you are about to get married," Ryleigh said with laughter. The look on her cousin's face was everything.

"You ready, Yani? Because I am ready to officially be your sister!" Kalia couldn't hold back her excitement.

Yanira blushed and replied, "Yes, me too! I'm ready for my big day and for my family to be complete."

The girls brought her breakfast in bed; she couldn't have been happier to share this moment with the both of them. The trio sat and talked through breakfast, then headed to the hotel to meet the makeup artist, accessories vendors, and others who had a part in making her day memorable for their prepping and pampering.

Yanira could feel her excitement building as they arrived at the hotel; she was ready for the pampering, starting everything off with a body wax, then her hair, nails, and finally her toes. Everything was going perfectly until she saw a woman that looked like Anais. Stopping in her tracks, she instantly became nervous and worried about Anais and what could go wrong. The woman turned around, and Yanira was relieved; it was not her. The last thing she wanted was to see or hear from Anais. Ryleigh touched her shoulder.

"Yani, I got you; nothing will happen. I am your shadow for the day, and I wish a bitch would! Not to mention, you invited all of Marshall's security to the wedding, and some will be at the reception, too."

Kalia said, "That part! We got you, so don't worry. She wouldn't dare do something stupid with my mom around. Besides, no one has told her the location. Kaleyla also told me that Clare is not even answering her calls, so we are good. Now, let's get ourselves together."

Yanira relaxed and cleared her mind as she prepared to walk down the aisle with her father. His presence was comforting as she turned and gave him a hug. On cue with the music, they began walking down the aisle. Smiling at everyone, she looked into the crowd, seeing both of Kaeo's kids, her best friend and cousin, and their families. As she got close enough to see the face of the love of her life, she knew in her heart it was worth all the drama and she was more than ready.

There were no interruptions as their family pastor assisted them in exchanging their vows. The ceremony was simple and beautiful. Yanira and Kaeo walked down the aisle finally as husband and wife. The family couldn't be more eager, and most importantly, Anais was nowhere in sight. The family gathered to take pictures while the other members and friends left for the reception. It took one full hour and twenty-seven minutes for all of the wedding photos to be taken with such a big family.

They rented the ballroom at The Prestige W for the reception and the penthouse suite for the honeymoon. After about thirty minutes, Yanira changed into her dress and refreshed her makeup. The ladies reunited with the men and walked into the reception ballroom so the DJ could announce the newlyweds. The wedding party danced and gave toasts as well as speeches. When it was time to sit down, Yanira asked for her flat shoes. Clariana left to grab them but realized she did not know where the shoes were with all the boxes and items in the car.

Clariana quickly powered on her phone to call Ryleigh. As soon as the phone powered on, she saw that Anais had called her over 57 times and left 36 text messages. She did not have time for any drama with her mother. She was still incredibly nervous about being alone with her and was now having a nightmare about the accident, picturing her mother being the one who tried to kill her was too much!

Ryleigh answered, "Hey Niece what's up?" Then explained, "I know the car is a mess! The shoes are in the trunk under the pink box." She began cracking jokes about how junky the car was. Clariana laughed as she made her way back to the hotel ballroom.

Around 7:30 pm, Anais pulled up to the hotel. When Clariana was in the hospital and sleeping, she had made sure to turn on her location and share it with herself so she would always know where she was. She asked for the Iosua wedding party at the hotel service desk, and they directed her to the ballroom. Anais immediately saw Yanira and Kaeo; his smile made her boil because he looked lovingly at Yanira. His eyes were locked into hers, his smile was bright, and his hands were all over her. She became simultaneously jealous and enraged as she realized it was the reception. The wedding was over, and she had not been able to stop it. They were taking pictures with the family, including her kids. Both hugged Yanira as if she were their mother. She could not and would not allow this nonsense.

Anais returned to her car, beating on the steering wheel, and talking to herself. She refused to let this bitch take her man; she would end her now and forever. Kaeo would fall back in love with her because Yanira would not exist. Just like all the times before, although it only took one time for the others. This bitch seemed to have nine lives! She was not scared of her like the rest; she fought back and challenged her constantly. That was a mistake for Anais; no one played with her.

Anais was livid as she exited the car and went back to the hotel ballroom. She entered the room, looking around for Yanira or Kaeo, knowing that when she found one, she would find the other. She glimpsed to the left, where she spotted Kaeo hugging all over Yanira. Fury ran through her entire body. As she slowly walked towards the couple, Kaeo's mother stepped in front of her, trying not to cause a scene or anger Anais.

"Oh dear, it's been so long. How are you, and what are you doing here?"

With tears in her eyes, Anais looked at Mrs. Iosua and said, "Mother, I am just going to give the new couple a gift they will never forget."

Gently, Mrs. Iosua responded, "No, not now dear. We have not reached the gifting part, Anais, and you know this is not the time or place for you to be here. Come with me. Apparently, we have a lot to catch up on; you have been very busy these days."

Anais was visibly agitated and became impatient as she had lost sight of Kaeo. As tears filled her eyes, she said, "Mother, No! I need to see Kaeo. Do you not understand what he has done to me? (She began to cry) This is not real; he belongs to me, not her. She has ruined my life. She has taken my children away. You don't understand. They shouldn't be celebrating them. It should be us walking down the aisle and getting married. Not a bitch like her!"

By this time, Anais was a little hysterical, but with so many people talking, dancing, and enjoying the music only a few people who were standing close could hear the words coming from Anais as the music was turned up with so much base. Kaeo's brother approached his mother.

"Mom, may I borrow you for just one second, please? It's about the cake. Anais, how are you?"

Anais looked at him; she hurt even more. He looked just like his brother, and she could not take this waiting any longer.

"Hey, little brother. Listen, take your mother. I need to find your brother, ok?"

"No, Anais. You must not do this; let this day pass. This is not the time, dear. You have moved on, and so has he. You

144

need to leave now. Do not disrupt this union," Mrs. Iosua demanded.

Anais became belligerent.

"I said NO mother! Kaeo can't move on without me. This is not a union, and they are not together. He belongs to me, and I will prove it. I do not want to harm you, but you keep trying to stop me. All I want is for Kaeo to come with me. I will not cause any trouble. Ok?"

By this time, Kaeo's other brother grabbed him and his father, and told them what was going on. Kaeo asked Marshall to escort Yanira and Ryleigh out of the venue, telling them to go and take more pictures and have the security guard go with them. Marshall did just that because he knew that Ryleigh would come for Anais.

As Kaeo and his father headed toward Anais and Mrs. Iosua, Kaeo wondered how Anais knew where to find him. The music continued to play as Kaeo approached her, in a demanding tone.

"What the hell are you doing here, Anais? You will not ruin this day for me, so leave now! We are already married, and there is nothing you can do about it."

Anais yelled, "No! I told you; you belong to me. I will not let you ruin our lives. You promised me you would always love me. You lied to me, Kaeo. It is you who is ruining everything."

Kaeo looked at her. "Anais, we were kids. You have cheated on me, lied to me, hit me, pulled a knife on me, threatened my now wife, and you disrespect me constantly. Why would I stay? You must leave. This is not the place to discuss this."

Anais pleaded, "Can we please talk about this? I have hurt you, but you know me. We were meant to be. If I had known that you would have done this, I would have stopped a long time ago. Kaeo, you must not do this to us."

People started to notice and listen to the argument. A crowd formed, and Kaeo noticed she had a gun. He quickly responded, "Yes, you are right. I know you, and yes, this is all a mistake. Let me let her down tonight, and I will meet you once this is over. OK? (He took his hand and rubbed it down her face as he looked into her eyes) Don't worry, let's just go for now."

He hugged her, then signaled at her purse, letting his dad know she had a gun. Mr. Iosua nodded. They all began to walk her out slowly. Kaeo held her hand to comfort her as they ushered her out of the building. He felt relieved when they reached her car; she was leaving peacefully.

"You promise? I knew you would come to me. I know you love me lover."

"Yes, you are right. It is you and always has been. I just needed you to see how badly you hurt me, ok? We are good now."

Kaeo said anything she wanted to hear just to get her to leave. He knew she had to leave before Yanira and Ryleigh came back. It would be hell to pay for everyone, especially him. He just wanted her off the property. He would not tell Clariana or Cordero she showed up; he didn't want the pain of telling them he had her locked up again. He just wanted this nightmare to be over and not to ruin Yanira's day.

Cordero, his wife, Kaleyla, and Clariana came running outside at that very moment. Someone told them Kaeo and his family had walked off with some woman who was yelling and crying, pointing to the door.

Just as they reached Anais's car, Cordero yelled, "Mom, what the hell are you doing here? Come on, man! You just keep fucking up; let this go!"

Clariana and Kaleyla noticed the car and immediately, Clariana began to panic. Just seeing the car hurt her heart and gave her flashbacks of the wreck and her mother telling her the truth that night at the hospital. It all came back, and to see the car was like death for her. She instantly burst into tears, crying loudly while staring at the side of the car.

Kaleyla approached her. "It's ok, Clare. Don't look at it; it's ok. Let's go back inside. It's ok, Clare. Come on please, it's ok."

Cordero looked at his sister and observed her body shaking. "Clare, what is it? You, ok?"

He noticed her glaring at the front and side of the car. He walked around and saw the damage to Anais's car. Cordero began screaming and lunged for his mother.

"No fucking way!!! You did this? You almost fucking killed your daughter. What fucking kind of mother are you? That's why Clare didn't want to be alone with you. This is why you kept yelling that it should have been Yanira, not her. You fucking drove the car. You didn't say anything, Mom. Damn! (Kaeo's brother grabbed Cordero as he continued to approach his mother.) Kaleyla, take Clare inside. Mom, what the fuck? What's wrong with you? I am done. I am done with you, man! You tried to kill my sister, and I will never forgive you! You sat talking and doing all that bull for no reason. We are no more. I'm done with you, you understand me. I am fucking done. You are a lunatic! I am her protector, and I couldn't have ever imagined I would have to protect her from you. Get the hell on man!"

He rubbed his head in anger and disgust. He was hurt and furious; tears were in his eyes. His sister was ok, but his mother had lost her mind. She needed mental help. Kalel hugged him and he broke down.

"Uncle, it was her; she tried to kill her own daughter. That's fucked up."

Kalel just consoled his nephew. He, too, knew it was horrible, but he knew Anais and what she was capable of.

Anais began to cry. "It's not my fault, son, please. I did, but I was only trying to stop this wedding. It is ok now because your dad and I have worked it out. He will tell Yanira it is over, and we will be a family again. Clariana knows that I love her. It's all going to work out. Kaeo just needs to be with us. We can all start over in California." Anais walked over to touch him, but he snatched away. Cordero wanted no part of his mother.

"Are you stupid? He is not ending anything with her. Look at his face, Mom! You just broke his damn heart, just like mine. Your daughter is shaking; she is fucking traumatized. Clare is scared to be near you! I'm done with you; this is it for me. You just admitted to attempted murder. You need fucking help." Cordero was in tears.

Anais looked at Kaeo. "Baby, tell him it's ok. You know me; it was a mistake. That bitch was supposed to be in the car. I only wanted to stop the wedding; that is all. I would never hurt our children, Kaeo. I asked Clariana for forgiveness." She began to hit herself on the head.

Cordero turned to Clariana. "What the fuck is she talking about, Clare? She told you she hurt you! I knew you were lying; I knew something was wrong with you. Why didn't you tell me? I would have protected you, Clare. What the fuck man."

Tears ran from Clariana's eyes. Kaleyla just held her niece and friend. She then spoke up.

"Cordero, Anais told Clariana when she thought she was sleeping. Clariana was not ok. She was scared to the point that she faked sleep until you and Kaeo arrived. That is why she refused to be alone with Anais. She wanted to tell you, but she feared ruining the wedding. And it's why she didn't want to talk to Anais. She fears her own mother. Please do not be mad at her, she only wanted to do the right thing."

Cordero ran to his sister; he needed to hold and console her. He did not protect her. He knew something was wrong and didn't push hard enough.

Kaeo couldn't believe it. "You are a monster, Anais! I am done. My feelings for you have turned into hate. What monster would go around blaming others for hurting their children? Faking as if you were looking for the person, but all along, it was you! Never contact me again. I'm done." Tears filled his eyes as well. He was hurt and needed to hold Yanira, but he couldn't let this ruin their day.

Tears rolled down his face. He went to Clariana and hugged her and Cordero tightly; she was shaking so badly. "Baby girl, I am so sorry; never be afraid to tell me anything. You will never ruin anything with the truth. Yanira and I would have understood and taken better precautions. She wanted to cancel, and I insisted, but had I known, I would have never; I am so sorry, love. Let's go. Cordero, let's go, son. It's going to be ok; we will be fine."

Cordero and his wife followed Kaeo. The rest of the family turned their backs in disbelief. Mrs. Iosua, Kaleyla, and their brothers walked away behind Kaeo. Anais was no longer a part of their family. In all the years of knowing her, they never once thought she was capable of hurting their daughter nor thought more about the things she had done to her children until now. They understood why he wanted so desperately to leave now more than ever. They also understood why he stayed; it was for the kids.

Anais stood there in shock, then became hysterical, beating on her car, crying and screaming for Kaeo. Mr. Iosua remained behind. He was a patient and gentle man, and Anais had always respected him and followed his instructions. He hugged her, saying, "My dear, things are not good. Your temper is elevated, and you are not thinking clearly; tomorrow will be different. The children need time to process this mistake that was made on your behalf. It will all work out the way it is supposed to, ok? Go home, and the kids will call you when they have calmed down. I will make sure of it."

Anais trusted his words; she thought he meant that he would make sure Kaeo returned to her. She nodded and said, "Alright, Makua. I will see you tomorrow. You are right. Everything will be ok."

Anais had snapped. It was obvious that she was mentally ill. Mr. Iosua stood there as she opened her car door and got in, making sure she pulled off and left the premises before he returned to the hotel. Security came running out, but they were too late. Mr. Iosua diffused the situation on his own.

Once inside, he saw the family speaking with Kaeo and consoling Cordero and Clariana. He told the family, "This is the time to pray; we must be solid together." The family gathered around and prayed in the reception hall.
Afterward, Cordero took his family, Clariana, and Kaleyla home. He would not allow his sister to be alone; he took her, where she felt safe, to Yanira's.

After prayer, Kaeo stood and cried in his dad's arms; he was upset and shattered. He wanted to press charges, but he knew the decision was up to Clariana. Although it was her mother, it was the right thing to do. Mrs. Iosua rubbed him gently, telling someone to find Yanira quickly so they could retire to their room because he could not guarantee their safety in the reception hall.

At that moment, Yanira, Ryleigh, and Marshall were walking in. Marshall kept them occupied for 30 minutes, taking pictures, and chatting to divert their attention. Yanira noticed her husband hugging his father and his mother rubbing his back. She casually walked up to the family, smiling until she heard his cries. Mrs. Iosua stepped away, tapping her husband to let him know to step away. Kaeo turned towards Yanira, and she saw his tears. He hugged her firmly.

"Baby, what's wrong? Where are the kids?" Kaeo couldn't speak. "Honey, whatever it is, just tell me. Where are the kids? What happened, are you ok?" Yanira asked with worry in her mind and fear in her heart.

Kaeo looked at her but said nothing; he couldn't ruin their special night for her. Yanira observed the pain he was dealing with, yet she saw the love in his eyes for her. Kaeo's love for her was amplified because of the pain Anais continued to deliver to him and the children; she kept pushing him into Yanira's arms.

He cleared his throat, "Let us enjoy the rest of this beautiful night, and I will explain things in the morning, ok? Right now, I just want to share a few more dances with you privately."

Yanira was confused, but she did not want to pressure him; Kaeo was always honest, and she would rather dance with him as he was officially her husband. She took his hand and queued with five fingers for the DJ to play a song for them, John Legend's "All of Me." Kaeo kissed her and forgot about the dance. He hugged her close through three more songs. Others joined in, some clueless about what happened and others who knew something happened but were unclear on exactly what.

Around 9:45 pm, they shut the party down. The couple took the elevator to the penthouse. Everyone agreed to meet tomorrow at the park near their house for a family Luau before Kaeo's family left. His father wanted to bring their tradition into the wedding, and Yanira's family helped. The couple would leave for their honeymoon in Italy on Monday morning.

Kaeo and Yanira were awakened for breakfast the next morning by someone knocking on the door of the penthouse suite. Kaeo kissed her sweetly, put on his robe, and opened the door. The spread was full of fruits, waffles, bacon, sausage, oatmeal, eggs, and toast served with orange juice.

Yanira finally asked, "So, do you want to talk about last night? I don't know what is going on, but should we not discuss it? I was worried about you."

Kaeo looked at her with uncertainty; why would she be worried? They were just married. She answered without him having to ask.

"When we made love for the first-time last night as husband and wife, you had tears in your eyes as you made love to me. I didn't know if they were tears of joy or regret. I am used to you making love to me, releasing your anger or passion, but last night it was different."

Kaeo looked up in dismay. "I would never regret meeting you, chasing you, loving you, and most certainly not marrying you. I cried because I was hurt and afraid of losing you. I can't imagine my life without you, and last night almost went bad."

Yanira asked, "What do you mean bad? It was perfect for me; I married the love of my life, and my kids were there, along with my family, old and new. Babe it was perfect in every way."

"Last night, I fear you would have left me had you known what really happened and why I sent you out for photos. I am grateful your night was not ruined, and you are still here. I love you, Yanira Iosua."

Yanira came closer, "Baby, please tell me what happened. I can handle it. You handled whatever it was last night, and I appreciate that because, for me, everything was perfect. Now is the time for us to fix whatever it is together."

Kaeo was hesitant, but he proceeded to tell her the truth because he vowed never to lie or withhold information. "Ok, well, Anais showed up at the reception last night. She spotted you and me, but my mother intercepted. My brother came to get me, so I asked Marshall to take you and Ryleigh outside to distract you from the commotion. I walked up to Anais, and she was on the same bullshit as always, but it was different last night; she seemed over the edge. I convinced her to leave the building by telling her that I would leave you. Of course, I didn't mean it babe; I just needed her not to ruin the most important day of our lives together. If I didn't, she would have done something stupid, because she had a gun.

When I finally got her outside, she was getting ready to leave. That's when the kids came out, and Clariana noticed her car; no one else had paid attention. The car was wrecked. Clariana had a panic attack, and her body was shaking. The fear that ran through my daughter's body was indescribable. Cordero demanded to know what was going on, but Clariana was so distraught she couldn't speak. Kaleyla told us that Anais confessed when she thought Clariana was sleeping at the hospital. My baby girl faked sleep for hours until we came because she was scared her mother would kill her. She didn't want to tell us because she feared it would ruin our wedding. (He teared up and choked on his words.)

She sacrificed her fear to ensure we were happy. She loves us that much. Anais had filled me with so much anger, but when we made love, I, too, felt anxiety when I lay with you last night. The thought of losing you put distress in my heart. I can't lose you, and I can't lose the kids I raised as my own. Baby, Cordero was so angry with her that he walked off with tears in his eyes. I have not seen my boy cry since he was a kid; he was hurt. Hell, we all walked off because she had gone too damn far. I want to press charges, but we are leaving tomorrow, and I am unsure if they will do it. I can't leave Clariana holding the bag without us."

Yanira's mind was blown. She felt anger build up inside as she processed what Kaeo had just told her. This bitch had lost her mind! She hurt Clariana, her own child, thinking it was me, then showed up to my wedding reception. I'm going to go to jail before this life is over for fucking her up. This man dealt with this alone, trying to protect his loved ones. How in the fuck did she know where the reception was? She cleared her throat and spoke.

"Baby, it's ok. We can handle this. We are married, and the wedding was not ruined. We will not leave Clariana holding the bag. I can't imagine what she has been going through, but now it makes sense why she refused to go to lunch or dinner with Anais and stopped receiving her calls."

"Yeah, it does. I just wish she would have told us. I mean, Clariana must have been tortured seeing that car."

"Kaeo, I have a question. How did she know where we were? I mean, Clariana is not speaking with her, and we know damn well Cordero didn't tell her, nor your family. Who else would have said something?"

Kaeo responded, "I honestly don't know. I want to go and see the kids to talk to them because Cordero took her to the only place where she felt safe."

Yanira asked, "Where is that?"

"Our house," he replied. Yanira felt relieved and honored that the kids found safety in their home over any other place.

"Then let's go home, get our kids, talk this out, and enjoy our Luau. We need them to see that we are ok and try to restore peace and happiness in their hearts. We can deal with whatever we need to do with Anais later. We may need to postpone our honeymoon until we are sure Clariana is ok."

Kaeo questioned her, "Are you sure, my love? It's our honeymoon; I can't ask you to do this. You need to be happy too."

"You didn't ask. This is our family, and we must protect it by any means necessary. We all have to be happy, not just me. Now, let's get going, baby."

Kaeo kissed Yanira and hugged her for what felt like an eternity. She didn't mind. He was her husband now, and she could enjoy him for the rest of her life.

# CHAPTER 10: THE LUAU SHOWDOWN

Kaeo and Yanira arrived at the house. Cordero and Clariana were talking as Kamryn fed Diego.

"Hey Clariana, are you ok?" Yanira gently asked as she sat next to Clariana to hug her, and she nodded yes. "I am happy to hear that, but baby girl, why didn't you tell us what you knew? Why would you feel you had to keep that to yourself? I thought we didn't keep secrets?"

Clariana teared up. "I am so sorry. I was trying not to ruin your wedding day, but it seems like it was ruined anyway."

Yanira retorted, "First and foremost, whenever there is an issue and whatever it is, we can always handle it as a family. And please know that it was not ruined. I never even knew what happened. I didn't know she was there until this morning. Your dad protected me just like Cordero protected you and brought you here. That's what family is for, we help and support one another. Your father and brother did what they always do, protect you, and I couldn't be happier to know that this is where you felt safe."

Cordero looked at her and Kaeo. "Thank you," he said. He was still angry from last night.

Kaeo began to speak, "So guys, Yanira and I have been chatting, and we were wondering how Anais knew where the wedding and reception were. We know neither of you talked to her, but do you have any idea?"

Both replied in unison, "No."

Cordero said, "Me and Kamryn were wondering the same thing. I asked Clariana this morning. What I do know is I

157

want nothing more to do with her, though. She is foul and should be locked up."

Clariana chimed in, "Yeah, at this point, I am good on her for a while. I need some space."

Kaeo looked at his kids. "You both take the time you need. I know it is hard, and I understand how you are feeling. It's difficult to cut off someone you love when they do wrong. Just remember she is still your mother, regardless of her actions."

Cordero spoke up, "I know dad. Right now, it's safer to stay away, but on another note, Kamryn and I have been talking, and we have agreed to stay with Clariana until you guys get back from your honeymoon. My boss told me he was ok with me returning when Clariana was well enough. Since Kamryn is not working, we will stay here if that is ok. We like MIA and need a break from Cali anyway."

Yanira and Kaeo were happy to hear they could go on their honeymoon after all. After two hours of talking and crying, Yanira decided to change their mood. "Well, let's all get ready for this big luau. There's no need to keep our family waiting; we need to live a little. Baby girl, you up to a little dancing?" They all smiled and laughed.

"We are officially a family: my wife, kids, sister, and grandson. Let's get to it." Kaeo announced, "This is just what I need to get out of this funk and have some family fun.

"Alright, ladies, let's go get us some dresses for this luau so we can show out!" The girls went shopping for dresses, meeting up with Kalia and his mother. Yanira was so happy and requested her daughter and daughter-in-law to wear white and pink just like her.

The luau was going great. Just as the kahuna pule was complete, they went on to the conch shell tradition and finally, the lei show. The washing of the hand's ceremony was the final touch. The couple had performed both ceremonies to represent their family traditions. It was time to see the fireworks and perform traditional dancing.

Kamryn left to grab baby Diego's diaper bag from Yanira's car. As she bent down to pick up the bag, someone snuck behind her with a gun pointed at her back and said,

"Bitch, you will not live long enough to enjoy marriage to my husband. I told you to just walk away, but no, you had to ruin everything. You are like a cat with nine fucking lives. You fight me like a man, put my daughter in your car, and it's your fault she was hurt. Now, my son will not talk to me, and my daughter is not talking to me. Do you know how humiliating it was for my daughter to know it was me who hit her? Can you imagine the look on her face last night? You stupid little bitch! You cost me my family. You tried to take them away from me, so now I am going to take your life and make sure that Kaeo's heartbreak is taken care of by stepping in when his dead wife is no longer around. Cordero is loyal to his mother; he is mad now, but he will soon get over it; he is too naïve to stay away. He is putty in my hands, just like Kaeo. I run the both of them. Now turn around bitch so that I can shoot you in the face."

Before Kamryn turned around, she asked, "Why are you doing all this? What would make you hurt the people you love, manipulate your man and your kids, and go so far as to kill?"

Anais snickered. "You don't get to ask questions bitch, but I will grant you that last wish before I shoot your face off. See, I remember you, but you don't remember me. Years ago, you cost me my job and my relationship with a wealthy man because you opened your big mouth. You messed with my money then, and now you are messing with my man yet again. That's why. You will never cost me anything else ever again bitch. And to answer your other question, I need Kaeo. He is like my dog and does whatever I say. Cordero is my firstborn, but he is stubborn like his real father. I can only control him within my reach. When he is away, he stays strong, but he will never leave his mother for too long. Cordero's wife doesn't fear me, but I will manipulate her in due time, too. I control people to get my way. Everyone is at my disposal. Don't you see that? My father did it before he died; he taught me, and now, I do it too. Hustling people has kept me alive. Now turn around bitch, and don't ask me any more questions."

"Anais I am sorry about that."

Anais snickered again. "No, you are not, you bitch! You think you can do whatever you want because you are young and pretty, but not this time, and not with Kaeo."

"Ok, I get it; you love Kaeo. I mean you must because you have been able to find us these last two days; you are really smart, and I can see that your love is true. I mean who would go through all this for a man unless you loved him, right?"

"I am, and I do love Kaeo. See you guys are not smart at all, because all I did was turn on the location app on Clariana's phone and share it with myself so I would always know where she was. The moment she turned on her phone, I found both the reception and now this place. See I am brains and beauty, so as long as she has her phone on, I can find her."

Kamryn turned around, and Anais looked as if she had shit herself. "I thought you were Yanira! I didn't mean those things. I mean you are my daughter; we are family, right? You understand. I was only trying to upset her. I would never harm my kids or Kaeo, and I would never hurt you. Let's keep this between us ok; you don't have to tell anyone."

"I get it, but why try to kill her? You can't have Kaeo if you kill her or harm anyone. Clariana was hurt, but it could have been deadly."

"Kamryn, I just wanted to scare her and upset her. I didn't know it was Clariana. I love you all so much. I just want my life back, that is all. You understand this don't you? You did what you needed to do with Cordero, which is why he is not talking to me. We are just alike you and me. See, we fight for what we want. We can work together, you know. We both just want to be happy."

Kamryn looked at her and realized this was her manipulation. She was damn good and convincing. If she snapped at her, Anais would kill her, but if she played along, maybe she had a chance.

"It's ok, Mom, I get it. Yanira is playing this sweeter-than-thou role and taking your life. I understand why you would think I would be doing the same thing because you have her on one end and me on the other. The two most important men in your life and women are screwing with them. I get it, but trust me, I am not. Cordero needs you in his life, and I know Clariana needs her mother. Stepmothers don't equate to blood. Trust me, I know."

Anais smiled, "Yes, yes, you get it. See, I just want that bitch out of my life, our lives. She will be no grandmother to my grandson; he has me. See, we have an understanding; you are not so bad after all. Our secret?"

Kamryn replied, "Sure thing. You should get out of here before anyone notices. I need to go back before Cordero comes. He is still mad, but I will help you, and I will make sure Clare keeps her phone on, ok. Diego needs changing so I will run but make sure you see Cordero so we can explain this to him ok."

In that instance, Cordero came around the corner. "Mom, what the fuck are you doing here? How do you keep showing up, and why?"

Anais said, "Son, listen it is ok. I am leaving. Everything's ok."

Cordero got closer and saw the gun. "Mom, why are you holding a gun to my wife? What the fuck are you thinking? Was it not enough for you to damn near kill your daughter? Did that not teach you enough? It's not ok! Give the gun to me now. You have lost your fucking mind," Cordero yelled loudly.

He walked up to her, holding his hand for her to give him the gun. Kamryn yelled, "Baby, no, it's ok. Just stay away from her!"

Anais realized then that Kamryn had played her by saying what she needed to make her leave. She used her, and she would pay. Anais held the gun up just as Cordero stepped in the way.

Anais yelled, "Move, Son! Your wife is a problem, just like that bitch Yanira. They both are trying to take away those I love. Move, you don't need her."

Cordero began to move in closer towards her while she still had the gun raised at him and Kamryn. The two wrestled for the weapon as people's heads were turning in their direction. Kamryn started yelling, "Stop! Please, someone!! Please help; someone please help!!" They continued to tussle for the gun.

Kaeo and the family heard the commotion. They realized it was Kamryn yelling, and they spotted Anais. All of them came running in her direction. Ryleigh was ready for action; and as always, Marshall was too slow to catch her. She was a track star and had legs for days. Both she and Yanira were running neck and neck. The gun went off, and both slowed down. Anais had shot Cordero as he tried to take the gun away. He moved back slowly.

Clariana yelled, "No, Dero!! Mom, what have you done? What have you done! Why?? Look at what you did!!" Tears rolled from her face as she ran to her brother. Then looking at Anais with hatred in her eyes, she screamed, "You are sick! Get away from him. Get away!! I hate you." Clariana cried in agony for her brother.

Anais cried, "No, no, no, it was an accident! I just wanted to keep the gun, but he was trying to take it away. I did not mean to shoot him. Please!!" She dropped the gun, as Yanira ran to Cordero, putting pressure on his wound. She asked Kaeo for his shirt so she could hold it against him to stop the bleeding, and laid his body down, allowing his head to rest near her leg.

Before anyone could say anything further, Ryleigh pounced on Anais, hitting her six times with direct jabs to the face. She fell back to the ground. Ryleigh continued to swing, connecting every time, then began stomping and kicking her, repeatedly. Kaeo and Kalia helped Yanira as she tried to put pressure on Cordero's wound. Clariana called 911. Marshall and Kaeo's brothers pulled Ryleigh off of Anais, but it took all five of them; she was now the one enraged and stronger than any one man they knew.

Her father called out, "Ryleigh Lynn White!" When she heard her father's voice and her full legal name, then and only then did she stop trying to wrestle her way back to Anais. Ryleigh was out for blood. Her dad raised his voice in a masculine tone, "Ryleigh, calm down; calm yourself now."

Ryleigh was huffing and puffing from trying to beat Anais to death. Her dad walked over and began hugging her; he knew how she felt about Yanira. He also knew everything that his niece had been going through with this evil woman. He felt the same way, but he could not let her kill another human being. He did not want his child going to jail or losing time on the street because of the ignorant actions of someone else.

The police arrived along with the ambulance. Immediately, they placed Cordero on a gurney, put him on oxygen, applied pressure to his wound, and got him in the truck. Yanira gave the proper medical advice as she recognized the EMTs. They thanked her and prepared for their drive. The police officer said he would need a statement from Kamryn. She refused, stating she was riding with her husband, and they would need to meet her there. The officer understood and permitted her to ride in the ambulance with her husband. Kaeo hopped in as well and rode in the ambulance with Cordero while Diego was in the hands of Mrs. Iosua. The other police officer cuffed Anais and walked her to the squad car.

The rest of the family were required to give statements about the altercation. They all took turns sharing their version of what had taken place with Anais. More importantly, the officer asked each of them if she had any previous mishaps or altercations and what had transpired to cause such a crazed outburst for her to shoot her son.

Each person was able to listen to all of the stories about the things Anais had done or what they had observed or heard. This woman had been terrorizing Kaeo and others for years. The brothers told stories of how violent she was when Kaeo left her before, how she broke into their house, and how she hurt and threatened other girls by cutting their hair and faces, bullying them, tampering with their cars, paying others to hurt them, and much more.

His mother and father chimed in and gave information about her father, who was a manic depressant and had been killed due to his violent streaks against people. Anais was tested psychologically, and they found her to be borderline, but more so an unreasonable person and premeditated.

The final blow was Clariana. She told the police that her mother confessed to running her off the road, causing her to be in a cast, and now she tried to kill her brother. The police had evidence going back for years, but what would send her away the most was the murder attempt and assault with a deadly weapon, along with a hit and run. The two crimes she committed against her children.

The police released everyone after questioning them, instructing them not to leave town as this was an active investigation. Mr. Iosua stepped in, informing the officer that they were only here for his son's wedding, but they would try to change their flights considering what had transpired; however, he could not make any promises. The police officer gave him a card, told him a flight change was not necessary, but told him to make sure the family prepared statements and get them to the police station; otherwise, if they left town, they must provide a notarized statement with the signature of a Notary Public in their respective county.

Ryleigh was livid. "This bitch better go to jail. She has attacked my cousin and her husband way too many times. I will not stand here and let her keep getting away with it. What kind of person runs her daughter off the road and shoots her son? She's a fucking lunatic."

Tears were in her eyes as her mother and aunt were holding her and rubbing her, trying to calm her down. Yanira was the only thing close to a sibling she had. Ryleigh was unwilling to lose her to the violence of a dumb jealous woman fighting over a man who didn't even want her. She knew this story all too well, always having to fight a chick over a man who wanted her and not the other way around. For that reason alone, Ryleigh stayed ready for war and would give it to Anais. She just needed five more minutes alone with her. If given the chance, Ryleigh would end Anais's life without hesitation. That was the difference between her and Yanira; she didn't have remorse, and Yanira was too remorseful.

The story is that Ryleigh had become the pretty thug in school because the girls hated her light complexion and perfect body. She was cocky and she knew she was the shit. Fighting had become her source of survival. On the other hand, Yanira was just as beautiful with a caramel brown skin complexion; one would have thought they were twins, one just lighter than the other. People were nice to Ryleigh because she was both a fighter and intelligent at the same time. Yanira was peaceful, but Ryleigh was all about that turnup. Their bond was solid.

As a kid, Yanira saved Ryleigh from drowning. When it happened, Yanira had no regard for her own life; she only considered that she might lose her cousin and best friend. Ryleigh, nor her parents would ever forget that dreadful day. She gave her mouth-to-mouth and chest compressions.

The girls were only 12 years old. Ryleigh's heart had stopped because her lungs were full of water, and Yanira started pumping all the water out, then turned her over until she began breathing again.

Back to the story: The officers on the scene found the bullet shell and noticed cameras on the light fixture. They had all the proof they needed to put Anais away, but that camera would seal the deal. The officer seemed to remember Anais from the last incident. He was the one who let her go the first time and later found out she was the perpetrator. This time, he would not make the same mistake. He, too, questioned why she was attacking so many people. Maybe she needed help, but she would not harm this family again because she would be gone for a long time.

*********************************************

The family arrived at the hospital with Cordero about three and a half hours later. He was undergoing emergency surgery because the bullet went in and was lodged in his abdomen. The surgeon on call was Dr. Thompkins.

Another 3 hours after their arrival, Dr. Thompkins came out to explain to Yanira that the surgery seemed to go well but was touch and go in the beginning. He would be held there for monitoring for several days before being released, but he was safe as the bullet was removed. Depending on how his stomach and muscles would heal would determine how long he would need to be off work, but she suggested somewhere around eight weeks. Yanira thanked her and entered the room.

Kaeo hugged her. "Baby, I am sorry for all of this. I can't imagine how you and your family are feeling. Anais has never gone this far with her antics. Kamryn told me all the crazy things she said when she thought it was you. She was threatening her with the gun pointed at her head. I don't know which was worse, her to hear it or you to be there."

Kamryn mouthed off. "It doesn't matter which one of us! What she said was deplorable. She is going to jail, and I am not playing around with her. Anais has gone too far: holding my life at gunpoint, shooting my husband, threatening Yanira, and damn near killing her too, playing with the livelihood of my son, injuring Clariana, bullying, and arguing with my mom. I am done with her; she is a psychopath, and I will not let this go by without her paying for the consequences of her actions. Yanira, if you could have heard the things she said! I asked her why, before she knew it was me, and she said because she could. Kaeo and Cordero were her dogs! Cordero would only be strong when he was away from her, but any other time, he was in her control. Cordero may be upset when he hears, but this is it for me. It will be our breaking point because that woman has no regard for anyone who gets in her way. She is a basket case; she has my husband fighting for his life!!" Kamryn broke down crying profusely.

Yanira could not believe her ears. Anais must have said some horrible things, but for Kamryn to have a gun pointed at her was news to her. She hadn't heard what happened until now. Yanira went to hug her.

"Kamryn, I am so sorry this happened to you. I had no idea. It was me that Anais was after. I hate you got caught up in her madness."

Kamryn in turn felt sorry that Yanira. "No, I am sorry you are going through all this drama because you love someone. It is all too much."

They embraced one another. Yanira wished she could say something to console her, but nothing would make this situation any better.

Kamryn said, "I feel sorry for you. You are one strong woman because I would have left him or killed her by now. No offense Kaeo, but Anais is freaking crazy."

Kaeo spoke up after quietly thinking about Kamryn's comments. "None taken; I fear every time something happens that my wife will leave me. I know you are right. My son's life is at stake, Clariana was endangered, and she is still going. She needs to be locked up. Otherwise, we will all be either hiding, looking over our shoulders, or never feeling at peace. I cannot live like this, neither can I expect any of you to. When the police get here, we will tell him everything."

\*\*\*\*\*\*\*\*\*\*\*\*\*\*\*\*\*\*\*\*\*\*\*\*\*\*\*\*\*\*\*\*\*\*\*\*\*\*\*\*\*\*\*\*

The police officer from the scene entered the room. "Mr. Iosua, I would love to get your statement now that your son is out of surgery, as well as yours, Mrs. Remhart."

Kaeo provided his statement, letting the officer know that he and Yanira already had restraining orders against Anais, and he wanted charges filed for terroristic threats, child endangerment, and whatever else he could do. When it came to Kamryn, she told everything from start to finish about the incident. The officer could not believe what Anais had said. He asked her many questions, trying to trip her up, but her answers all aligned. Kamryn was able to repeat everything verbatim from her incident with Anais. Kamryn even included how she had threatened her mother and even her when she refused to leave Cordero back in California.

After taking notes, the officer said, "Well, it looks like this woman is going away for a long time. Since the accident, additional charges have trumped up against her. Taking into consideration this, along with all of the statements, she may do several years. We have her for vandalism, harassment, failure to comply with a court-ordered restraining order, hit and run, evading the police, reckless and egregious conduct, endangerment, failure to follow traffic signs, intent to kill, terroristic threats, assault with a deadly weapon, and attempted murder on two accounts. Most of these charges are felonies, and it looks as if there are multiple causes. We were able to get footage from a camera across from the park, so we will uphold the charges whether Mr. Remhart agrees or not. Here is my card. It has my mobile number on the back; please call me if you think of anything else."

The family looked in dismay; they could not believe all the things that had gone on without their knowledge. Mr. Iosua was beside himself. He was an honorable man, but never thought Anais would stoop this low. Mrs. Iosua sat and shook her head as the brothers and sisters all took turns whispering and chatting amongst themselves about Anais and her actions. They were glad their brother left her, but now they too wanted her to go to jail.

Kaeo took Yanira's phone, locked his number in, and then sent him the video of Anais attacking him at his job as the officer had requested earlier. They were done with her.

# CHAPTER 11: THE SENTENCING

All the family waited patiently to hear of his status and to confirm he was ok. Everyone was still in disbelief over what had happened. They only wanted to have a family gathering and celebrate the couple, yet it seemed Anais was hellbent on ruining any and everything for them. Luckily, the hospital staff kept everyone updated as a favor to Yanira. Her connections continued to be of value; she knew the chief medical officer of this hospital and the nurse on duty.

Once they confirmed Cordero was awake after his surgery, they called the officer, and he came to see him and take his statement. Kaeo interjected, "Listen, he has had a long day. His surgery took several hours, and I am not sure how much he can or is willing to answer at this time. He has just woken up within the last 2 hours and 30 minutes."

"No worries, sir, I understand. I will get what I can, and I will respect what he has been through. You have my word."

Kaeo then stepped out of the way for the officer to enter the room, but he stayed with his son. No one was going to trick or hurt him.

The officer walked close to Cordero and introduced himself. "Good day Sir, my name is Detective Bronson. I understand that you have been through quite an ordeal today, but I was wondering if I could ask you a few questions regarding your accident."

Cordero quickly gave his side of the story; Cordero did not hold anything back. After hearing it all, Detective Bronson knew he was telling the truth. His story was consistent with what Kamryn had told him several hours before. He knew they had not had an opportunity to speak or tell one another what to say because Cordero had been sedated and on medication since the accident. The detective took several pages of notes and prepared to head out.

"Thank you for your time. I really appreciate you and I know this has not been easy. If you remember anything else or need anything, I will leave my card on the table. Take care of yourself and I will be in touch soon, but whatever you do, please do not leave town until you have spoken with me."

Cordero nodded. He was high off medication and still angry that his mother held a gun to his wife; however, he remembered it all. He quickly closed his eyes and rested, feeling a little better, knowing that she would get some help. At this point she had damn near taken out both of her kids and she was still blaming an innocent woman. He would no longer allow his mother to manipulate or disrespect either of them.

Kaeo walked the detective out and shook his hand. "Thank you, officer."

"No problem, sir. I have what I need and as I said, I will be in touch with you all as we make progress on this case. Have a good one and stay safe."

Kaeo went back in to sit while Cordero slept, still not wanting to take his eyes off his son.

Later that evening, Yanira and Kaeo decided to postpone their honeymoon trip, deciding it was best that they stay and monitor the kids. Both were distraught, as well as mentally and physically hurting. Neither returned to work even though the trip was canceled, agreeing instead to take turns rotating their schedules to stay at the hospital with Kamryn or to watch the baby.

Cordero was released into their care after one week, but he was unfit for travel. In addition, Yanira found them a family therapist. She even made virtual visits with Cordero until he was released. The therapist made great progress with Clariana in a short period of time. She was able to recall a lot of stories and signs that she missed growing up about her mother. After each session she would talk with Yanira about them, trying to keep her in the loop and never holding onto any secrets.

Often Yanira was quiet and just listened and let Clariana vent, but she told Kaeo all the stories that she had heard. The more she heard, the more she despised Anais. She was a witch by all means, but oddly enough, she only loved kids so she could influence them or their fathers. Everything was a means to an end with her. She always seemed to have a plan to get something out of every situation.

After two weeks, Yanira returned to work, while Kaeo worked from home to help Kamryn care for Cordero, the baby, and Clariana. Her mother and aunt took turns three days a week with lunch and dinner, as well as cleaning up the house for them due to their schedules. Ryleigh pitched in by sending lunch and stopping by to help out when Kaeo needed to run out or to get a break.

\*\*\*\*\*\*\*\*\*\*\*\*\*\*\*\*\*\*\*\*\*\*\*\*\*\*\*\*\*\*\*\*\*\*\*\*\*\*\*\*\*\*\*\*

Two weeks after the accident, Clariana decided not to return to school. Due to the two major incidents, the dean allowed her to attend school from home for the remainder of the semester. She was a remarkable student, and her grades were up to par so he allowed it with rules that all assignments be turned in on time and any labs could be coordinated with a local university lab and results would be sent over. This was a weight off her shoulders, and with therapy she seemed more relaxed and happier.

During this same time, Kaeo also returned to work full time while Kamryn stayed with Cordero and Diego. Cordero had follow-ups and rehab for three additional weeks with the previous physician before he would be able to be released and return home. Kamryn was happy to sit in on the therapy sessions. The more she learned of their past, the more she understood her husband. He was fighting a never-ending battle with his mother; he wanted to be good, and she needed him to be something different. He fought with himself for years and was now realizing he had to become his own man so his children would not feel the way he felt, nor be treated as pawns for others good.

The court date was scheduled three weeks after the incident. Kaeo's family provided letters as their statements and had them notarized in Hawaii as they could not return for the court case. These letters were read in court, along with camera footage of Anais attacking Kaeo at his job, Clariana's accident from the bystanders who had thought it was a random incident and posted their videos to social media, and lastly, Cordero's shooting. Anais had nowhere to run nor lies to be told that would keep her out of this disaster she had called a normal life.

The Judge was not lenient on Anais at all and admitted that the psychological exam showed she was a narcissistic woman with no regard for others, including the children she birthed. Additionally, she advised she viewed her as selfish and motivationally driven for self-preservation. The Judge stressed that plenty of women in this world could not have children, and here it was that she had come close to killing not one but both of her children to keep someone else from being happy.

The prosecutor had one more witness who would definitely put Anais away and seal the deal. What they didn't know was that Anais was convicted of violent outbreaks on her mother, family, school kids, and others, but she was a minor, so her records were sealed. One of Cordero and Clariana's aunts on their biological father's side testified that Anais was responsible for their father's death and his girlfriend's disappearance because of her anger. At the time of this incident, she was over 21 so her family covered it up and moved her to New York. Apparently, her family had special ties with an elite group that kept her from being incarcerated; this infuriated the judge even more!

In the end, Anais was charged with every single charge detective Bronson mentioned previously at the hospital, with an added charge of domestic violence, which all collectively carried a sentence of 35 consecutive years without a chance of parole. The last piece of evidence was crucial as it upset the judge, but it also led everyone to believe there was some sort of mental inconsistency and treatment was needed. Still, there was no remorse for her penalties, so the judge tacked on an additional ten years, totaling her sentence to 42 years.

As an adult, Anais had been convicted of assault on many others and threatened them before they could testify. She had been charged with assault in Atlanta, California, and three times in Hawaii, which is why she stayed in Miami. The most recent charge in Miami stemmed from her fighting a woman at her residence for sleeping with her own man. The Judge called Anais a menace to society, a sorry excuse for a mother, and she prayed that her children did not adopt the inhumane streak that she did, adding she never wanted to see her in the courtroom again.

Anais went nuts. "You bitch! You can't do this to me. I was only protecting what is mine. I love my children. They were just in the way of me trying to get Kaeo back. I would never hurt them intentionally; it was an accident. They were all accidents, and you are making a mistake based on these lies. I am not a bad person; I just don't like it when people take what is mine. If that is what you call self-preservation, then yes, I am guilty of that and no more. These were accidents, neither child was killed."

The judge interjected. "Ms. Remhart, I will not tolerate these outbursts! Do you understand you could have killed your daughter had she went 5 more inches, and you shot your son point blank range and held his wife at gunpoint. These are not some simple accidents."

"It was not meant for them. That bitch Yanira has convinced my children to hate me so she can take them away from me. She was meant to be in the car, and I only wanted to scare her at the park. I would not have killed her. Listen to me; this is all a mistake. Clearly you and I can talk about this; you just need to listen to me."

The Judge replied, "Ms. Remhart, you see, this is exactly why you are being charged. You just admitted that you intended to harm, scare, and intimidate Mrs. Iosua. Sadly, you stand here and deliberately want to jeopardize the life of another human with a deadly weapon, one that weighs over a ton and one that is meant to kill. However, I will show you a little leniency by sending you to receive continued counseling and mental health evaluations. There is something totally wrong with you and how you process your anger. If that is correct, you will be sent to a mental institution for the remainder of your time served. If the psychologist deems you not mentally ill, you will sit in isolation until released. I want to ensure you never have the opportunity to kill, assault, threaten, intimidate, or hurt another human being."

Anais looked at the Judge and said, "You dirty bitch! Have you lost your mind? I am not going to a crazy house. This is not what you call leniency." Then, she turned around. "You are both ungrateful ingrates. I have cared for you and loved you, and this is how you repay me? You let her turn you against me. I love you, and you love me too. This was a mistake. Arielle, you bitch! You know it was an accident. I told him not to upset me; I warned him. You have no right to tell anyone or to be here, you ignorant bitch! I killed him by accident. Yanira, I swear I will kill you for stealing my life! If you had never met him, this would have never happened. Kaeo, you will never be happy without me. You will see. I know you will!"

Cordero shook his head while Clariana shed tears; they hated seeing their mother go through this, but she had gone way too far. Ryleigh sat back laughing as she enjoyed this ignorant woman being put away for the rest of her life. Yanira felt sorry for the kids. She could only imagine what it must have been like growing up with her. No wonder Kaeo was so timid and easy to have a good relationship with. He just wanted a non-confrontational relationship with someone who loved him unconditionally.

"Order in the court; order in the court! Mrs. Remhart, you have now tackled on another year for your outburst and disrespect shown to the courtroom and to a Circuit Judge. Your sentence total is now 43 years to serve. Bailiff, take her out of here. Get her out of my courtroom now before I lose my cool." The Judge ordered, then banged the gavel for the last time.

Once the court was adjourned, the crowd exited the courtroom, and everyone chatted briefly outside. The friends Anais had who showed up to support her apologized to the kids, claiming they had no idea what kind of person or mother she had been before their friendship. They also apologized to Kaeo, Yanira, Ryleigh, and Marshall for their part in her foolishness at the club that night.

Ryleigh didn't want any parts of it. She walked off in the middle of their conversation after saying, "Fuck y'all too. Luckily, I couldn't do more that night. Y'all knew that bitch was crazy, and she had nothing to do with your participation towards my cousin. She didn't ask for help, but all of you bitches jumped in. You did it on your own and got dealt with. Fuck all that!" Cordero just laughed; they knew by now that Auntie Ryleigh was nothing to play with.

Arielle walked up to the children and hugged them both. Once she heard about what Anais had done to Clariana and Cordero, she reached out to the officer to make a statement and promised to testify in person. Arielle apologized for holding out on the truth about their father and revealing it in court, advising that she was sure it was not easy hearing that story for the first time there. Still, she needed closure, and telling the truth was the only way she would receive it. Her brother, their father, could never be brought back, and before Anais harmed them or someone else any further, she did what she had to do.

Clariana seemed relieved after hearing her aunt; she was glad her mother was going to be locked up. Cordero thanked his aunt because he was the one who called her and shared the news on both occasions. Cordero communicated with his family often and was partially raised by his Aunt Arielle once when he ran away and then when he left Miami. Arielle always knew something was off about Anais and took him in every time he ran away. She promised her brother if anything ever happened to him, she would ensure their safety. This was her keeping that promise.

As they walked out, Kamryn smiled for the first time in weeks; she was so glad to rid her life of Anais. The sentence of 43 years wasn't enough for all the horrible things she had said and done, but it would do. Cordero noticed her smile as he looked at her while sitting in his wheelchair, holding their son. He took her hand, squeezing it tightly, without saying a word.

That was their confirmation that they would start over; he knew she was right before, about Anais, but it was hard to let go of his mother. Anais controlled and manipulated him all his life, but she no longer had control over her life or his. They all could live happily ever after now in peace. The family went to Sea Spice for a change of scenery and to have a good meal, after spending all day in court. It took a lot out of them.

*************************************************

A few weeks went by, and things were finally getting back to normal for Yanira and Kaeo. Clariana returned to school, and Cordero, Kamryn, and Diego returned to California. Yanira was back at work as an anesthesiologist by morning, a Nurse practitioner in the afternoon, and wife in the evening. Kaeo was making moves and working hard to make a new life for Cordero. The plan was to have Cordero and his brother Kalel run the business as Manager and Assistant Manager of their location in California.

Anais called several times threatening Kaeo, so he changed his number, and when she couldn't reach him, she called threatening the kids. Eventually they changed their numbers too. Neither wanted to hurt her, they only wanted her out of the way so they could live a happy life. In jail she was safe, she had a room, three meals, and had no control!

# **CHAPTER 12: JOYOUS MOMENTS**

Three years had passed since Anais's sentencing and the dreadful day in court. With Anais in jail, they were much happier. When they finally stopped accepting her calls, she began writing letters to the kids. First threatening, then asking them to come and see her, and to love her because she was still their mother. Also adding that what she did was for the good of their family and things had just been turned around. It was the same old story; she was never in the wrong. It was always someone else.

Yanira and Kaeo were doing well since her incarceration. Their communication was great; they fell back in love like nothing had ever interrupted their flow. Most recently, they had been trying to get pregnant for almost eight months and it finally happened. There must have been something in the water because Ryleigh and Marshall had found out only three months before that they were expecting, yet they were not planning as long as Yanira and Kaeo. By the time she figured out what was going on she was already two months pregnant at the time.

The two cousins couldn't be more excited to share the same childhood bond with their children. Both were planning baby showers, setting up nurseries, and shopping proactively without even knowing the sex of the babies. They were a few months apart, with Ryleigh being five months and Yanira being one month.

On Friday nights, instead of club night, it was dinner and conversation surrounding their new bundles of joy or business. The two were conforming to a normal life, often joking about turning into their mothers. They were more aware of their feelings, opinionated, and firmer with their expectations and decisions, all characteristics of their mothers.

Clariana, on the other hand, was dedicated to completing her master's in nursing. She worked hard over the years to keep her life moving in the right direction in Anaias's absence. Clariana attended summer classes and doubled up when she could to ensure she didn't stay in school longer than necessary. Not to mention, her education costs were being paid for by Yanira's hospital team, grants, and personal funds of Yanira and Kaeo to ensure she did not have any debt once she graduated. Kaeo was proud that she had pushed through her adversities to achieve this great accomplishment. He knew that Yanira was the driving force behind her excelling. While other kids were partying their way through college, Yanira encouraged her to enjoy her college years but also made sure she took advantage of her somewhat free education while she could.

While in school, she tried dating, but it didn't seem to fit well with her schedule. She had given herself to a gentleman who was two years older than her, and he broke her heart. He transferred to another school his senior year and she vowed not to date until she was truly mature and met someone who knew exactly what they wanted in life. She needed to step back and focus on school. Boys were a distraction and did not fit in at that time. Just like Yanira, she wanted to finish school, get residency at a prominent facility, and then find her true love.

Clariana was a smart girl and knew exactly what she wanted. Her mother placed a sour taste in her mouth when it came to men, love, manipulation, and tricks; she wanted no parts of anything other than true love. In her free time, she was with Cordero and his family, babysitting while they worked or went to school and hanging out occasionally with her line sisters.

Cordero was working at the newly opened store, raising his children, and loving his wife in peace. He too had made big strides in his life since Anais departed. Kamryn had just had another baby, another boy named Carmelo, and Cordero couldn't be happier without his mother there to get him off track. His marriage was great, and his family had purchased their first home. In his free time, he learned how to build things; he built his boys a playground, and a mini swimming pool in the backyard. Kamyrn had also moved up in life. Deciding to shift gears, she graduated culinary school and was now a Master Chef. Their lives had done a complete 180 degrees.

Kalel, Kaeo's brother even found him a girlfriend, Zoey, in the short time he had been in California. She was a business major with a minor in marketing. They were two peas in a pod, both introverts who loved small crowds, and they loved to eat even though both were slim. Often, they came to Cordero and Kamryn's to be taste testers for her meals and new dishes. Zoey and Kamryn were in talks about opening a restaurant. Zoey would run the day-to-day operations, while Kamryn would run the kitchen and staff. Kalel loved that they were creating their own relationship and planned to pop the question soon.

Finally, Clariana was graduating, and that weekend Yanira, Kaeo, Ryleigh and Marshall were traveling to California. Everyone wanted to be there to attend her graduation ceremony in person. Both ladies made sure to sit in first class because neither wanted to be in small seats or seated next to anyone they didn't know. Being pregnant had made them both paranoid. Kaeo and Marshall laughed at how they had become overprotective of their space and germs since becoming pregnant.

When they arrived in California, Cordero informed them that Clariana would be graduating with honors and was ranked in the top 10 of her class. On top of that, she was offered a job at UCLA Medical Center with Yanira's old colleague who had become a Chief Medical Officer and previously mentored Clariana during the summer for internships.

As Clariana walked down the aisle, her eyes were glued to the crowds to make certain that Kaeo and Yanira were there. Much to her excitement, Ryleigh had Marshall holding a sign which said, "Congratulations Clariana! We are proud of you!" Marshall couldn't be more delighted to hold the sign. Clariana shook her head and smiled. Her friend patted her on the back, as she mouthed, "That's my uncle and aunt; they are wild."

All who heard laughed. She was satisfied with knowing her support system was all there, Cordero, Kamryn, the boys, along with Kalel and Zoey. Clariana walked across the stage, gracefully taking a bow just as she reached the center. Once the diploma was in her hand her entire family made a hell of a lot of noise; there was no question who they rooted for.

After the ceremony, the group drove to Skylights to dine and celebrate Clariana's triumph. After about two hours her phone blew up. Her friends and line sisters were calling for her to appear at social events. Once she left, everyone migrated to Cordero's to visit the kids; mainly Yanira and Ryleigh wanted their motherly bonding time, while Marshall wanted to throw a ball with Diego, and Kaeo caught up with his brother and Cordero about the store.

After Marshall tired out Diego, and Carmelo went down for the night, the gentlemen indulged in drinks with Cordero chatting about business, parenthood, and life. Kamyrn couldn't wait to share her new red velvet crunch bars. The ladies ate half the pan and told her they needed her to make a mixture of snacks before they left for the plane ride, including telling her she needed to begin shipping her creations so they could be a part of the taste test group like Zoey! Kamyrn had not thought of that idea but loved the sound of it. She could definitely add shipping to her business for desserts and special items.

On Monday evening, Kaeo's mother called and asked if he and the children had heard the news that Anais was presumed dead after an accident transporting several inmates to another facility. In that instant, Cordero's phone began to ring, as well as Clariana's; both were told the same news by two different officers at the State Prison. The day was bittersweet; they all knew she deserved to be in jail, but to burn to death in a fire was a bit much, even for her. Hurt by the news, the kids cried, sulked, and held one another.

They still loved their mother, just not the things she had done to them, Yanira or Kaeo. Neither had spoken to her since her incarceration, although Anais continued to reach out over the years. They had both changed their numbers and social media sites after hearing about her killing their dad. Cordero would write "wrong address," on her letters so they were sent back. Eventually she got the idea or assumed he had moved; he did, but it was almost two years later.

The dinner went silent while everyone processed their grief; even Ryleigh had a moment of silence. She didn't give two shits about Anais, but she would soon be a mother, and the thought of having a bad relationship with her child or none at all caused her a little sadness. The look on the kids' faces was even worse. She hurt them; their pain was her pain. She had enjoyed being an auntie and getting the late-night calls for advice from Kamyrn and Clariana.

After dinner, Yanira broke the ice and asked Ryleigh, Kamryn, and Clariana what time they would be meeting up to shop for Clariana's new condo, which was close to Cordero and Kamryn. The items would be donated from Kaeo, Cordero, and Kalel as her housewarming. The arrangement was for the women to pick out new furniture while the gentlemen moved her things out of the dorm, and had her security system, motion detectors, and ring doorbells installed. There was much work to do, and they all had a role to participate in.

Clariana sat that night looking through the catalog to see what type of furniture style she liked; she was stuck on conventional versus modern. Looking at patterns, color schemes, and rugs all night gave her a migraine. In the end, she decided she would go with neutral colors and mix the modern and conventional look. The only person who had to like it was her, she thought. Not too many people would be allowed in her home anyway; she liked privacy and did not trust many people. Two of her line sisters, who were actual sisters, had recently purchased a condo in the same building which made Clariana give it some thought, so other than them, she didn't plan on visitors.

The next morning, while at the family furniture store, Clariana picked a new bedroom set that was fit for a queen. It had a velvet headboard and footboard, with mahogany wood finishing, matching nightstands, a dresser, chest, and a seat at the foot of the bed for when she wanted to take off her shoes or relax outside of the bed. For her guest bedroom, she went with a regular mahogany finish as well; the bedroom came with one night stand, dresser, and chest. She picked out a beautiful six-piece living room set; it was a small sectional. Her kitchen table was all wood and her velvet seats had buttons on the trim. Clariana chose plenty of décor for her walls and bathrooms. The ladies were impressed with her taste because everything turned out nice.

The drivers loaded each piece as they picked them. Clariana couldn't be more excited to live on her own; the roommates and dorm life were too much, and she wanted out! In addition, she was starting a new job the following week. Yanira and Kaeo agreed to pay her rent and bills for the first three months to allow her to stack up some money and see how she could manage the bills on her own after their support stopped. She knew they would still assist but she wanted to do it on her own. They had also done the same for Cordero, giving him furniture from the store and paying their mortgage for the first four months since Kamryn was pregnant and on FMLA from work.

# CHAPTER 13: RANDOM INCIDENTS

One month had passed, and they were back in MIA. Yanira was so excited for her and Kaeo to attend their first appointment together; she was finally two months pregnant. Kaeo worried about twins since his family had two sets of twins: Kalia and Kiron, then Karo and Kalel. He was secretly hoping for twins; they could have it all done at one time, and each would have someone to play with. Yanira, on the other hand, did not want two. She knew the child's cousin would be just as close as she and Ryleigh were.

At the monthly checkup appointment, Kaeo did not get his wish; there was only one baby. Still, Kaeo was as happy as ever. He would finally get what he always wanted: a biological child of his own, and he was hoping for a boy. Yanira was relieved there was only one. She was scared to have two babies at one time.

Ryleigh had some different news the month before; she was having twin boys. It seems that twins ran on both her and Marshall's side of the family. Marshall was excited. He had so many girls on his side of the family, and now he was finally getting his boys. The couples had dinner at Marshall and Ryleigh's to celebrate their news.

\*\*\*\*\*\*\*\*\*\*\*\*\*\*\*\*\*\*\*\*\*\*\*\*\*\*\*\*\*\*\*\*\*\*\*\*\*\*\*\*\*\*\*\*\*\*

One day during her 2nd trimester, Yanira decided to go to the grocery store after leaving work to pick up a few items for dinner. As she was walking through the grocery store, she had a feeling that she was being followed but didn't see anyone. Turning on the last aisle, she had the feeling again, so she turned and hid in the next aisle over, waiting to see if the person would follow.

Much to her surprise, it was one of her college friends. She told Yanira that she was trying to get close to see if it was her but didn't want to alarm her. Yanira admitted she was indeed startled but glad it was someone she knew. They laughed and chatted for a few minutes and parted ways.

*********************************************

On another late evening, Yanira didn't leave until 7 pm due to paperwork, two walk-in patients, and being asked to prepare a patient for emergency surgery at 5:45 pm. Kaeo knew not to expect her early. She stopped by the donut shop as she had a craving for some honey-glazed donuts. When she returned to her car, another car was coming at a high speed and almost hit her. It missed her by an inch, thanks to the gentlemen parked next to her car. She thanked him after gathering her composure.

Arriving at home, she told Kaeo about it. He told her not to worry; it was probably some maniac trying to rush home to eat hot donuts. But honestly, he was worried and didn't want to stress her out. A sequence of weird things had been happening to them both over the last couple of months: flat tires, scratched cars, feelings of being followed, calls to the job for him and her but no one on the line, and now the car incident. It felt like Anais, but she was dead.

Marshall called Yanira to tell her Ryleigh went into labor at 4 am. He asked her to stop by when she was in the building. Around 8:30 am, Yanira strolled in to take a look at her cousins and godchildren. They were precious, and she was as happy as she could be. She was ready for her bundle of joy but would have to steal these two in the interim. The boys were adorable, with beautiful caramel melanite skin tones and a head full of hair on both of them. Ryleigh was so happy to see her beautiful boys and deliver them healthily. She had lost her twin during birth and was very paranoid about the same thing happening to her. Her parents and Yanira's parents were at the hospital bright and early, taking turns holding the babies, excited as if they were the parents and not grandparents or aunt and uncle.

*******************************************

A couple of months later, on a Friday afternoon, Ryleigh called to check on Yanira to make sure she was still stopping by after work. Confirming, she told Ryleigh she would stop by as promised to check on her and visit the twins. Leaving work at 5:45 pm, she called Ryleigh, letting her know she was walking out the door in just a few minutes. Traffic was heavy; she arrived at Ryleigh's around 6:20 pm and sat with the babies until 9 pm, when Kaeo summoned her home. She hated to leave, but Marshall's mother and sister were there to tend to Ryleigh and the babies, along with her mother stopping by daily. The twins were two months old and already spoiled by everyone.

As Yanira drove home that night, she had a craving for hot donuts, so she stopped by to grab a box on the way home. She was a little hesitant as the last time she went there, she was almost hit, but Kaeo assured her it was a freak accident. Still being cautious, she parked on the other side of the parking lot just to be safe.

Leaving out of the donut shop with a dozen honey glazed and another half of Tiger Twist donuts for Kaeo, she pulled the handle on her car door, and boom, she was attacked from behind and pushed into her car. Her belly instantly began to hurt, and their child's safety ran through her mind and body as she felt the pressure. Her head was rammed into the car door four times, then jabs to her ribs and back, one after the other, with blows to the back and sides of her body. Suddenly, a knife went through her side, and her body fell to the ground. Yanira couldn't fight back; she was in pain, trying to protect her stomach and hold the open wound from the knife.

Feet began to trample her body. She couldn't protect her baby, nor herself; the person stomped her repeatedly without saying a word, just laughter coming from each side of her. Her belly was being targeted, then her body and her head. It was hit after hit, then more kicks and stumps, like it was on repeat. The hitting was so vicious that it had to be a man. The pain and blows came quickly, and every hit stung like metal. After several minutes of this beating, the feet continued to pound Yanira as she lay on the ground, fading. "Die bitch, just die," Yanira heard as she withered away, then lost consciousness.

\*\*\*\*\*\*\*\*\*\*\*\*\*\*\*\*\*\*\*\*\*\*\*\*\*\*\*\*\*\*\*\*\*\*\*\*\*\*\*\*\*\*\*\*\*\*\*\*\*

Yanira woke up four days later in the hospital. Kaeo and her parents were there. He saw her eyes flutter first and immediately began calling, "Nurse, Doctor, anyone, she is awake! Please come quick, please!"

Yanira was confused. Her body was in pain; her head, legs, stomach, hell, her entire body was hurting. She felt everything. Dr. Lawson came through the door, spoke to everyone, and addressed Yanira.

"Dr. White-Iosua, you gave us quite a scare. I need to check your vitals; bear with me, please." After a few short minutes, he asked, "Dr., do you know where you are?"

"It's Yanira, Dr. Lawson. Yes, but I do not understand why. What's going on?" Yanira asked.

"Well, you were attacked several days ago, and you have been unconscious for four days. You were beaten pretty badly and stabbed. The wound was not life-threatening to you, but considering the circumstances, it cost you. Your vitals seem fine, but..." He tried to continue, but Yanira cut him off. She knew something had happened.

"What do you mean it cost me? I do not understand what it cost me." She began looking down, moving her arms and legs. She couldn't move much, but she felt them all. She rubbed her belly.

"Dr. Lawson, my baby, where is my baby? Is it ok? Where is my baby?"

Kaeo stood, "Baby, calm down. Please do not elevate your blood pressure; please just calm down. We can discuss the baby later. It's ok, we just need you to relax."

"Kaeo, I am fine. Just get my baby, and it will all be ok. I am not worried about me." Yanira was in shock but could not move her body; she was hurting, and now her heart had joined in.

Tears rolled down Kaeo's and her mother's faces. They both agreed not to tell her about the baby until she was well, but their hearts hurt as she called out for her unborn child, not caring about her own life. Her father had to walk out; he was a proud man and could not handle seeing his daughter go through this tragedy, nor would he allow anyone to see him break down.

Yanira asked Kaeo, "Why? Why did this happen to me? What is wrong? We finally got rid of Anais, and now this!" She felt her stomach, and her mother lost her composure. She walked up and held her daughter, nodding to Kaeo to tell her the truth.

Kaeo spoke up. "Baby, you were robbed and beaten pretty badly. As Dr. Lawson said, you were also stabbed. You umm, you, well, umm…" (he choked up as he began to speak the words).

"I lost our baby," she confirmed for him. She already knew. "Kaeo, I am so sorry. I went for donuts, and I..." Yanira cried profusely; she was heartbroken.

Kaeo nodded and broke down even more. He was at a loss for words for her and himself. He was in pain; he didn't protect his wife. He felt horrible. What kind of man doesn't protect his wife, he thought. Why did she stop? Why did this happen? All his thoughts were piling up at one time. The tears poured down without a sound.

Then Yanira cried out in agony, regretting that she stopped for donuts. She wished she had just gone home. Instantly she felt sorry for Kaeo because she had lost the one thing neither she nor any woman had ever provided. This was all too much for her; she cried for an hour until she fell asleep.

While Yanira slept, the detective came in to see if he could speak with her, but Kaeo and her father shut it down, saying "NO." They explained that she had just found out she lost her baby, and now was not a good time. The detective was very understanding. He apologized to Kaeo copiously, telling him that the weapon she was stabbed with was left at the scene and they were waiting for prints, but it was too dark for the camera to actually see the perpetrator.

Without assuming, it looked as if two people attacked her, but they could not be 100% sure if they were men or women because of the clothing and darkness. He would update him when the prints came back and advised when Yanira could speak to contact him, even if it was when she returned home.

As the detective approached the door, he stopped and asked, "This may be a weird question, but does your wife/daughter have any enemies? Anyone who would want to harm her?"

All three answered unanimously, "NO."

Kaeo said, "If you knew my wife, you wouldn't have to ask. She works here; ask anyone around. My wife is humble, caring, thoughtful, and selfless. Even when there are those deserving of something other than kindness, she always gives them the benefit of the doubt."

Her mother spoke, "I'm just trying to understand why someone would be so vicious to a pregnant woman, let alone a doctor. She saves lives, and someone tried to take hers."

The detective replied, "Thank you, Mr. Iosua & Mr. & Mrs. White; I have heard the same from others around. Sometimes, there is no real reason or explanation, people are just vindictive, but make no mistake, whoever it is, we will do our best to capture them and make sure justice is served. You have my word."

Mrs. White cried in her husband's arms; he stood firm and tall. He was determined to hire a private detective if no one gave him answers, and soon. He had already reached out to a friend who was a District Attorney and advised him to keep this incident on his radar and if there were any leads or information to update him immediately, as his daughter was barely hanging on. At the time, she was unconscious, and that statement was true, but today, only heartache overwhelmed her.

Roughly two hours later, Yanira woke up to see her family still there, along with Ryleigh and Marshall. Ryleigh couldn't bring the twins as she could only imagine how her cousin and best friend was feeling after carrying a baby for five months and losing it. When Yanira saw her face, she cried. Ryleigh rushed to her side, and they cried together for another 12 minutes. Yanira asked about the twins. Ryleigh tried not to discuss them, but Yanira insisted, stating they were her nephews, and she needed to make sure they were safe.

Ryleigh pulled out her phone to face time with her mother. Both boys were awake and eating. Yanira smiled; they had gained a few pounds in just a couple of days. Marcelo, one of the twins, smiled at the sound of her voice; Marcos then smiled just seconds later. Yanira cried again, but this time, because she was happy laughing at their big smiles. They recognized her voice. Her aunt told her she loved her before ending the call and advised that they were praying for her to return home safely and soon.

The following morning, Yanira was taken for X-rays, CAT scans, and other tests to make sure the swelling didn't leave any permanent damage. When she returned, Kaeo had brought her a salad, a few chicken wings, and a slice of cake from her favorite cake place. Yanira told him she was not hungry but maybe later. Her mother told her she needed to eat something solid, and the hospital food would not cut it.

Yanira did not want to argue with her mother; she would just wait it out and eat if she said anything else. An hour later, she was eating. Her father came into the room with Clariana and Cordero. They had flown themselves in and refused to keep waiting.

Clariana cried intensely upon seeing Yanira, in disbelief as to how someone would hurt Yanira other than her mother, who was now dead. She was bruised in the face, and on her arms. It was hard to see how the once beautiful face of perfection was now bruised and battered.

Cordero asked Kaeo, "They haven't found out anything? This is some bull..." He stopped as he saw G-Ma White in the corner.

She looked over and said, "Baby, you get a pass from G-Ma on this one. I want to know the same thing. Say it for me."

"It is G-Ma; it's some Bullshit for real! I mean, look at her." Cordero said as he let out a tear. He knew then his grandmother was just as angry. Mrs. White never cussed or allowed cussing in her presence unless she was upset. She must have been really upset because she had let out a few since Yanira had been awake.

Cordero looked at Yanira. "Ma, I am sorry about all of this. You know I am here for you, and I am not leaving until we get whoever did this."

Yanira replied, "It's ok, I am fine now. I am so glad to see you both. I missed you. Where are my babies and Kamryn?"

"They stayed. Once Dad told us what happened, he insisted we stay home, but when we heard you woke up, we booked the first flights we could so we could lay eyes on you."

Yanira shed more tears. "Thank you. I appreciate you both caring so much. It kills me at the moment, but I will get past it."

They hugged her tightly. The family sat together, talking, and catching up for another two hours. Dr. Lawson came in to discuss her test results.

"I see we have the whole family in the room this evening. Are we comfortable sharing results?"

Yanira nodded. "Yes, these are my kids, well, young adults. But yes." Both smiled at the sound of her calling them her kids.

"Ok then, well, honestly, Yanira, much to my surprise, everything looks great. There was no scar tissue damage, no abnormal reading on the CAT scan or MRI, and all other test results came back normal. I want you to stay here for another 48 hours and within that time I need you to do the following: have a bowel movement, hold down solid food, and walk around on your own with minimal assistance. If you can do that then you will be released."

Mrs. White spoke up. "You are late, Dr. Lawson. Momma is here; she had chicken wings, salad, and she had a bowel movement 2 hours and 22 minutes ago. The only thing she needs to do is walk around, and between my son and grandchildren, we can make that happen tonight."

Dr. Lawson chuckled, "Now I know who the real boss is and where you get your drive from, Dr. Iosua. Momma is in charge. (He laughed) Ok, so I stand corrected. If you can walk about, shower, and have no complications overnight, then late tomorrow evening, I will have Dr. Rodriguez release you when he rounds your room, ok?"

Yanira thanked him and told him she appreciated his treatment and support. Cordero shook his hand. "Thanks, we appreciate you taking care of her."

Clariana piped in, asking, "Yes, thank you. Does she have any guidelines she must follow? Days away from work, medications, or any symptoms or areas of concern we should look out for? Any permanent damage? Are the stitches dissolvable, or will they need to be removed?"

Dr. Lawson shook his head and laughed. "We taught you well, young lady. Yanira, no pulling the I am a doctor card. You have two bosses at home who seem to have things covered. To answer your question, yes, Nurse Remhart, stitches are dissolvable, no permanent damage as far as we can see but I would suggest a follow up visit in roughly 6 to 8 weeks, just to perform an ultrasound for the bruised areas, and no areas that show a need for concern."

"I see. Thankfully, my mini-me doesn't live here, and the other one has her own home," Yanira responded.

Her mother looked and said, "She is wrong. My grandkids have me on speed dial, and neither are going anywhere for a couple of days. I know how to reach you if I need to."

The room laughed because Mrs. White didn't even look up from her puzzle book as she spoke. She was stern and confident that everything would be under control. Dr. Lawson could not help but laugh loudly. "I have no more words and I think I can exit as I know you are in good hands." He exited the room and said he would see them soon.

\*\*\*\*\*\*\*\*\*\*\*\*\*\*\*\*\*\*\*\*\*\*\*\*\*\*\*\*\*\*\*\*\*\*\*\*\*\*\*\*\*\*\*\*\*\*

Back at home Yanira couldn't help but sit in the nursery. She was saddened and determined to understand why she had to lose her baby. It was for a reason, and she respected God's choice, but she was grieving. The thought of carrying a life just for someone to take it was unbearable and too much for her to deal with. The swelling had gone down, but she was bleeding as if she had delivered the baby.

The detective scheduled time with Kaeo to visit Yanira and hear her side of the story. He also stated he had some strange news to share. He arrived on her 4th day of being home. Kaeo, Mr. White, and the kids all made sure they were present to hear her side of the story as no one had heard it yet.

"Good day, Mrs. Iosua. Not sure if you remember me, but I am Detective Bronson. If you are up to it, I would like to ask you a few questions, ma'am. Would that be all right?"

"Yes, I do, and sure," Yanira stated as she nodded.

"Alright, so, can you tell me what you remember about the night of the attack?" He asked.

"Well, I got off work and went to my cousin Ryleigh's house to visit with her and my nephews. Sorry, I know that is confusing. Biologically, they are my cousins, but we grew up like sisters."

"Ok, that is understandable," he said.

"After I left her house, I had a craving for donuts. It has been my weakness since being pregnant." She began to choke on her words. Before Kaeo could do anything, Cordero jumped over to her and rubbed her back. She touched his hand and held on to it. "I pulled up to the shop, went in, grabbed a dozen of our favorite donuts, and when I walked out, I just remember someone pushing my head and belly into my car hard. He was hitting me, and the fists hurt. I was stomped, kicked, punched, and..." She paused and started to cry; it was too painful. Yanira had mentally started to relive what happened to her.

Kaeo rushed to her other side, and her dad stood behind her.

Detective Bronson said, "Let's take a break, Mrs. Iosua. I know this is a difficult time for you. I am sure this is not something you would want to think about ever again, and I can understand that. I will give you just a few minutes, and if you cannot continue, we can try again tomorrow or the next day. I am at your disposal."

"Ok, thank you. I just need a minute, please." Yanira was in tears as she walked off to gather herself.

Clariana offered the detective a bottle of water and a granola bar. He obliged and thanked her. Kaeo and her father took her to the outdoor living room. Both told her to calm down and try to remember but not to force herself.

Yanira told Kaeo, "I am very sorry. It was my fault this all happened. If I had not stopped in the first place after you told me to go home, we wouldn't be in this situation. I never expected something like this to happen, and I am just so deeply sorry. I let you down and lost our baby, and your grandchild, Dad. I am so sorry. Every day, I pray that you will forgive me because this is all you wanted, a baby of your own, and my greed cost us that."

Mr. White wanted to speak, but it was Kaeo's position to step up and say the right thing. If he didn't, it would be hell to pay. But his words were better than Mr. White could have expressed himself.

Kaeo looked at his wife. "My love, this is not your fault at all. This is the fault of someone else. There are times when something we want is put on the back burner; this is one of those times. If I had to choose between my unborn child and my wife, it would be my wife every time. I need you here, with or without a child; I need Yanira Catori White-Iosua, nothing more. We will try again when the time is right, but for now, you are my focus. I pray every day that you will forgive me for not protecting you. It seems we are praying for one another, and it's clear that we are doing the right thing, putting Him first, that is through prayer. So, let's not discuss forgiving anyone; it's already done. Let's focus on your health and finding this person so this never happens to anyone else, ok? I love you with all my heart. Nothing or no one will ever change that!"

Tears were in Mr. White's eyes, but his tears were one of joy. Kaeo loved his daughter, and he, too, was happy they had faith in a higher power. The drama that his daughter went through before with the crazy woman was all for a good man. She had chosen well. He patted Kaeo on his back and walked away. No one needed to see an old grown man cry.

Kaeo and Yanira walked back into the room. "Ok, Mr. Bronson, I am sorry about that. I just needed a minute," she said, still holding Kaeo's hand as she spoke. "So, I remember my head being shoved, the blows, then as I faded out, I heard someone say, "Die bitch." The voice was familiar, but (she paused) it was just familiar because it was a woman, not a man. Had I not been in pain with my stomach hitting the car, I could have turned around. The first hit was my head hitting the car, and it dazed me. My stomach was shoved into the car as well. It was intentional. It was aggressive and rough. I can't remember anything other than the fight."

Detective Bronson countered, "Fight? No, that was an attack. You had no room to defend yourself, nor any time to prepare for what was happening. I have already asked your family, but I will ask you, by chance, do you have any enemies or people who would want to harm you? Has anything out of the ordinary happened lately that you can't explain?"

"Sir, the only person who hated me this much is, well, she is no longer with us. No one else would do this. I only go to work, come home to my husband, or associate with family, no one else outside of my co-workers."

"This person that you speak of is your husband's ex, correct?" He asked.

Yanira was puzzled as to how he would know this; she would never say the name in front of the children. Detective Bronson spoke up and said, "Your children told me it was your husband's ex that would have done this, ma'am. I do not mean to pry or ask questions that make you uncomfortable; I just want to get the person who committed this crime. So, I assume she was before you."

Yanira smiled. The kids no longer looked at Anais as their mother; they claimed she was an ex, not their mother, and they were embarrassed by her. It warmed her heart. "Yes, it was his ex, but as I said, she is no longer living. She was killed in an automobile accident some time ago."

"Yes, that is what the children told me. Ok, well, let me do a little more digging into this, and I will be in touch. If you think of anything else, please, by all means, contact me immediately, ok?" As he rose to leave, he asked, "Mr. Iosua, can you walk me out, sir?"

Kaeo stood, as well as both Mr. White and Cordero. They all walked him to the door.

"Mr. Iosua, I wanted to speak with you privately. I have a question you may not like, and I'd rather ask you…" Before he could finish, Kaeo cut him off without hesitation.

"You can ask or say anything to me in front of my son and father -in-law. I have no secrets, not one. And honestly, I already know your question is, have I ever cheated on my wife, or do I know of anyone who would have done this as retaliation? And the answer is hell no! I love my wife, and under no circumstances would I ever cheat on her. If you knew how long I waited for this woman, how I chased after and courted this woman, man, you wouldn't have to ask, but I understand why you do have to ask. Truly, I say to you, I would never. Yanira is perfect, and I would marry her a thousand times over and never have to stray from my marriage."

The detective looked at him seriously. "Mr. Iosua, you are my kind of guy. I believe you; I do. Most men would show a sign of a lie or give me a reason not to believe them, but not you. I see that you are genuine. Thank you for answering so I did not have to ask you a ridiculous question, sir."

Kaeo nodded. "You said you had some news. What was it?"

"Well, your wife already told you some of the news; the perpetrator was indeed a woman. The shop's camera was dark, but we zoomed in, and we could see fingernail polish on one of her assailants. The metal or heavy beating your wife mentioned was due to her being hit with brass knuckles. Both are considered deadly weapons and are punishable, but your wife almost lost her life, so we are going to pursue attempted murder and murder. Your child was a human being and was murdered, and she attempted to murder your wife. The video shows they would have beaten your wife to death had someone not yelled out and walked closer to her. The assailants ran before they could finish the job. I am quite sure that was the intention; it was too orchestrated not to be."

Cordero burst out, "Then you need to fucking find their ass. My mom doesn't deserve any of that shit, and my baby sister or brother didn't have to die because of some ignorant ass person."

Mr. White took his hands and placed them on the shoulders of Cordero. He felt his passion and love for his daughter. Whether she had given birth to him or not, he was her son, and nothing else mattered. He loved both Cordero and Clariana himself; they had become remarkably close, and no one would have ever known they did not belong to Yanira or Kaeo biologically.

"I understand your frustration, Mr. Iosua. I will make sure that I do my best with this case and bring your family closure. I am terribly sorry to deliver that news. You all have a blessed day. I will be in touch."

The men stood outside talking, all in disbelief about the brass knuckles. They discussed whether or not to tell Yanira or Clariana, as it would only make them emotional. Kaeo knew that Yanira would ask, and if so, he would not lie to his wife, ever.

Cordero spoke up, "I swear this feels like something Anais would do. I can't blame her from the grave. Whoever it is, they will be fucked up if we catch them first."

Mr. White replied, "No worries, grandson. We will allow them to do their job, but if they can't, I have a private detective working on it as well."

*******************************************

One week had passed, and the detective called Kaeo. "Mr. Iosua, we were able to do a little more digging. It seems the perpetrator was indeed a woman. She followed your wife into the parking lot, then circled to the store parking lot in the next building across from the donut shop and waited for your wife to exit. We were able to get footage of the car but because it was too dark, we could not see faces. We are trying to locate the vehicle and registrar. I just wanted to keep you posted. Please make sure to take every precaution possible until we catch these assailants because this was premeditated."

Kaeo called Mr. White immediately. He told him the exact words of the detective; it was premeditated. Mr. White stated he had already heard. The DA had called him and told him the news just now. Both men agreed that Yanira did not need to return to work; it was not safe. But both knew keeping her home wasn't safe either. Yanira went into the nursery every day, and now she was having bad dreams at night.

Talking to the detective had made her more and more nervous. It had been almost a month since she had been home, and the kids had finally left. The kids were a big help for two weeks, and then her mother took over for the third and now the fourth week, while Kaeo traveled to work for a couple of hours each day.

# CHAPTER 14: DIGGING DEEPER

Kaeo was making enough money to stay home permanently since opening the new store and getting the new truck. Pratt called to check on Yanira, and the two discussed business and rehashed how he had already opted out of driving the trucks three years prior. Pratt was ready to spend more time with his wife; they were always busy and never traveled together. He dreamed of early retirement and told Kaeo to put it on his radar because he and his wife wanted to enjoy a life well-lived while they still had a few good years left.

After much thought, Kaeo decided to have Kendall stay in the store. He had earned their trust and was loyal. Kaeo made the decision to start training him as store manager while he handled all the paperwork from home. Yanira needed his support while she attended therapy weekly, and he joined her.

On the third day, he called Pratt with a proposed plan. Kaeo started by saying, "Listen, I have a proposal. I have been thinking about your retirement and how we can make that happen without too much disturbance to the business."

"Ok, I'm listening. What do you propose?" Pratt asked.

"Well, I was thinking I could handle all the paperwork from every furniture store and for the trucks since I am not ready to slow down or retire. This change would save a lot of money and, by doing so, allow us to keep over six figures in the house to divide equally as we have been doing everything else."

Pratt countered, "No. Since you are doing the work, you should get 70/30, if not all."

Kaeo was humbled and said, "It's not about that. We are a team, and had it not been for your dream, I would not be in this position."

Pratt retorted and urged, "Kaeo, understand you will still be working. It is only fair for you to receive additional money. It may have been my idea, but your brains and plans have kept us afloat over the years. Plus, I'm making enough from the other income and was already planning to retire. I have a better idea. Let's agree to purchase two more trucks with the additional money."

Kaeo agreed. "I am glad you said that. I have already found two and went ahead and contacted the dispatchers, letting them know to plan on increasing the loads and I made a decision I hope you are ok with, to promote my guy here in Miami. I know he is not family, but he has been very loyal and with my support he can do it."

Pratt's excitement was coming through the phone. "Well, now I can retire immediately, effective within the next 30 days. Kaeo, I will follow your lead and promote my nephew to run the store in Arizona. With this 30% split and an extra 35k in my pocket from the additional trucks, the rest of the added income would be a decent amount for an increase and promotion to manager for my nephew. So, if you agree to take 70%, we got a deal."

"If you insist, sounds great to me!" Kaeo was so happy. Previously, responsibility of the business was equal, regardless of whose family worked at what facility. It was based on a split between the east and west regions. This is how they handled personal trucks, joint trucks, and the stores. They didn't trust anyone with their business or paperwork, so it fell on the two of them. Every other position within the company was held by a family member until now, with Kendall in the picture.

Now that Kaeo would be doing all the paperwork, he would keep a close eye on everything. He had recently purchased a new program to handle his paperwork, and it worked flawlessly. Every piece of equipment was scanned, and all business was electronic. As long as the managers kept inventory updated, the data, metrics, inventory, and business information would be in one location, visible to him and Pratt. Adding Pratt's West region would keep him working the same hours each week that he was already putting in, and he could do it all from anywhere.

As far as the trucks were concerned, Pratt's sister did some of the work for the operations, while the dispatchers (Kalia and Renee, both Kaeo and Pratt's sisters) handled hiring, firing, other personnel issues, and business items. This area would change as he would have his new brother-in-law running it as he was a human resources guru. Pratt's cousin Angela was the Broker, but they would add another person, Kaeo's other brother, Kiron to assist with her broker's business.

At this point, they owned six trucks (four jointly), five furniture stores, and they were adding two more trucks. Pratt was not missing out on any money and loved the plan. He celebrated on the call as he explained to his wife that this meant he didn't have to do anything but collect a check. Pratt was ten years older than Kaeo, so retiring before 50 was his plan; he just did it ten years earlier than expected. He had been driving trucks since he turned 18.

Nile, his wife, was overjoyed. She was a hairdresser and owned two shops, so she was ready to relax a little, too. Her celebrity customers kept her rolling; just seeing 15 celebrity clients had her financially satisfied. The Pratts thanked Kaeo for being such a loyal friend/brother as well as entrepreneur.

Kaeo and Pratt had known one another since Kaeo was in grade school and had been best friends since day one. Pratt's father was stationed in Hawaii for 12 years before the family moved to Arizona. They lived next door to the Iosua family. Even though Kaeo was younger, he was mature for his age and looked the part because of his size and height. The two men had stayed in touch and always agreed to help each other make it big one day. They did just that by working together to build a rising business; luckily, they made two successful ones.

*************************************************

Kaeo walked in on Yanira. She was in the nursery, packing it up.

Kaeo asked, "Baby, what are you doing? Why are you packing up the nursery?"

Yanira explained, "Baby, the room makes me remember, and at this point, I only want to forget. I need to return to work soon, and this has become a distraction. I refuse to continue hiding out at home."

Kaeo didn't say another word; respecting her feelings and wishes, he began helping his wife. Once the entire room was packed, he asked, "Hey, what do you say we get out of the house for dinner tonight, maybe we could go and see Ryleigh?"

Marshall had already called Kaeo to check on her and told him Ryleigh missed her. Yanira agreed to go and see Ryleigh, but she was not in the mood to dress up or be around too many people. She pulled a sweat outfit out of her closet and headed to the shower. Kaeo texted Marshall, and they decided to have dinner at their place.

Ryleigh was snapping right back into her figure; the weight she gained from the twins was slowly fading away. Yanira, on the other hand, had snapped back because she was not eating; she had lost weight. The ladies hugged one another for 5 minutes without breaking, letting go, or saying a word; they shed tears together. Their bond was indestructible. It seemed as though they felt each other's pain. Yanira went upstairs to see the boys. They were laying peacefully, yet smiling as if angels were playing with them.

Ryleigh asked, "So, really, how are you doing? Kaeo told us about your nightmares, sitting in the nursery, and your therapy."

"I'm ok. I packed up the nursery room today; it was killing me. I am ok with my nephews, but I can't stand to see the room every time I walk down the hall in the house. I will never forget, but I don't want the daily reminder of what happened and what I lost. I plan on going back to work on Monday. I have already called Dr. Rodriguez and Dr. Simon; they are excited because they need relief, and I do too. He said it has been hell without me," she smirked solemnly. Yanira was sad as she spoke to her cousin; her heart was hurting, and she felt like a piece of her soul was taken away from her. However, she was ready to push forward.

"That's great, Yani. I mean, you need to shake it off. It was a horrible incident, but you are a fighter. You are my blood, and we don't lay down or scare easily," Ryleigh stated. She believed her cousin was a fighter; better yet, she knew it. Yanira had always been a silent thunder; her hands were just as vicious as Ryleigh's, yet her temper was more controlled.

"Thanks, cousin. I have been working out at home, trying to build my strength, and you are right, I will not lie down or hide. I told Kaeo that today. It's not who I am, hell, who we are. We were not raised to get beat down and stay down. We rise up and regroup, right?" Yanira smiled at her own words.

"I think you should try again when the time is right. In the meantime, these little guys right here are up for grabs for you."

Yanira replied, "I will, and I am open arms to the world's cutest baby boys." Marco and Marcelo must have heard their voices because they were getting fussy. Ryleigh grabbed two of the bottles she had pumped earlier just before Yanira came. Together, they fed them, and they both fell asleep right after.

Kaeo and Marshall were there sipping and discussing business when the wives came downstairs. They had been upstairs for an hour.

"You beautiful ladies ready to eat?" Marshall asked.

They took a seat as their men served them, providing them with water because neither could drink due to breastfeeding and medication—steak alfredo pasta with spinach, cherry tomatoes, and broccoli with garlic bread, a Caesar salad, and his famous plantains.

Once they sat down and started eating, Marshall opened the conversation. He asked, "So Yani, I hear you are returning to work. Will you be accepting new patients? Cleo needs to come and see you."

Replying with a smile, Yanira stated, "Absolutely! I need to see every patient I can. I need to get back in the swing of it.

Have her call Resha first thing Monday morning and I will let her know to make her a priority."

"Will do," he replied. "So, did your cousin tell you we are opening a new restaurant, lounge, and bar? I am excited about it."

"Yes, I heard. Getting to the money, I see. You guys are trying to retire early." Yanira was proud of both of them.

Ryleigh chimed in. "Yes, these boys need a future. Our goal is to do what Kaeo is doing: make it a family business across the states and Jamaica, of course. I have already done the paperwork and found locations, menus, legal business names, trademarks, décor, suppliers, and everything. We are both eager to just build and create residual wealth. With Marshall already owning two clubs jointly, we need something separate for us. I'm ready to stop punching a corporate clock, too."

"I love it, and I am so proud of you two. You have not been doing corporate work; you have been building an empire. I'm with it." Yanira's mood changed as she congratulated her cousin for her ambitiousness.

Kaeo added, "I agree. That is fantastic man. Ry, you are definitely on the ball with all the legal aspects. I'm glad you got all that handled first. It took us a while to realize what we had to do. When we first started, we were clueless."

After dinner, they talked for another two hours and fifteen minutes. The boys were on a schedule and would be waking up soon for their last feeding for the night. Kaeo and Yanira left, then proceeded to check out at the security gate around 11 pm. The houses where Marshall and Ryleigh lived were gated and secured, and no one could get through without checking in and out with security or being seen on camera.

Kaeo disclosed his new plan to Yanira as he was not able to share his news with her earlier. She was elated to hear what Kaeo and Pratt were doing, and proud of her husband for turning his business into a family business as well, providing generational wealth. The promotion of Kendall was music to her ears because he deserved it; as he said he had been loyal to Kaeo, and Kishida had been just as loyal to Ryleigh. They were considered family; it didn't always have to be blood.

The two of them were so involved in the conversation that they did not realize they were being followed once they exited the gate. They pulled into the garage, unaware that they had led the assailant right to their home. Around 3 am the dog next door started barking loudly, and the camera in the backyard was alerting them there was motion. Yanira said it was probably the dog, but Kaeo told her he was going to check it out and to stay in bed while he went downstairs.

Kaeo went to the kitchen without turning on any lights and saw someone in the yard. It was dark, and he could not see a face. He went back up to grab his phone and flashlight without letting Yanira know that someone was in the yard, instead telling her to stay calm and remain in bed. Everything was ok; he just wanted to take a look.

He heard the door handle jiggle from the outdoor living room as he made his way downstairs. That startled him so he ran back upstairs to grab his pistol; Kaeo would not let anything happen to Yanira after what she just endured. The door handle was still jiggling, so he turned on the light to see if he could see a face, but the person ran. He was not fearful that someone could get in because they had it on camera, and the alarm would alert him and the police if it went off. Unfortunately, by the time he reached the back door again, no one was there. He surveyed the entire back yard. Pistol in one hand and flashlight in the other.

On Sunday evening after service, Yanira's parents invited them to dinner. Kaeo couldn't wait to tell Mr. White what happened on Friday; he wanted him to get the private investigator involved as soon as possible. He also planned to let Detective Bronson know what had transpired first thing Monday morning.

Mr. White beat him to the conversation. "Hey, I have some news for you. The cops found out who the car belonged to. It seems that Gloria Deploy was the owner. Do you know her? Or ever heard of her?" He asked.

Shaking his head and rubbing his face, Kaeo replied, "No, not at all."

"Well, my private investigator has been staked out at her house for four days now. There are two women who have been going in and out of the home. I am waiting to get photos for each. Tomorrow, or the day after, the police will search the house with a warrant and take fingerprints. I hope to find out more details. One of the women in that house is behind a recent incident and robbery, that's all I know so far, but more to come."

"Thanks, and just so you know, I was planning on calling the police in the morning. Around 3 am the other night, someone was trying to get into the house. The camera alerted me. I went to the kitchen and found someone trying to break through the door. Went upstairs to get my pistol and the flashlight, but when I turned on the light, they ran. I am not sure if the person was male or female; whoever it was, they were in all black with a mask on," Kaeo alerted him.

"What? Why didn't you call me? This is getting out of hand! You all need to find somewhere to stay, either with us or somewhere secure," her father replied in frustration.

Kaeo replied, "Dad, with all due respect, I didn't want to alarm Yanira after the nightmares she has been having. She is just now ready to go back to work. The other day she packed up the baby room, and she is finally smiling again. Telling her this would put her right back where we were before. Besides, our home has a camera in every corner of the house, inside and out. The person was just in dark clothing. I will be installing additional solar lights tomorrow while she is at work. I just couldn't scare her."

Mr. White retracted by saying, "No, you made the right call. She would be on pins and needles, as well as her mother and Ryleigh. We do not want those two alerted just yet. I will keep you posted. If it happens again, shoot to kill with the lights on or off; it is your property."

*********************************************

Work was going well. Yanira felt good administering medication to save lives and seeing patients. She felt normal for the most part, but Resha checked on her every hour; she was such a great employee and an honorable friend. It just reminded Yanira that something happened, and they worried about her.

Lunch was brought in daily by Kaeo or a vendor, not to mention Kaeo dropped her off and picked her up every day. He told her there was no driving for her, at least not alone until she was off medication, no longer having nightmares, and 100 percent back to normal. Yanira knew none of what he said had anything to do with one another, it was just his way of protecting her.

By Thursday, she was ready for a break, but news broke that there was a shootout between the police, a homeowner, and others inside the home. Just as Kaeo was delivering lunch, Yanira was headed to the ER to support the trauma team.

"Code Red, Code Red, all trauma one team members needed in the ED. Code Red!"

Yanira and Dr. Simon rushed to the units. Two women were shot, one in the chest and leg and the other in the arm and stomach. Additionally, four policemen were wounded: one hit in the leg, one in the neck, the other two in the torso. All anesthesiologists were needed. Yanira and Cameron were swamped prepping each of the patients. It turned out to be a busy four hours. Yanira didn't finish until 6:45 pm. Kaeo returned to pick her up and Yanira apologized as she entered the car.

"Sorry I couldn't see you for lunch, baby. The victims and perpetrators from the shootout were admitted to the hospital and I had to help out in the ER."

Kaeo replied, "It's ok. I gave your lunch to Resha; I figured she would enjoy it." Yanira smiled. She was happy to do anything for Resha because she did so much for her.

Kaeo asked, "Have you eaten anything since breakfast this morning?"

"No," she exclaimed. "It was so busy that I didn't have a chance to think about it."

"Well, dinner is waiting, and as soon as you shower, it will be on the table for you."

She kissed him then entered the garage and headed to the shower. Once done, she made her way back to the dinner table to tell Kaeo about her day.

"So, the shootout was between some ladies and the police. They all had so many wounds, but we were able to save everyone who arrived at the hospital. Two were in critical condition; it was touch and go for a moment."

Kaeo nodded. "That was a hectic day, but I am glad you were able to participate in saving the officers' lives. That's crazy! I bet those ladies are going under the jailhouse." Yanira laughed, sometimes his foreign sayings were just too funny.

Later that night, the cameras started buzzing. Someone was in the yard again; this time, there were two. One noticed the camera and lights and ran off.

The next day, Yanira went in and performed her normal anesthesia for surgery, but before leaving for appointments, she visited with the police from the previous day's incident just to check in on them. One police officer thanked her. He remembered her putting pressure on his wound to stop the blood and administering his medication to him and talking to him. His wife also thanked her. Yanira was grateful, telling them she was doing her job and glad he was still with them. The women, on the other hand, were being held with security and chained to the beds. They were definitely going to jail for shooting at the police. There were two officers assigned to each room, one in and one out.

Detective Bronson called Kaeo and told him he needed to see him immediately. Kaeo told him he was 5 minutes from the hospital to deliver lunch to Yanira. The detective advised him to stay at the hospital and to get Yanira, insisting on seeing them privately as soon as he arrived. Kaeo called Yanira and advised her to meet him before seeing patients; it was critical.

When he got to her office, Detective Bronson explained, "The car that was driven in your incident belonged to Gloria Deploy. She is the sister of Marla Deploy, a woman who was incarcerated and presumed dead, but much to our surprise, four of the women escaped and have been hiding out at Gloria's house. We were able to capture Gloria, Shirley Gaines, and Rebecca Linley, but Marla and another woman are still on the loose. Do any of these women sound familiar to you?"

"No, not at all; I do not recall ever meeting them or treating them unless it was in the ER."

"Well, I am heading there to speak with them now. They are awake. I will try to get what information I can and update you as soon as possible. I do not know the connection, so just be careful, ok?" Detective Bronson instructed.

Kaeo ate lunch with Yanira. As they racked their brains trying to find out who the ladies were, and what it had to do with them, Kaeo's phone rang. It was Yanira's dad, asking if he could talk. Kaeo replied he was with Yanira having lunch, but he would call once he left to head back home.

Yanira asked, "My dad, ok?"

Kaeo said, "Yeah, just man talk. You know how we talk about so many things. He just wanted to run something by me."

Yanira smiled and then kissed him. It felt so good and relaxing. It was at that moment she realized she hadn't had sex with her husband since before the accident nor pleased him in any way. He had been completely focused on her and not himself and had not asked or hinted. Looking at her watch, she noted she had 25 minutes before her next patient. That was time enough.

Yanira locked her door, walked over to her husband, and mounted him, kissing his neck as her hands rubbed through his hair; she felt Kaeo rise below from her touch. He smiled. "Baby, please don't tease me; it's been so long."

Yanira slithered down to his bottom half, unbuckled his pants, then began to put her mouth to work. She had to be quick, so she began sucking, tugging, licking, pulling, and nibbling. She pleased Kaeo with her tongue and jaws. Oh, how she missed the feeling of his dick being down her throat. It didn't take too long; he was truly backed up. Three minutes and he poured out like a waterfall.

Yanira chuckled. "I guess it has been a long time, and for that, I am sorry. More to come tonight. I promise."

Kaeo looked at her. "Nah, you still have 15 more good minutes before you have to clean up. I need just a few of those minutes."

She smiled and knew he missed her and the inside of her. Kaeo let his pants fall, grabbed Yanira, and pulled her pants down as well. He bent her over her desk, as she slid her paperwork to the side, and he dug in slowly, not wanting to hurt her. He also wanted to take his time and feel her insides; too many weeks had passed by, and he just needed to feel her.

Yanira panted instantly upon his entry. He growled as he entered her, took a deep breath, and then glided inside, barely moving because he felt he wouldn't last another minute. She was tighter than ever before. Yanira was wet as water at Niagara Falls. Five strokes and she was counted out.

"Umm," Kaeo called out. "Damn baby, I have missed you so much."

"Me too; I have one more. Want to match it?" She asked.

"Hell yes," Kaeo said proudly as he began to pick up a little speed and dig deeper into her walls.

"Ahh, shit," Yanira called out, and Kaeo followed behind her.

"Damn," he pumped and poured out once more inside her.

Yanira quickly went to her restroom to clean up and shower before her afternoon patients. She loved having a full bathroom in her office and always kept extra scrubs and a toothbrush. Kaeo cleaned himself as she showered. Once they were finished, he kissed her.

"I love you so much. Welcome back, baby, welcome back."

Yanira laughed out loud. His words caught her off guard. It was corny but cute and that was the reason she married him. Besides being a sweet and generous man, he was fine as hell. Kaeo always made her laugh, and he cared enough about her to sacrifice and put her needs first. That's love and respect. The fight was definitely worth it back in the day and long as she still had him.

# CHAPTER 15: THE SETUP

Kaeo reached the car and called her father once he was on the highway.

He asked him, "Are you still with Yanira, son?"

Kaeo told him, "No sir, I just left her. I took her lunch and now I am headed home.

Her father yelled, "No, No! Go back Son! Go Back! That girl was locked up with Anais. They didn't die. It's all connected! There was a three-car accident, and one car left the scene. The bus with the inmates and the other car were the only ones left. Those ladies escaped, took the bodies from the other car, and swapped them. Anais was locked up with Marla, Shirley, and the other one. Anais was the one who did this to Yanira…"

"What? What do you mean?"

"Listen son, turn around! Anais and Marla. Marla was the one who stabbed Yanira and helped Anais beat her, and they stole the money from her wallet. Don't tell Yanira; just get her now, please! And don't leave her alone until this heathen is caught," he demanded.

Kaeo exited the highway to turn around and get back to Yanira. He was speeding, thinking there was no way he would let Anais or anyone else kill his woman. He called Detective Bronson and said, "Hey, are you still at the hospital? If so, get my wife, please. I am on the way; I'm speeding and will not pull over for anyone, so warn them. I am heading to get my wife."

Detective Bronson said, "Yes, and I just got some crazy information. Your ex is not dead. I am headed to find your wife now. I promise to call your vehicle in to make sure no one stops you and request they escort you if necessary. "

Yanira was with a patient when Kaeo reached her office. Resha saw the look on his face. She yelled, "Patient room 5... she is with a patient," and began walking towards the room.

Kaeo knocked on the door, and Resha walked in. "Dr. Iosua, we need to speak with you briefly. It's urgent." Detective Bronson met them in the hallway. Yanira was there with Marla and had no clue.

In an attempt to keep Yanira alone, Marla spoke up, "Can she not treat me in peace first? What kind of place is this where the doctor is called out before they get to work on you?"

Detective Bronson pushed through the door and interjected, "Marla Deploy, you are under arrest."

"No, no, my name is Nancy Bridgestone. I am just here to see this doctor; I am not who you are looking for."

Detective Bronson said, "I will not ask you again, Marla, to get on the damn floor now. If not, I will shoot you without hesitation."

Marla did not look like she was going to lie on the ground. He gave her one last look and then, without hesitation, due to the location, Detective Bronson took out his taser and tazed her.

Marla dropped to the floor, shaking from the tase. There was a gun at her side. One minute longer, and Yanira would have been dead. Bronson grabbed the weapon, placed cuffs on her, and lifted her from the ground. A unit officer arrived just as he handcuffed her to take her to the station.

Marla yelled, her voice slurred from the tasing, "I'm telling you that you got the wrong woman. My name is Nancy. It's on my ID; check it out. You got the wrong woman, man. Come on. Take these cuffs off, dammit. You know I'll fuck you up if you do; that's why you won't. You chicken shit. Take them off!" She wiggled trying to escape from their grasp as the officer shoved her out the door.

Yanira was in shock. "Baby, what is going on? Detective, why did you just take my patient away? Please don't bring drama to my workplace." Yanira was pleading because she had already been embarrassed enough by Anais.

Detective Bronson had a serious look on his face. "Mrs. Iosua, we need to speak privately." They walked off as the detective directed Yanira back to her office.

Resha calmly spoke to the people who had congregated around to see what was going on. "I am sorry, patients. We just had an unruly character here. Please return to your rooms, and we will be with you shortly. Everything is ok now, please, and thank you." She was such a ride-or-die employee.

In her office, Yanira was shaking and unsure of what was happening. Whatever it was, she knew it was bad. She was afraid of being fired, but what she didn't know was that Resha blamed it all on the patient, and the other physicians bought it.

Kaeo looked at her. "Baby, I need you to relax because we need to tell you something but please be calm. Let me get us a bottled water, ok? Detective, you can explain." She nodded, nervous and anxious at the same time.

Bronson got straight to the point. "Ok, Mrs. Iosua, here we go. Anais is alive and well; she never burned to death in that accident. The other ladies have confessed to switching the bodies from the third vehicle that crashed into the bus a while back and purposely setting it on fire. No one ever knew it existed because no one ever knew to follow up on the third vehicle. This allowed them to have people think they, too, burned to death along with the rest of the inmates.

In the other car, there were five bodies, not one, but only they knew that. They stole the bodies of the four girls and dumped them near the bus fire where they also burned. Marla's sister was the one who intentionally caused the accident in the first place. The disappearance of the girls who were in the car was closed because bodies were never found.

One of the other ladies you treated the other day from the shootout, Shirley, recognized you from the pictures Anais kept. She had a picture she kept and posted up in their living quarters with, excuse me, but "Die Bitch" on it. Apparently, she painted an awful depiction of you with the girls, so they were willing to help her.

See, they have been hiding out in different places and saving to get out of town. However, the night you were attacked, the others heard of what Marla and Anais did to you, so Shirey made them leave town and they have been hiding ever since.

Once Anais found out you didn't die, they returned. Unfortunately for them, they did not have the money, so they agreed after Anais said they would leave for good. Anais had all the money, so they followed her lead. They only left with $600 and the money she and Marla stole from you the night of the attack. The money ran low since neither of them could get a job without IDs. Anais told them she could get the fake IDs once they returned, and when they got here, Anais got the fake IDs but was holding them until she finished the job of killing you. When it was done, they would all leave again. Apparently, Anais threatened them that if they did not help, she would not give them the fake IDs she had gotten them."

"What?? This is all crazy! Why even stay together?"

"Well, they all just wanted to start over, so they promised to sit tight until they could leave, but they refused to kill. Marla, on the other hand, loved to kill. She was being transferred to the mental health institution because she had attacked too many inmates and staff; they deemed her as mentally incapable, crazy and a risk to society.

The lady is quite the character and has failed all psychological testing. She is not the sharpest tool in the bunch, if you know what I mean. She has a rap sheet 5 miles long. Both Marla and Anais had ways of getting money, so the others stuck close to them. Those two became the ring leaders and are the reason they have been able to survive thus far. Going to their families would have been too dangerous. So, they have been waiting for you to return to work. The plan was for Marla to pretend to be a patient and kill you because you would recognize Anais. The appointment had been set since last Monday. Apparently, that is when your schedule opened, I am guessing it had been closed."

"Yes," Kaeo announced, "We just let her back on Monday. I drop her off and pick her up."

"That makes sense. Well, once it opened up, they all knew the plan and knew when to be ready to hit the road. That is how we knew the name and appointment time. Marla used the name Nancy Bridgestone."

Kaeo was in shock, shaking his head and knee profusely. Why was Anais doing all of this? Even if he did want her, they could never be together; she would be in prison. All she needed to do was to hide and never be found, but her vengeance had to supersede.

Yanira asked, "So, is she the one who has been coming to my house for the past week trying to break in?"

Kaeo looked in confusion. "Baby, you knew? Why didn't you…"

She replied before he finished. "Because I knew you were trying to keep me from being scared. I felt safe with you there, so I didn't make a big deal out of it. I can't hide Kaeo. I have to work. I can't live in fear. This bitch is crazy. I mean, what does she want? Detective, even if my husband leaves me for her, what does she expect? For them to live in hiding? For him to leave his business for her? I don't understand. You are one hell of a damn lay!"

Detective Bronson couldn't help but laugh at her humor in this situation. It made his job a little bit easier. "Mrs. Iosua, we need you to be careful. We are going to keep this connection under wraps because we do not want too many people chatting. You never know who knows who. I am sorry to say that Anais is still at large, but I believe she will be in a rage and will mess up soon. She knows the girls are in custody and that we know she is alive. I need to see what I can get out of Marla.

Mr. Iosua, I will keep you posted. I will also have an undercover at your place tonight. Unless you have somewhere else to go?"

Yanira spoke up with confidence. "No, we are not leaving our home. The security system and your undercover will be fine. I will tell you now, if she shows up again, I will fucking shoot her, so you better arrest me now if that is illegal."

"Ma'am, as far as I am concerned, anything you or your husband do to this woman is self-defense. Be safe, and I will be in touch. I am sorry to drop all of this and leave, but I need to get everything situated before nightfall."

Kaeo asked her, "Baby, are you sure you're, ok?"

She nodded, stating, "Yes, I need to see the rest of my patients, if I still have them. I am only scheduled for six more, and I am behind schedule."

Kaeo shook his head. "Baby, do you have to? At least can Resha go in with you?"

"No, my love, she cannot. She has a job to do. I will be fine. I will see you when you return." Yanira needed to stay busy.

Kaeo replied, "Hell no, I am not leaving you. I am going to stay and wait for you. I am not asking, nor will we discuss it." Yanira headed for the door, and Kaeo called her dad and filled him in on what had transpired. He also let him know that Yanira refused to leave their home.

When Yanira came out, Dr. Simon and Dr. Rodriguez were just stepping out of their patients' rooms. "Are you ok?" They asked.

"Sorry about the patient, Dr. Iosua. Boy, they sure can't seem to keep their control when they want medication. I hear they had a shootout too. Sadly, we can't keep drug addicts from coming into the office." Rodriguez said.

"Yes, we need to figure out a way to vet our new patients better. Are you good? We heard you kept her in the room to avoid hurting any of the other patients and she had to be tased by the police. That was extremely dangerous but thank you."

"Definitely, you deserve a bonus for that one." Dr. Simon added.

"No worries, I am ok. I didn't want to bring any attention to the office. I apologize. Resha is the real MVP, for sure. She called the authorities immediately."

In her head she thought, "What she did was make up a good lie, and they bought every word." Her actions were spot on and Yanira just played along. She was definitely going to ask about a raise for her even if she had to pay for it herself.

They departed from the hallway, and Yanira went in to see her next patient and apologized for the delay. She did that for all the remaining patients for the day. They all said they heard about the crazy patient, it was not her fault, and it was ok.

Once she was finished for the day, she thanked Resha. "Girl, I owe you one. The lie was very clever. How did you think of that so fast? I never condone lying but you are saving my job, and I am sorry to bring it all here. This is so embarrassing. I can't thank you enough!"

Resha laughed. "Not at all. I know you don't, but this is not your fault. I had to be quick because I didn't want everyone in your business, and I don't know it either. I mean you have told me a little, plus what I know from the calls and other foolishness, but you can't be held liable for someone else. I needed them to believe something; however, moving forward, I will check any new patients and make sure I am in the room if they are ok with it, to ensure they don't have anything on them and if so, we will signal each other and call security."

Yanira commented, "Thanks again. You have done enough, so that is not necessary unless you want to learn. Just notify me if the Remhart lady returns; she is the reason for this all."

Resha agreed. "Well, I want to learn, so I am all in for new patients." She smiled and showed a little excitement for the opportunity.

In her office, Kaeo was waiting patiently for her. "I have some paperwork to do before leaving, if that's ok, unless you want to drop me off early tomorrow," she told him.

Kaeo looked at her and laughed, but not in a good way. He said, "I will not be dropping you off. I will bring my work here and stay with you until they catch her. It's not an option or up for discussion, and I mean it Yani, so you make the choice, either let me come with you or you go back to being at home and seeing patients virtually. Not to mention your dad knows what is going on, so you won't be fighting with just me, it will be him, your mom, Ryleigh, and everyone else."

Yanira rolled her eyes; Kaeo was stern. He didn't flinch, nor was he willing to budge, but she understood why. In addition, her father knew, so there was no point because that was a battle she did not want or need. Yanira sat and completed her files and paperwork as he watched TV. It took an hour, and around 5:45 pm, she was ready to go. They walked out hand in hand, talking about dinner. They agreed to pick something up from the Japanese steakhouse.

When they reached the house, her parents were there waiting for them in the driveway. It was only 6:12 pm. Her dad stated, "Baby girl, I just needed to lay eyes on you and make sure that you are safe. Oh, and there is an unmarked car waiting on the other side of the street. So, if Miss Anais comes back, she will be arrested."

Knowing Kaeo would not leave Yanira, her mother brought dinner: fried chicken, mashed potatoes with gravy, and mac n cheese. Her mother made the best mac n cheese. They decided to eat the dinner her parents brought and save their Japanese for lunch tomorrow. The Whites left around 8:25 pm, and the two of them cleaned the kitchen, packed up their food for tomorrow, and went upstairs with a bottle of wine around 9 pm. They were going to finish what they started earlier, just a longer version.

Kaeo took her right there as they showered, kissing, rubbing, and loving one another. Lifting those thick thighs and round ass, he couldn't help but raise her so she could feed him dessert. He was powerful with it, and she leaked her juices on his tongue twice. His sucking game was everything.

Lowering her body, he carried her out of the shower and to their bed. He licked and sucked a little more, then climbed her body and inserted himself, howling (ouugghhh) as soon as he entered. Yanira's skin was like velvet, so soft and smooth. Kaeo made sweet passionate love to her causing her to cum three times. She smiled as he got excited, knowing he was nearing his peak. He pumped hard and went deep inside while she squirmed as she felt it in her gut and back. He released and kept driving through her walls, orbiting in and out of her with force. Their love was incredible. She had missed his smell, his warm body on top of her, and especially his manhood making her deliver all sorts of warm splashes.

Two hours later, they were fast asleep, naked. Kaeo was so tired he didn't even wait for Yanira to fall asleep first. Yanira dozed off fifteen minutes later but woke up after an hour of sleeping because she had a dream about the beating. Remembering the voice, she knew it was Anais but didn't understand how or why she had that feeling. Today was eye-opening to find out how that bitch had escaped. Now she was thinking how she could trap her to get her back in jail where she belonged.

Suddenly, Yanira heard the buzzing of the motion detectors. She looked at Kaeo, but he was sound asleep. Something or someone was in the backyard. Keeping the lights off, she got up, put on pajamas, grabbed her gun, and went downstairs. She rested on the bottom stairs, waiting for Anais to try and enter.

Twenty minutes later, Kaeo turned on the light and saw her sitting there. He made his way down, asking, "Baby, what happened? Are you ok? Did you hear something?"

She explained, "No, I had a dream and couldn't sleep, so I figured if Anais came by, I would be ready." Yanira lied. There may not have been anything, but she was ready to catch Anais.

Kaeo came down the stairs. "Come on, baby, let's go back to bed. It will be ok."

She went back to the bedroom as he requested. As they lay in bed, Kaeo asked, "Baby, are you sure you are, ok? I know this is a scary situation, and I wish I could fix this all."

She replied quickly, "Yes, I am ok. I am not even scared. Now, I am just annoyed with it all. I mean, when is enough going to be enough? I want this to be over so we can have our life back. Plus, I am pissed she killed my baby. I want to get her, and I know I shouldn't, but I will just have to repent."

Kaeo countered, "I fear that one day you will walk off and leave me because of all the foolishness Anais keeps doing. I feel you might blame me for us losing our baby and all this damn drama."

Turning to face her husband, she said, "Honestly, I don't blame you for any of this. Our relationship is solid. I love you with everything in me, and I will never leave unless you give me a reason to. My prayer is that you will not resent me when I kill her because I am."

Kaeo looked at Yanira. Never would he ever have thought she would say anything like that, but he didn't blame her. "Baby, I will never resent you. I want this to end, too. This is what Ryleigh meant when she said you are just as vicious as her, but you had to be pushed, right? You have been pushed to a point where I know I can't even imagine what I would have done so I understand."

Yanira came clean. "I am not a vicious person, Kaeo. I am not pro-violence, but she has pushed me way beyond being nice, patient or understanding. She killed my baby and tried to kill me yet again. Had that man not come out when he did, they would have taken my life."

"Baby, what do you mean? I thought you..."

Yanira interrupted. "Truthfully, I knew it was Anais then. I heard her voice when she told me to die. In my dreams, I heard her voice loud and clear. The night they attacked me,

I thought I was going crazy because I couldn't understand how it could be her. I thought my mind was playing tricks on me by thinking that the only person who would attack me was her; it was impossible because I knew she was dead. I thought I was crazy or going crazy because it felt so unrealistic. But now, this coming to our home and our businesses trying to intimidate me, having her friends make a fake appointment, trying to get me to leave you, or attempting to kill me so she can live out some sick fantasy of hers is over. I am at the point of no return with this situation."

"Baby, why didn't you tell me? You have been dealing with this all this time and you have said nothing. When did we start keeping secrets babe? You could have talked to me." He caught himself, trying not to start an argument and putting himself in her shoes. He corrected his words and tone. "My love, listen, I am so sorry. I hate that you remember. I can't stand that you knew all this time and dealt with it alone even though you didn't have to. Wow, this is all fucking nuts. I wish I could make this all go away or do something to make it stop."

With a look of absolute seriousness, she responded, "Kaeo, it's cool, because like I said, I am going to kill her. So, brace yourself. When she comes for me, I will be ready. That sick bitch is going to pay for killing my baby and messing up my mind and body. She will remember me, but for a different reason this time."

Kaeo just looked and listened to Yanira. There was nothing more for him to say. He couldn't kill Anais, unless he absolutely had to, but he was definitely going to make sure she didn't hurt his wife nor another child if they could even have one. Yanira took a brutal beating, and it would be nothing but a miracle if they had another one thanks to Anais.

## **CHAPTER 16: GETTING TO THE BOTTOM OF IT**

While driving to work, Yanira told Kaeo, "Listen, I have been thinking and I want to set a trap for Anais. I know it sounds weird, but I know she is coming to our house soon, and I want to be the one to end it. She thinks she is going to show up and catch us off guard, but she won't. I want her to think she will. I am hoping to catch her off guard; I want to make her think that she has won by letting her get in and seeing what she does. We will be faking like we are in the bed but then capture her if she does anything violent and beat her ass as she did me. Afterward, we will call the police and make sure they lock her up for good."

Kaeo did not like the plan at all. It seemed premeditated, but it was just like she had done to Yanira. Detective Bronson called before he could reply.

"Mr. & Mrs. Iosua, we spoke with Marla. Marla offered to give Anais up only if they reduced her time. So, we are going to set Anais up with the help of Marla. We are still looking at Gloria's house, but she caught wind and hasn't returned. Since the arrest of Marla, however, the two have been in communication via mobile phone, so we are going to see if we can catch her by arranging to have them meet up."

Yanira interrupted, "How do you even know this will work? How do you know you can trust her, this Marla woman?"

Detective Bronson replied, "We don't. We are hoping it will."

"Well, I have no faith in that plan. When she came to our house last night, your detective was parked outside in the front. She, however, came through the back. I plan on letting her in tonight and shooting to kill. I am no longer doing this with her, Marla, or any fucking one else. I am not sure if you have read or viewed the case before this, and if you haven't, you should, then you will understand why I am not taking any chances with this woman. I need to move on." Yanira was pissed, and both Kaeo and Bronson could tell.

"Well, I tell you what, Mrs. Iosua, since you want to bait her, I can't stop you, but I will have an undercover in the front and the back parked in a space hidden yet accessible. When we spot her, we will arrest her, but that does not mean you should not protect yourself if you catch my drift."

Yanira replied, "I caught it, say less. Thank you!" Yanira disconnected the call.

Kaeo saw that Yanira was all worked up. He just wanted to protect his wife so they would both be carrying protection from here on out. Yanira told him, "I want to park in private parking so Anais will think I came to work by myself if she is watching. I want to create the illusion that I am comfortable and careless."

As the day went on, Yanira worked and saw patients. Kaeo stayed in her office, handling paperwork, and making his calls. An officer was waiting for them outside the private parking deck as they exited the building after her shift was over. They decided to go to the grocery store and then home to cook dinner and watch a movie.

Everything was quiet for the next two months, with no Anais and no issues. They still walked around protecting themselves, but now it all seemed in vain; she never surfaced. She must have finally gotten the picture. In the third month, with no activity, Detective Bronson decided to cut the surveillance.

In the 5th month, Kaeo finally stopped taking her to and from work, but he still brought her lunch every day. Whether they had leftovers or a surprise, he was her daily lunch date. Kaeo was a loving husband, and still waited patiently to discuss her giving him a baby of his own to love. For the next four months, she thought about it daily. With no signs of Anais, she decided to stop her birth control and planned on surprising Kaeo.

Within weeks, Yanira found out she was pregnant but didn't want to announce anything to Kaeo until she had to. She feared that Anais would come back and repeat the same ferocious beating and kill this baby, too. By the time she turned 2 1/2 months, her belly was starting to show, and it was evident that she was gaining weight. She didn't think she could keep it a secret much longer. Kaeo, being sweet, never asked; he just loved her body as if she was the same size as before. Assuming since she was not running daily that maybe this was the reason for the additional weight.

One day, Yanira asked him to meet her at their old lunch space near the hospital with the benches, telling him she thought it was cute to finally enjoy the sun and fun again without any distractions. April always brought out the best weather, not too hot, but just right.

When Kaeo arrived, he brought her a sub, just like old times. Yanira smiled without even knowing she was smiling so brightly. They enjoyed lunch, talking, and remembering previous dates and chats. Once they caught up, she asked him a few questions: Are you still in love with me?"

He answered, "I love you more today than I ever have, and tomorrow that love will be even stronger."

"Question 2…How do you feel our marriage is going?"

He was now confused, but answered, "I am madly in love with you and with us. Everything is perfect; both of us are well, and there are no signs of Anais."

"Question 3…Do you ever think about us trying again to have another baby?"

Kaeo put his head down and grabbed her hand. "I cannot deny that I want you to have my child. Considering what you have been through, I couldn't ask for anything else, but if we were blessed to have one, I would be through the roof."

Yanira spoke loudly, "Well, Mr. Iosua, I think it's about time I tell you that we are indeed pregnant, and I am already 2 ½ months. I have been waiting to make sure I get past the scary stages, and so far, so good."

Kaeo jumped up, pulled Yanira into him, and kissed her ten times. "Seriously?? We are pregnant!! I mean, you are pregnant; we are having a baby??? Hot damn, I am going to be a dad!"

The bystanders all clapped and yelled congratulations! Kaeo was so happy. Smiling from ear to ear, he wouldn't put her down; he just held her. Finally, he released her and asked, "Is it safe to tell the family? We need to celebrate with Ryleigh and Marshall tonight."

"Babe, please, let's wait one more month before telling anyone; I want to make it a little further along."

Kaeo agreed. "Ok, Babe. We will hold off. Thank you!" He kissed her once more.

The following month, Yanira arrived home, took off her medical coat, showered, and put on a casual oversized fleece suit to lounge in. Kaeo looked at her and said, "Baby, how much longer are we going to keep this a secret? You are showing a lot for 3 ½ months. Your baggy clothes are not baggy anymore."

Yanira rubbed her belly. "Yeah, you are right. Let's share with the family soon and my job as well. Let's see if everyone is free Sunday evening for dinner. If so, we will tell them all then. We have to make sure Kalia gets everything together for your mom and dad to get on the line, too. I know they meet for Sunday brunch anyway."

That next night, when Yanira came home, Kaeo had redecorated the baby's room. He had the room staged just as it was before, but with different colors and décor to make sure he did not make her sad or remember the first one.

Yanira's heart melted. "Have I ever told you that I love you more than anything in this world?" She gushed, blushing, and planting a kiss on her man with all tongue and juicy lips. Kaeo loved to feel her, and when she planted that kiss, he rose below.

She smiled, "Shall we take care of that, my love? I think you deserve to get all the loving you can while it's quiet." He smiled, and they headed to the bedroom for a shower and celebration sex.

Kaeo lifted her up and carried her to the bedroom. He sat on the chaise lounge and gently pulled her pants and panties down. He slid out of his basketball shorts and placed her soft body onto his, as he lay relaxed on the chaise. Yanira smiled as Kaeo told her, "Well, you said you were going to give it to me so why not let you drive." She grinned, sliding down on him. Taking him all in caused a chill down her spine. She was wet and slushy. Holding onto his neck, while he held her waist, she grinded her hips into his pelvis. Kaeo moaned out loud; her pregnant sex was so intense and needed.

He needed to be inside her every chance he could. Kaeo started to rise more and more. Yanira became more ingrained in his body as he pulled her into him so deep that his nuts grazed against her butt cheeks. He was so deep inside her she felt he touched her tubes. Yanira let out a slight scream as she released her orgasm, and this caused Kaeo to pour out his. She collapsed on his body and fell asleep naked from the waist down clinging onto her husband.

Kaeo let her sleep as he watched the TV. When she came around, he joked, "I still got it! Rocked that ass to sleep, didn't I?"

Yanira rolled her eyes. "Yes, you still got it baby. Now come on, lets shower."

Everyone came over for Sunday dinner: her aunt, uncle, parents, Ryleigh, Marshall, Marshall's mom and sister, and the twins. The family mingled throughout the main floor and outdoor living room. Kalia texted that she would Facetime in 45 minutes to an hour; she had to wait for everyone to come over, and some of the family members were late. Yanira gathered everyone together, telling them it was time to eat. Her dad blessed the food, then they ate and later cleaned the kitchen.

Just as they finished cleaning and Yanira was putting up the dessert dishes, the Apple TV in the kitchen rang. When Kaeo's family came on the screen, everyone was happy, greeting one another, smiling full of joy. By now, everyone had become one big happy family. Kaeo couldn't wait to open his mouth about his bundle of joy.

"Alright, family, we have you guys here and, on the phone, because we have an announcement to make. We are not sure about how you guys are going to take this, but we figured it's time we let you all know." Their faces went from happiness to curiosity. They knew they were in love, but had the mess with Anais corrupted their relationship?

Kaeo's father said, "Son, whatever it is, we are still family. Speak your peace."

Yanira's father agreed, "That's right, Chief."

Kaeo looked at Yanira. On cue, she unzipped her sweater and rubbed her big pregnant belly. They announced together, "We are pregnant!"

The family went wild. They were so happy. It had been so long since she had lost the baby, but they knew she wanted children. Hugs, kisses, and joy filled the room and the TV. The dinner was indeed a celebration. It was so loud the twins woke up crying. Marshall went and picked them both up and held them, both returning to their good sleep.

Mother Iosua smiled. "Oh, there are my grandchildren," she said, referring to Ryleigh and Marshall's boys. "My goodness, they are getting so big. Ryleigh, my darling, Marshall, what are you feeding them? They are Hawaiian babies for sure." They all laughed.

The family mingled, celebrated for an hour more, and ended their Sunday with a blessing and prayer. After everyone left, they decided to FaceTime the kids. As soon as everyone picked up, Kaeo announced, "Hey, you guys, Yanira and I have to tell you something."

Cordero began to get worried. The last time they announced they had something to tell them, Anais was alive and terrorizing Yanira after killing her baby. "Oh man, you guys, ok?"

They both shouted, "We are pregnant!" Clariana, Kamryn, and Cordero were ecstatic. Even the boys were clueless clapping. The family talked a little more, and then they ended the call after 30 minutes.

# **CHAPTER 17: BABY? ON BOARD**

Three weeks passed, and it was time for a prenatal checkup with Kaeo. This would be his first appointment. This time, they would get an ultrasound and learn the sex of the baby. Yanira had gotten so big in such a short time; she looked six months pregnant instead of 4 1/2. They walked hand in hand as she escorted him to the OB/GYN practice across from her office.

As soon as she reached the front, the receptionist gave them a cheerful greeting. "Dr. Iosua, welcome. Dr. Yasmine is expecting you; room 2, please."

Yanira walked into the office and sat with Kaeo right next to her. "Baby, I am so excited to be in this room again; you have no idea." He hugged her gently around the neck.

Yanira smiled and said, "Me too, baby."

Dr. Yasmine knocked on the door and walked in. "How are you, Dr. Iosua? Good to see you again. Mr. Iosua; how are you, sir?"

Kaeo replied with a huge smile. "Good, I think."

Dr. Yasmine laughed. "Well, let's see if we can make this a sure thing."

"So, any new complications or concerns Dr. Iosua?" The doctor asked as she prepped the tools.

"No, nothing new. I just feel like this child is going to be a big one. I have gained a lot of weight in such a short time, and I get winded easily. Not to mention, I'm constantly craving ice cream."

Dr. Yasmine laughed and performed the ultrasound. When they saw the baby's leg move, Kaeo asked, "What is it? A boy or girl?"

Dr. Yasmine laughed, "Well, Mr. Iosua, that's your son."

Kaeo started to celebrate. "Yes, a boy!" He took another look at the screen and his face changed. Yanira then turned to look at the screen fearing the worst.

"Wait, what is that? What is behind my son? Is something wrong?" Kaeo was about to panic.

"Well, let's take a closer look. It looks like what you see is another baby's arm. He has a playmate in there with him. Let's see if we can find out by having you move around a little, Yanira. Ok, let me see...well...well, it looks like he is a protector. It's a girl," she expressed with cheer. "Look at her; she is hiding behind her brother."

Yanira was not as cheerful. "Well dang! That is why I have gained so much weight, and I am so big. This is unbelievable. Our first and last."

Kaeo gave her kiss after kiss after kiss. He was happy, and this was the best news he could ever have. Kaeo asked a million questions to Dr. Yasmine, so many that she told him they had run out of time, but she would be sure to give him a host of books to read. Kaeo had already read every book she mentioned, but this time, he was so excited he couldn't keep his composure.

They left full of joy from their appointment. Yanira went back to work, and Kaeo went home. The more he thought about the twins, the more he realized they needed a new house. They could not have a boy and a girl in one room, nor could they have one downstairs and one up. He needed to start looking for a house or build one. Marshall called at that moment, interrupting his thoughts.

"Hey, Bro, I wanted to see if you guys wanted to go out for dinner tonight. We are leaving the babies with Ryleigh's parents."

Kaeo said, "Sure, man, I'm game. Seaspice?"

Marshall replied, "For sure."

Kaeo held him from hanging up. "Hey, I have to ask you, do you know a good realtor? We just found out we are having twins, and I think I want to surprise Yanira with a house when the babies get here."

"What! Twins? You too? Man, oh man... Congratulations. Girl or boy?" Marshall asked.

"One of each! I am so excited that I don't know what to do with myself. I'm blessed and happy."

Marshall continued, "They are going to open up phase two over here in the next couple of weeks. The houses are just as big as ours, with the same amenities, gates, and all, you know. If it is something you would be interested in, I am sure we can link up and get you a sweet deal. If you get in before the properties start to sell, you can pick your lot first. I'm cool with the builders."

"Hell yes, man! Yanira would be so happy to be near you and Ryleigh, and the kids would be close. If you are good with that, I am for it!" Kaeo couldn't keep his excitement down.

"Ok, let's plan for Tuesday next week. I will get with the builder now, and I am sure he can get you something righteous. Quick question. Do you want a basement like mine, and do you want them to finish it? If so, they may make you a good deal on that, as well."

"For sure, that would be ideal! Good looking out," Kaeo replied.

"Cool, I will make sure he is prepared to show you the best lots with basements and something in a cul-de-sac too like mine."

"Bet, I appreciate you! Remember it's a surprise so I don't want her to know just yet. This will be that push surprise thing she kept telling us about."

"No doubt, I got you covered."

\*\*\*\*\*\*\*\*\*\*\*\*\*\*\*\*\*\*\*\*\*\*\*\*\*\*\*\*\*\*\*\*\*\*\*\*\*\*\*\*\*\*\*\*\*\*

The following Tuesday, they met as planned. Kaeo did a walk through with Marshall and the builder. They drove and viewed every lot and floor plan, then picked the biggest lot they had. He requested a two-level house with a finished basement. Kaeo told them to start building the house asap and made Marshall promise not to say anything to Yanira.

Kaeo put down $150k earnest money on the house, all from his savings, not their joint account, because he didn't want to alert Yanira. The house would have six bedrooms, two offices on the main floor, a basement with a theater, game room, bathroom, kitchen, a kid's playroom, an outdoor swimming pool, hot tub, and outdoor grill.

Their master bedroom would come with a sitting room, his and her closets, and two fireplaces, one in the bedroom and one in the bathroom. Every other room had its own bathroom as well. This would serve as a Christmas and push present. He was so excited; Marshall was as well. Few people could afford their type of houses. Most of the people in that community were entertainers, lawyers, or CEO's.

# CHAPTER 18: HOME ALONE

Just two weeks before Yanira's 8th month, Kaeo had to rush out of town for business. One of his stores ran into some issues with a leak and damage to most of the furniture due to a unit above them flooding. Pratt was not available as he had gone to New York with his wife for a hair show. Yanira gave Kaeo her blessing to go, stating she and the babies would be fine for five days without him. She suggested to him to allow Cordero to meet him there to assist with getting everything arranged and then spend a little quality time together. He agreed as long as she promised not to make any stops after work and to go straight home, parking in the garage.

When Cordero found out, he was so happy to spend some male bonding time with his dad. They would handle business during the week and then chill on the weekend. Cordero posted pictures all over social media of every restaurant and bar they attended. He even posted photos of the damage done to the store. When all the work was completed on Saturday, they planned to go to a ball game and catch a flight back on Sunday morning.

Kamryn and Clariana were also on a girl's trip with Kamryn's sisters and friends while her mom watched the kids. Both of them posted their fun times on social media, celebrating life. While everyone was out living their best life, Yanira, on the other hand, worked her last week in the office, seeing patients. Kaeo called as much as possible, checking on her and the babies. He loved for her to put the phone to her belly so the kids could hear his voice. He wanted to make sure his children knew who he was.

\*\*\*\*\*\*\*\*\*\*\*\*\*\*\*\*\*\*\*\*\*\*\*\*\*\*\*\*\*\*\*\*\*\*\*\*\*\*\*\*\*\*\*\*\*

Friday, her last day at work, seemed to have gone by so fast. The team gave her a small baby shower/ farewell since she would not be returning to the office for the next seven months. During her last month of pregnancy, she would provide telehealth support to her patients. Once she delivered, she would be off for three months, then work the next three performing more telehealth support for her patients.

After work, she went straight home. Kaeo had gone to the grocery store, purchasing every snack she liked, including microwavable meals, cutting the grass, checking the alarm system and fire alarms, everything he could think of to ensure she was safe and could relax for the week and weekend without leaving the house.

Yanira did just that. She showered, ordered a pizza (she had a craving for a turkey pizza), then made some homemade brownies and watched movies. Around midnight, she woke up on the couch; the brownies had put her to sleep. Laying there, she realized she hadn't set the alarm. She picked up her phone, and the system showed "Armed Stay." Kaeo had already set it. She checked the perimeter; all was quiet. By the time she had made it upstairs she was out of breath and tired, she didn't even bother to turn on the TV, she dozed off immediately.

Saturday morning, Yanira woke up and went for a walk. She didn't get far, only ten houses past hers, before she was stopped by a few of the mothers in the neighborhood asking when she was due. The ladies kept her hostage for an hour, chatting, giving her tips about motherhood, and offering their services if she needed anything. Yanira didn't mind; she enjoyed seeing the kids in the neighborhood riding their bikes and scooters and playing with one another. Letting her imagination run, she visualized what her kids would be doing at that age. After their conversation, she retreated to the house, tired from standing and shifting with her big belly.

She spent the rest of the day cleaning, changing bed linens, and planned on making herself a four-course meal. After cleaning, she noticed a car across the street she didn't recognize, so she closed all the blinds and made sure to set the alarm back. Yanira was slightly concerned because no one ever parked directly in front or across from their house.

After ensuring everything was secure, she started cooking dinner to occupy her mind and relax; she cooked two bruschetta slices, a house salad with lettuce, spinach, croutons, bell peppers, onions, and cheese, small pan of lasagna, and oatmeal raisin cookies. Once she finished cooking and cleaning the kitchen, there was a knock at the door. Yanira froze, then grabbed her phone to look at the camera; she saw it was Ryleigh and the twins. She quickly turned off the alarm and opened the door to let them in while peeping to see if the car was still there.

Just as she was closing the door, she saw her neighbor's teenage daughter walking her friend to her car. The friend must not have known which house was theirs and parked wherever she could. Yanira was so paranoid earlier, and this gave her a little relief. She relaxed and welcomed her guests into the house.

Ryleigh said, "Hey, I was out shopping nearby and needed somewhere to let the boys use the bathroom and use it myself. I tried calling you, but you didn't answer, so I decided to come over to check on you."

"Oh, I am sorry. I was cleaning and cooking. Let me help you."

Yanira helped her take the twins to the restroom. She took Marcelo to the downstairs restroom and Ryleigh took Marco upstairs. When Ryleigh came back down, she asked, "Hey, do you want to stay for dinner? Or do you guys have to rush off?"

It was already 5:20 pm, so Ryleigh agreed. "Nah, if you have enough, we can stay awhile. I appreciate you because I was going to go to someone's drive-through. These boys are a handful, and I am tired."

"Where is Marshall?" Yanira asked.

"Oh, Marshall is at the club handling business, and he will be out for most of the night. You know how they have to do inventory, then they have special performances, so he has to do his thing."

The cousins enjoyed the meal, watched a movie, and caught up on Ryleigh's business plan. Everything was running smoothly, and their second grand opening was up and coming within the next 30 days. The restaurants were a hit, and Ryleigh was glad not to be in corporate America anymore, working on building someone else's pockets. She was stacking hers.

Around 9:30 pm, Ryleigh decided to leave and take the boy's home. They had played themselves out, crawling and trying to run around. Ryleigh knew the car ride would put them at ease and right to sleep. Yanira helped her get the boys in the car and headed upstairs.

As soon as she turned on the water, Kaeo called. "Hey baby, I just wanted to tell you goodnight before you dozed off and let you know I set the alarm when Ryleigh left."

Yanira smiled. "Thank you. I was heading to shower and forgot all about it. How is everything? Are you guys ready for your big game? It starts in less than an hour."

Kaeo told her, "Babe, I am having such a great time with Cordero; he is turning into a responsible man and becoming very mature and less hot-headed than before. The responsibilities he and Kalel have taken on helped them to become better men. Both of them seem happy to be able to provide for their families."

Yanira smiled at him and said, "Well, they have a phenomenal role model and mentor. It was inevitable."

Kaeo's heart was full of love as he smiled back at his beautiful wife, seeing her glowing face and full cheeks. He spoke to his babies as Yanira held the phone to her belly, then Kaeo told her he loved her, and they ended the call.

# CHAPTER 19: THE MASSACRE

Around 2 am, Yanira woke up to a loud beating on the door. She looked at the camera, but it was blurred and partially blacked out. She got up and began walking downstairs to the door, asking, "Who is it?" She didn't hear anything, so she asked again, "Who is it?" Again, nothing. Yanira began to walk away, and the loud banging started once more. She said, "I have already asked who it is; I will not ask again."

The voice rang out, "You know who it is, Yanira. Let's not play this game. It's me bitch."

In disbelief she realized Anais was at her door and knocking at that! Yanira scolded the unwanted quest. "Anais? What the hell! Why are you at my house? What the fuck is wrong with you?"

"I want you dead bitch. That is what is wrong with me. You have crossed me three times now, first my job and my lover, second my man, then my kids. I want you dead because no one takes anything from me and gets away with it."

"Your job...what job, Anais? I have never worked for or with you."

"Oh, you don't remember now? Well, let me help you. See, years ago, you treated a boy who had an allergic reaction, and he had fallen off those bars. I was fired because of you that day, and my lover left me. Then you fucking took Kaeo away from me, my one true love, and turned my kids against me. You thought you could because I let you get away with it the first time. Not anymore bitch."

"What?" (Yanira began to think back. Thinking hard. Still, she did not know what she was talking about.) Anais, what the hell are you talking about?"

"They called me Anna back then. The boy fell off the monkey bars, remember? My lover dumped me because of you. I know you are in there alone, and Kaeo can't protect you now. All I want is for you to die and that baby of yours, too. I have had enough of you; you have run out of luck tonight, and you will never give him a child. I will kill them all so you might as well die this time."

Yanira could not believe Anais was at her home and holding a grudge after so many years. Why in the hell was she still at this? It had been over a year since she bothered them. This woman was relentless; all she had to do was stay hidden, but she hated her that much. She was so stupid to do all of this over a man who didn't want her.

Anais started banging again, and Yanira just walked away. Calling Kaeo wouldn't do her any good; there was simply nothing he could do. She ran to the alarm and hit the silent panic button.

Anais yelled, "There is nowhere to run bitch! You will be dead before anyone gets here."

"Anais, go the fuck home or wherever you have been. Leave me alone! I didn't do anything but tell them the truth back then: it was an accident. Why are you holding on to this? Why are you here?"

Anais screamed, "I told you before, you don't get to ask questions bitch! I want you and that baby dead. Open the door!!"

"And as I have told you a million times, you fucked up with Kaeo. I took nothing from you, and I am not opening my door. Now leave before I call the fucking police."

Anais didn't respond. Figuring that she had left, Yanira checked the peephole, but no shadow was there. She was annoyed that she couldn't fight Anais because she was too far along in her pregnancy. She planned on just going upstairs when Anais came back. The police would call soon or be on site and she would just ignore her until they arrived.

Suddenly, as she headed for the stairs to grab her cell phone, she heard a glass break, then another, which startled her. She ducked down as much as she could with the big belly. Then she went to take a look and noticed Anais had thrown two bricks into the living room window. Once she could see Yanira, she started shooting through the broken window into the kitchen and living room. Yanira ducked behind the couch just in time, trying to hide. The door started rattling immediately as Anais began kicking on it, and then she shot at the door handle four times.

"Bitch, open up," Anais demanded. "I have nothing to lose. You made a fool of me."

As Yanira started crawling to the stairs, Anais began shooting. She ducked down again until she heard the gun click. Anais was out of bullets, so she dashed for the stairs to grab her phone to call the police.

Anais loaded the gun quickly and let off three shots as she walked up the stairs. Yanira stopped in her tracks, trying to dodge the bullets. One hit her leg. Looking around, she noticed Anais had begun breaking through the glass with her gun handle and started to climb through the window.

Yanira was trying her best to make it up the stairs, running as fast as she could with her big belly. When she made it up to the top, she turned to see Anais right behind her at the foot of the stairs. Anais took another shot at her just as she turned the corner, hitting Yanira's arm this time. The adrenaline was pumping, and she didn't even feel it. She ran to her bedroom, locked the door, threw her sitting chair in front of it, and then hid on the other side of the bed as she called 911. Another shot rang through, and a hole appeared in the bedroom door.

"I need an officer here right away! A known assailant has broken into my home. She has fired shots at me and is trying to kill me. Please hurry; I am pregnant, home alone, and need assistance as soon as possible."

"Yes, ma'am, we have your location. Please stay calm and stay on the line until the officers arrive. Have you been hurt? Is there anywhere you can go until the officers come?"

I am locked in my bedroom, but I cannot say that it is safe. She can come in if she breaks the door down. Please, can you call Detective Bronson? He is aware of my case. The attacker is a known criminal at large. Please get him here now. Hurry! I cannot fight anyone pregnant."

Initially, Yanira was calm, but then the alarm started beeping, which caused her to panic. Anais was kicking and banging on the door, yelling, "Bitch, either way, you are going to die. I will keep beating on this door; either you let me in, or I will break in and kill you. Stop hiding behind the door. There is nowhere for you to run. I am going to kill you this time. Open the door, you stupid bitch! I told you I would be back to get you, but you didn't listen. Now, it is time to pay. Open the fucking door!"

The dispatcher said, "Ma'am, stay clear of your assailant, and please stay calm. I have called someone. Do not engage."

Yanira was startled; she was not scared of Anais, but fighting her was not an option, or she would lose her babies for sure. The police were taking too long to get there. Anais had begun hitting the door with a hammer, hatchet, or something heavy. Yanira was in shock and froze—the thoughts of Anais getting in and what she had done to her before started flooding her mind. Memories of waking up in the hospital without her baby in her belly and hearing that Anais was the culprit made her emotional as she feared endangering her unborn children.

Anais continued to hammer at the door, bringing Yanira out of her trance. She was having a panic attack and hyperventilating, so she opened the bedroom window. Suddenly, the phone beeped. It was Detective Bronson. She told the dispatcher, "I have to go. Detective Bronson is calling on the other line."

"Ma'am, please do not hang up. You may click over. I will wait. Please do not hang up the line." Yanira clicked over.

"Mrs. Iosua, are you there? What is going on?" Detective Bronson was yelling loudly on the phone.

Panicking, Yanira told him, "She is here! Anais is here! She threw bricks through my living room window and shot at me. I'm trapped in my bedroom, and I am 8 months pregnant. She is hammering at the door, and it's about to cave! I need help!"

Detective Bronson told her calmly, "Mrs. Iosua…Snap out of it! You are not some scared, helpless woman; you are one tough cookie! You have to protect yourself and your baby. You can't lose control. Now, shake it off and do what you have to do! If you have a weapon, use it; I am on my way. A fire rescue team has been called, and the police are three minutes out."

"Three minutes out! Please hurry," she called out.

Anais laughed. "You don't have three minutes Bitch! I am coming for you."

Yanira was hoping that if Anais heard the police and dispatcher, she would become scared and run away. She was far from that. She had become unhinged and ready for war.

Something snapped in Yanira at that moment. She gathered herself and grabbed the gun from her nightstand, double-checking to make sure it was loaded to capacity with as many bullets as it could hold. Anais let off more shots but could not get the knob off because the chair held it up.

Anais put a hole in the door, then stuck her hand through it, trying to push the chair out of the way. She reached all the way in, then suddenly let off three shots through the door at the door handle and chair, missing Yanira by inches. Yanira heard sirens and the fire truck from a distance. She stuck her head out of the window to get some air and calm herself.

Yanira began crawling into the restroom to create more distance. Anais saw Yanira making her way to the bathroom and let off four more rounds. She was determined not to let this bitch get away and prepared to light her up with bullets.

Yanira's phone started ringing. When she answered, it was Kaeo, yelling, "Yanira, what is going on? What's happening?"

Yanira got scared and dropped the phone as Anais tortured her with more gunshots, and then she stopped to reload. Yanira let off one shot as she continued to make her way into the bathroom. She felt a sharp pain in her arm and noticed blood. Looking down at her arm, she realized Anais had shot her, and she was bleeding. It was evident Anais was determined to kill her, but she had no idea how many bullets she had left. This was now clip number two. Yanira wanted to make sure she didn't waste her bullets.

The door finally opened with a kick from Anais. She looked around and didn't see Yanira, but then, out of the corner of her eye, she saw the bathroom door shut. She started shooting bullets into the bathroom door and walls until her gun clicked. Anais took a few steps, and Yanira thought she was leaving because she had no more ammunition. Instead, she was waiting to see if Yanira made a sound, but she was lying down in the tub. Anais went to get her hatchet/hammer and started trying to break into that door as well to make sure she was dead.

The phone rang again. This time, Anais answered and turned the phone on speaker. Kaeo heard Anais chastising Yanira. "Hey, Bitch! Tonight's your last night on this earth. If I don't get in, I will set this bitch on fire with both of us in it before I let them kill me."

Kaeo yelled at her. "Anais, what the hell are you doing? Don't do this, please. Anais, listen to me, please!"

"No, Kaeo, you have run out of chances. This bitch dies today. I told you she has taken too many things from me, and I will not let her live any longer. I will not go back to that jail or mental institute. I am not crazy, but this bitch has pushed me too damn far."

Cordero yelled from the background, "Mom, what the fuck is wrong with you. You fucked up, not her. Just run. Don't do this, man! Please."

She began to cry. "Son, it's ok. When she dies, we will be a family again. I just can't let her take everything. That is what your dad's girlfriend did. That is why she had to go. I loved him, and she took everything. These young girls with their perfect bodies always take from me. She even took you, Cordero. You don't love your mother; you are a traitor." She would not let them get in her head.

Pounding on the door, she said, "I got you bitch! I told you tonight was your last. Are you dead? Say something."

Yanira took two towels as she hid in the tub and wrapped her arm and leg while Kaeo and Cordero distracted Anais. Quietly, she climbed out. Anais continued to pound on the door, drowning out any sound Yanira made. Silently, she stood in front of the door. Anais swung with the sharp tool one last time in an attempt to cave in the bathroom door.

Pop, Pop, Pop, Pop was all you heard. Yanira fired the gun from left to right at the bathroom door. Anais screamed and fell to the floor. Yanira reloaded the gun and took three more shots from left to right at the bottom to ensure Anais was no longer standing.

Yanira waited a few more moments to see if she heard anything from Anais; she heard nothing. Cautiously, she opened the door and saw Anais lying there with bullet holes and blood leaking from her body. She caught her in the abdomen, stomach, and shoulder.

Feeling relieved that it was finally over, Yanira rested her body on the bathroom sink. After five minutes she walked out, stepping over the body so she could go downstairs, when Anais grabbed her leg. Yanira screamed and tried to move but fell to her knees. Anais scooted over to her. Yanira struggled, using only one leg and her arms to reclaim the gun.

Yanira let off more rounds at close range to ensure Anais was dead and gone, hitting her in the face, head, and chest, clicking until her gun signaled it was empty. She moved against the wall, watching as blood leaked onto the bedroom floor from Anais's body. Yanira was in shock and sat in silence until she heard footsteps making their way upstairs. What if it was Marla? She had already shot all her bullets into Anais. Yanira was scared and started to cry.

"Mrs. Iosua, this is Officer Bryant. I'm coming in. It's ok. The assailant is down. It's ok, please lower the weapon." Yanira couldn't stop crying. "Mrs. Iosua... Mrs. Iosua, please, ma'am, lower your weapon." He would not come closer because he was unsure if she had more bullets, but the tears and her body language let him know she was in shock and intended to kill no one else.

"Ma'am, are you ok?"

The police officers began to come closer to Yanira with caution. "We are coming closer, ok? Please lower your weapon."

Officer Bryant yelled, "Get a medic up here and call a bus."

Detective Bronson came up the stairs running, "Mrs. Iosua! Mrs. Iosua!"

Officer Bryant shouted, "In here, Detective."

He was scared to ask, but he did. "Is she alive?"

"Yes, sir, just shaken. I couldn't get her to move, talk, or lower her weapon."

The detective yelled, "She is not a danger! Do not shoot her, do not."

They removed the gun from her hands as she sat on the floor shaking, crying, and nervous. The officer who retrieved the weapon gave it to his partner. Noticing the blood on her arm and ankle, he said, "Mrs. Iosua, I am Officer Bryant. It's ok. You are going to be ok. It is over now. You are bleeding, so I am going to get you medical attention. Please sit and do not move."

Yanira didn't say a word.

"Detective, I'm not sure if the baby is hurt or if she is just in shock, but she has been shot in the arm and leg; there is blood surrounding her ankle."

Detective Bronson walked up and bent down eye level to Yanira. "Mrs. Iosua, it's me, Detective Bronson. Look at me. Hey, hey, it's ok now. It's ok, you did it. She can't hurt you anymore. It's over, ma'am." He touched her hand.

Yanira cried out; she was so relieved, but she couldn't move her body. She was indeed in shock and pain. The detective stood as the medic arrived, and the four of them removed her from the floor, carefully placing her on the gurney. They began to place oxygen on her as she was hyperventilating, strapping her down, putting pressure on her arm and leg, then carrying her out.

As they reached the front door, the neighbors were all outside staring. Her parents pulled up, and her father rushed to the gurney. "Yanira baby, it's daddy. I am here, baby. I am here. You are going to be ok."

Seeing her child on a gurney and blood all over her clothes, her mother became terrified. Scared of losing her daughter, she let out a scream. Mr. White held his wife in his arms as she cried. She thought Yanira was hurt and prayed out loud at that moment for protection for her daughter; she didn't want her to suffer. Mrs. White hopped in the ambulance with Yanira while her husband told her he was right behind them and would meet them at the hospital.

A few minutes later, Ryleigh, Marshall, and her aunt and uncle pulled up just as the ambulance had taken Yanira away. With all the commotion, the neighbor called Ryleigh as she had instructed long ago. When Ryleigh was moving, she gave the neighbor her number and advised that if anything ever happened to her cousin, to call immediately, and she did. Yanira's mom called her sister to let her know they were heading to the house because Kaeo was scared something had happened to Yanira.

Ryleigh was in a rage, jumping out of the car before it was in a parked position. "Yani, Yani, where is my cousin? Where is my cousin?" Looking around as the coroner brought out the black zipped back, she fell to the ground, screaming, "No! No, please, Yani get up! Please No!" Marshall and her father grabbed her. She was heartbroken. They all thought they were too late.

Detective Bronson came out the door, immediately yelling, "Hey, no, no, that's not her. She is in the ambulance, and she is going to be ok. She was injured, but she did what she had to do and eliminated the intruder. It's over. Please go to the hospital. I am sure she will want to see you when she comes around. Her parents are on the way there as well."

Ryleigh needed that reassurance. She just knew Anais had hurt her cousin. His words sent chills down her spine, causing rage because she knew Yanira could not suffer losing another child at the hands of Anais. Ryleigh called her aunt and uncle as she made her way to the car.

"Hey, how is Yani? I am on the way. Is she ok? How bad is it?"

Her uncle answered, "I don't know anything right now. They took her into surgery, Ry, so just be calm and pray. I will let you know as soon as I hear something, or I will just see you when you arrive." In his heart, he knew she wouldn't be calm until she put eyes on Yanira, and at that moment, he was no longer calm himself. Both Yanira and Ryleigh were his family and losing them was not an option.

Ryleigh cried hearing her cousin was in surgery. Their connection was deep. She hurt because Yanira hurt.

Just five minutes after they got into the car Kaeo phoned Marshall, and he answered. "Hey bro, I don't have any news on Yani. They took her to the hospital, but Anais, well she is gone.

Kaeo yelled, "Fuck, Fuck, Fuck! How in the hell did she get away?"

Marshall interrupted, "No, bro, I mean like she died. Yani shot her several times, they say. Anais did a number on the house. She shot through and beat down the bedroom door and almost through the bathroom. That's when Yanira shot her, but Anais shot her as well. We are not sure where exactly, but she is in surgery. We are headed there now. I promise to call you as soon as we lay eyes on her or hear some news."

Kaeo was worried. The unknown status of his wife and children was too much to take lightly. He was filled with pain, sorrow, and emptiness.

Ryleigh began to cry. Hearing her cries, Kaeo knew they wished for the same thing: that they were there to protect her. That feeling of failing to keep the one you love safe was unforgiving and cruel.

Marshall consoled Ryleigh. "Ry baby, it's cool. We are going to see about her; it's ok. Have faith. You need to calm down, baby, please. We are almost there. Kaeo, my brother, we are exiting the highway in 3 more exits. I will give you the same message. She will be fine; your babies are going to be fine. No worries. I will call you soon."

Kaeo caught his breath after a few more seconds. "Thanks, man, I appreciate you. Ry, be easy. Love you guys."

# CHAPTER: 20  THE AFTERMATH

When Ryleigh and Marshall arrived, her parents, aunt, and uncle were all sitting in the waiting room. Her father told her Yanira was fine. She was out of surgery and stable but sedated due to her being in shock. They retrieved the bullet from her arm, and she also had one that went in her leg; it pierced her and went straight through. Ryleigh was in shock and didn't say a word; she just cried. Her father, uncle, and husband surrounded her; she loved Yanira just as much as she loved herself.

By 9 am, Marshall headed to pick up Kaeo from the airport while the family went in to see Yanira. Since she was a physician there, they allowed all five family members to go in at once. Yanira's mother and aunt stood at a distance, crying, afraid to touch her or wake her. Their men held them tightly. Ryleigh broke down in tears and hopped into the bed next to her cousin. As kids, anytime something happened to the other, this was their ritual even when the other was sick and contagious, they expected both to become ill because only they could relax and calm one another. It was them against the world.

Yanira came around after another hour and a half, opening her eyes looking at her belly to make sure they were still there, then looked at her cousin. She tilted her head resting it on Ryleigh's.

"Ry, she came for me and my babies. She shot me, so I had to kill her."

Her mother and aunt approached the bed. "It's ok. Nothing else matters as long as you are still here with us." Her mother could barely speak those words. Her sister-in-law had to hold her and keep her composure.

"Yani baby, what happened?" Her aunt asked.

"Tia, (the name she had called her aunt) Anais came to the door, beating on it and threatening me. She threw bricks inside through the windows, then she shot at me and chased me into the bathroom. I didn't realize I was shot in the leg because my adrenaline was high, and I could not see the blood because of my sweatpants. I was just in pain, and I thought it was from running up all the stairs. I was so scared for my babies that I froze; she just wouldn't stop."

"All this for Kaeo? I mean, she wanted him so badly she was willing to kill for him. I can't deal with this anymore." Her mother said.

"No, she said that I met her years ago. Ry, remember when you first moved in and I told you about the nanny who was so busy texting the husband that the child was given candy that he was allergic to and it caused a reaction, and he fell off the monkey bars?"

"No." She paused, "Wait yes, I do. Yes, it was when I was moving upstairs. She called you a bitch right, she got dumped by the husband at the hospital right and we laughed about it for days."

"Yes, that one. Well, that was Anais. I haven't thought about it in years. Her hair was different, and she was smaller back then too. She blamed me because she got fired and because the child's father dumped her. The mother was the one with the money, and he was not willing to leave his wife for her, so he ended it with Anais. She blames me for that, Kaeo and the kids."

Ryleigh replied, "Wait, What! You are kidding me. Did you know all this time it was her?"

"Ry, no, I didn't remember until she told me. I mean, that was years ago, before I even met Kaeo. Do you know how many patients I've seen in that ER? And back then, they called her Anna, short for Anais. Kaeo was not the reason; it was me. He just added fuel to the fire. It was all because I was young and took two men from her."

"Well, you don't have to worry anymore. She is gone, and you made sure of it. This woman has hurt you, the children you have come to love, killed your unborn child, and now tried to come for you and your new unborn children. It was the right thing to do, Yani. Now you and Kaeo can live in peace."

The On-Call physician, who just so happened to be Dr. Yasmine, walked in.

"Dr. Iosua, I need to check your vitals, and then I want to take you to the ultrasound room so we can perform one last check on the babies. This was a rough night; you lost a lot of blood due to the two bullet wounds. We need to make sure the babies are ok." She checked her vitals.

Ryleigh moved off the bed, and the nurse came in to assist Yanira in getting into a wheelchair and to the ultrasound room.

For a moment, Yanira forgot about the babies. Reliving the story and piecing it together made her only think of Anais. "Hey, Dr. Yasmine. I would like my cousin to come with me. I just need some support should anything be wrong. Without my husband, I want someone around."

The physician nodded, "I understand totally. Let's get going."

As they made their way down the hallway, Yanira shared her feelings with her cousin. "Ry, I'm scared. I can't deal with another dead or undelivered child. I mean, I took from her, but no one died. She has taken one person from me already." She began to cry; her nerves had gotten the best of her.

Ryleigh replied, "No, you didn't take anything from her. She fucked up, not you. Don't let her get in your head, Yani. It is not your fault. Everything will be ok; just relax for the babies. Besides, together, we can get through anything. We always have and always will."

Yanira held Ryleigh's hand and said a quick prayer before getting started. She closed her eyes and took a deep breath.

"Ok, Dr. Iosua, it will be a little cold. Are you ready?" the physician asked.

Surprisingly, both heartbeats were pumping, although their rates were elevated compared to normal, but nothing to worry about. Yanira could also see their legs, hands, and faces in the sonogram. She was relieved that no harm was done to her babies.

Dr. Yasmine, however, was not so easily appeased; she took her seat and a deep breath. "Dr. Iosua, you must rest. The babies seem a little excited. Considering what you have been through, that's understandable, but we need to make sure you do not deliver prematurely—no more drama and stress. When you are released, go home; you need to be homebound and on bed rest as much as possible, with a little exercise if you're able to. We will check them again tomorrow morning and in another couple of days."

Yanira began to cry again. She still felt she was to blame. "Yes, ma'am. I understand, and I will try my hardest to keep them safe. I appreciate you coming in."

Ryleigh chimed in, "See, I told you everything would be fine. Now let's get you out of here so you can go home and relax, ok? You have one more month."

When she entered the room, she was pleased to see Kaeo there. He instantly engulfed her with a big hug. "Baby, baby, are you ok? I am so sorry I left you alone. I am so sorry." Kaeo didn't give her a chance to say anything. He held on to her tightly as if he would never let go. Her family had filled him in on what happened.

Yanira responded, "I am ok. I am glad you made it back safely. I needed you, and I was so scared, but it's ok. I told you to go. Ry and I saw the babies. They are fine, and I get to go home possibly tomorrow after they observe me overnight and there are no complications."

Kaeo continued to hug her. "Baby, I am so sorry about all of this; I promise I will never leave you unsafe again. You can't imagine all the things that have been going through my mind: the thought of losing the babies or losing you." A tear rolled down his eyes from love, fear of the unknown, and happiness because his family was safe.

Yanira smiled. "Baby, we are ok. The babies just have an elevated heart rate due to what has been happening and the blood loss, but they are fine."

Kaeo kissed her five times on her cheek. She could tell he was feeling bad, so she cracked a joke. "Baby, I love you, but I tell you what though, there had better only be one Anais, no evil twin or twisted sister, because if so, we are divorcing today, and I'm moving to Japan."

The room laughed in relief for both a healthy mother and children. That good news kept everyone in good spirits.

Her mother said, "I know that is right. We all are."

He smiled, "Baby, I promise there is not. I don't think there is anyone else in the world that is that crazy or petty to stoop low enough to kill someone or their baby because they got dumped. If there is then we need to buy our own island and be the only living creatures around."

"Facts! Make sure we are included in that too. I can sit on my own island and collect a check." Ryleigh laughed at her own words. They had to let Kaeo know he was not to blame nor responsible for Anais, but also that wherever her cousin was, she would be too.

Yanira was finally released two days later. The family agreed to meet them at the house to assist with cleanup and doing what they could. Kaeo had not seen the house and had no clue what he was in store for because once he arrived at the hospital, he never left Yanira's side.

The family waited patiently in the driveway for them to arrive. The appearance of the outside alone was different. Anais did a number on the door and broke two windows. All the glass shattered between the inside and outside, and everything was taped off by the police.

Kaeo helped Yanira out of the car. He saw the boarded window and thought nothing of it. The front door had several dents from Anais trying to kick it in. As they walked into the house, the downstairs was a mess. Yanira rubbed her belly as she walked in, trying to walk slowly. The women immediately started cleaning up the glass and reorganizing the items that had fallen over.

Kaeo and Yanira stood and looked around their house. She was disgusted, and Kaeo became angry and upset that Anais had destroyed all their belongings. Yanira needed rest, so she sat on the couch as Kaeo helped her. The women walked over to her, consoling her. After a short break, she decided to continue upstairs.

Kaeo and Yanira walked upstairs slowly. She was afraid to touch the railing, thinking about how she had to run up to protect herself. As she reached the door, she began to cry, seeing the bullet holes in the wall, the door, and the dents where Anais tried to force her way in. Kaeo was in disbelief. He could not imagine what his wife had endured that night. The hatchet did a number on the bedroom and bathroom doors.

Yanira entered the room and immediately noticed the blood from Anais on the floor all over the carpet. It had spread from her wounds and leaked, making a huge puddle. Yanira couldn't help but think she could have died. Having the gun saved her and her unborn children.

Kaeo walked behind her, then her father and uncle behind them. Kaeo covered his face. Anais had demolished their bedroom. She was so ignorant that as she lay there dying, she inscribed the word "Bitch" with her own blood as Yanira hid in the bathroom. They all were in shock. Her uncle let out a deep sigh. "Baby Girl 2, I'm glad you are ok; this young woman had anger problems. She was truly insane, dying with all that hate in her heart."

They walked into the bathroom and noticed the blood all over the tub. Yanira never knew she was bleeding from her leg. The sink, floor, toilet, and tub were all full of blood from Yanira. Kaeo just held her from behind.

For Yanira, it was all bittersweet as she looked around, seeing where all the bullet holes had come through the room. Bitter because she was traumatized, chased, and had to hide in her own home. On the other end, Yanira was relieved; she didn't have to live in fear of Anais coming after her or her children any longer.

When she finally noticed the blood and inscription, she became nauseous. Even in death, this woman was still haunting her. The house would be a reminder of everything she had gone through with Anais, and she couldn't stand to be there, not one minute more. Tears began to fall as she spoke. "I can't stay here. Please, I need to get out of here. Just being in this room is too much." Her uncle was the closest one standing to her. He escorted her out of the room.

Yanira walked back downstairs as she could not relive that moment. It brought on stress and anxiety. She reached the stairs and told her mother she was going home with them for a few nights. She needed to be comfortable, and staying in this house was not conducive or safe for her mentally, as her emotions were high.

Yanira left with her mother and aunt. They took her for lunch at The Steakhouse to clear her mind and help her relax after being in the house. Ryleigh met them there after her aunt texted, requesting she join them. The four ladies enjoyed lunch together and strolled to the ice cream parlor across the street. They parted after 2 ½ hours of spending time with each other.

# CHAPTER 21: CHRISTMAS

Yanira and Kaeo stayed with her parents for one week while the team worked on the house, fixing all the doors and windows, and renovating the bedroom and bathroom. Yanira refused to go back until everything was completed. Kaeo hired the contractors who had previously added the outdoor living room.

When the house was ready, they did a walk-through. The front door had been replaced, the glass door was restored, and things were back to normal; some of the finishing touches made the house look better than it did before. The kitchen had fresh paint, new flooring, new décor, and new countertops. Yanira could finally smile, but only temporarily. She went upstairs into her bedroom and had visions of the bullet holes and the blood. The room just didn't feel right to her, and she began to tear up. Her hormones were high, and she was emotional.

"Kaeo, I can't handle staying here. I don't want to raise my kids in this house—the place where Anais was killed and tried to kill me and them. I just can't. Maybe I need a few more days or weeks at my parents' house." Yanira was saddened. The house she once loved was no longer a place she wanted to be.

Kaeo saw the look on his wife's face. He had never seen her so bothered before. Grabbing her and holding her tight, he said, "Ok... it's ok, baby, we do not have to stay here. Let's stay with your parents through Christmas. Maybe we will find something by then."

The two of them packed a few more items and all their necessities for a couple of weeks, then returned to her parents. No words were spoken when they arrived, just hugs; her father knew why. She went up to take a nap and tried to rest, determined not to stress, or cause harm to her babies.

By the time Yanira woke up, it was dinner time. "I hope you don't mind, but we are going to stay with you guys until we sell the house. We are going to put it on the market and find something new. Is that ok? Can we stay until then?"

"Baby, I am your father; you don't ever have to ask. Kaeo, you can continue to use the guest room as an office for now. We will work through this, don't worry!"

Mrs. White chimed in, "Baby, you know you are welcome. I wouldn't have it any other way. I love you both being here!"

Yanira delivered the babies two weeks later. The baby boy was named after his father, Kaeo Iosua II, and the girl was named Kaori Leigh Iosua. She named her daughter after Kaeo and Ryleigh, her two favorite people outside of her parents. Yanira delivered without complications, and after three days, she was able to go home.

## CHAPTER 22: THE HAPPILY EVER AFTER

The two months of living with her parents had been a blessing; her mother helped with the babies every day. Having two was not as easy as Kaeo had thought. Yanira sold their house for $547,500K, which was more than what she had bought it for, leaving all the new additions, repairs, and furniture. The value of her house and the market had changed and increased. She had gained over $370k in equity. That bad omen was now out of her life.

After all the presents were opened on Christmas afternoon, Kaeo told her he had one last gift for her, but he wanted everyone to be present. He stated that it was too big to bring to her, so they had to drive to it. They packed up and headed out. Yanira was blindfolded. Arriving at the gate of Marshall and Ryleigh's place, the security guard said, "Mr. Iosua, how are you doing today? Welcome."

Yanira smiled, "Now that we have arrived, can I take the blindfold off? I am anxious now."

Kaeo replied, "No, not yet, my love, just a few more minutes. We have to wait just a little longer. Kaeo pulled up at a house that sat far back off the street and by itself in a cul-de-sac.

Yanira heard Ryleigh's voice and the babies. "Ok, Ry is here, and the boys. Baby, I have to take this off. This must be some present if Ry is here."

Her uncle snuck up behind her as she spoke, "Hey, Baby Girl 2."

Yanira laughed, "Uncle C, you are here too? Babe, I'm ready. Please let me take this off."

Kaeo stood behind her and took the blindfold off. Yanira opened her eyes and was in disbelief. Her husband had built a home in the same neighborhood as Ryleigh. They had three acres of land and plenty of living space for the kids and their adult children. The house was fully furnished with new décor from Kaeo's furniture store and a few other stores. To pass the time, Yanira would always look through his catalog and circle new furniture she liked so he knew just how to decorate their home and exactly what to get.

Yanira was in love with her new home, it was more than she could ask for. The house was astounding from top to bottom. Kaeo had added a man cave, kid's cave, and a lavish living room for Yanira in the basement, along with a gym, sauna, sitting room, game room, and kitchen. The outdoor patio was fantastic for entertainment. With all the amenities and a huge backyard, the kids would have plenty of room to run around.

Life would be well for the Iosua's now that Anais was dead and gone, leaving no unwavering feelings about their future and safety. Yanira could finally live and rest peacefully with her husband and children.

**THE END**

## *Epilogue: Lesson*

Sometimes we are so quick to give up on love or life in general when we really should be more patient. Somethings will never be on our time, but they are always on His time; and that is the right time.

Yanira went through so much with Kaeo; I am sure as a person who has been in love, we can all relate; however, she found an undeniable bond and love that she was not expecting. Although she struggled with Anais and with the children, in the end, her resilience made her stronger. It gave her an opportunity to change the lives of those around her who may not have had the chance if she was not available, faithful, and giving.

Yanira's patience turned out to be a blessing and was fulfilling to others, even though that love came with baggage it morphed into something more than she bargained for.

Just like Anais, there will always be people you encounter who will hate you for reasons that truly have nothing to do with you or things you have done to them; it will be for their own jealous and ignorant reasons, but you have to stay focused on you.

Never seek revenge! Yes, I do know it is hard because we are human and deserve better but allow the higher power to have the last say. He will never leave you nor forsake you, no matter how long it takes. No matter how many people try to break you. Stand and Stay Strong; You are your greatest asset!

# About the Author: Cherokee Grey

Cherokee Grey is a writer from the Midwest, residing in Atlanta Georgia. Growing up her passion was poetry, being infatuated with love and conversation. Her first public debut with writing was January 13, 2023, with the release of "Nefarious Triangle of Love." Her writing style is narrative, writing books from a narrator's point of view.

Cherokee favors fictional stories that are relevant to us all. Either you or someone you know can relate to trials and tribulations with loving others, family, friends, or lovers. She believes that Life is a journey and we all have experienced a love story that we will never forget.
When Cherokee Grey is not writing, she serves as an advice columnist offering her personal guidance and outlook on situations at hand regarding Life, Love, and Relationships.

.

Made in the USA
Columbia, SC
01 February 2024